SOUTHERN
pleasure

kaylee ryan

Cover Design: Perfect Pear Creative Covers
Cover Photography: Golden Czermak, FuriousFotog
Cover Model: Mac Robinson
Editing: Hot Tree Editing
Proofreading: Kim Ginsberg, and Proof This, Jennifer Singh
Formatting: Integrity Formatting

Kaylee Lovering (Kaylee 2)
You asked for a country boy.
I hope you fall in love with Evan.

EVAN

My heart pounds against my chest as I watch the tears running down her face and struggle to process what she just said.

I hate tears.

I hate my girlfriend, Misty, for what she just said, the words still ringing in my ears.

"Evan, I just don't want kids. I don't want to be a parent. My own parents sure as hell weren't role models, and it's just not something I want. I'm getting out of here," she says through her tears.

"Don't I have a say in this? That's my flesh and blood." I point to her belly. "This is my baby, too." My voice is pleading. She's just dropped a bomb on me.

Fuck that!

"Evan, I just . . . I don't want this."

"This is not just about you!" I roar. "This baby is a part of me, dammit. Please don't do this," I beg her. I'm not above pleading to save my unborn child.

"Evan," she sobs.

"How did this even happen? I wrap it every damn time. You're on the pill?" I say it like a question, even though she has always assured me she is, indeed, on birth control.

"Nothing is 100 percent. I don't know what happened. I take my pill religiously. All I know is I'm pregnant and I don't want to be!" she

screams.

I'm twenty-four years old. Old enough to be a father, although this is not how I'd planned it. I always thought I would be married to the love of my life when I started a family, but the fact of the matter is I'm not. Misty and I have been together for almost a year. I knew she wasn't the love of my life, but I didn't care—until now. I always figured we were having fun together and I had time. Time to find that one girl who consumes me and make her mine. Build a life together. I even thought, with time, Misty could be that girl.

Life has other plans, or maybe I should blame this on my swimmers and the damn condom company, or even the pharmaceutical company, but I know she's right. Nothing is 100 percent.

"Evan, you know I want out of this town. Small town life is not for me. I've been saving. We've talked about this."

She's right; we have. I think that's a big part of why she was never the one. I love being on the farm, living in Kentucky. This is my home. Misty has always been honest about her plans to move on. Her parents are both big shot business moguls, who never paid any real attention to her. To hear her tell it, she was never good enough for them.

Running my fingers through my hair, I take a deep breath. "Please don't do this." My voice cracks on my plea.

"I just . . . I don't want to be a mother." She cries harder.

"How long have you known? Give it a few weeks to sink in. It's a shock for sure, but that's our baby."

"I found out four weeks ago. I'm two months along. I've thought about this, Evan, and it's always the same answer. I don't want this."

"I do," I say with conviction. That baby is a part of me. My mind races for a solution and before I know what's happening, words are falling from my lips. "Sign over rights to me."

"What?" She's looking at me like I've lost my mind.

"Have the baby, then sign the rights over to me. I'll never ask you for anything. You don't have to be a part of his or her life, just . . . please, Misty."

Silence grows between us. The only sound is her soft cries and the rapid beat of my heart against my chest. I know she needs to process what I've just said, so I bite my tongue, giving her time.

"You really want this that badly? We've never talked about having kids."

"Yes, and I know we haven't, but that doesn't change the fact you are now carrying a part of me and I want that, more than I ever thought possible. Please don't do this."

"So, how would this work? You'd just take the baby and what? Go on with your life?" she asks.

"Yes. I'll make sure you have whatever you need during the pregnancy. We can go to a lawyer and have it written up. You sign over all rights to me and that's it. You can leave and go wherever you want. I won't ask you for anything else. Please, Misty." My voice is soft and pleading. I want to scream at her and demand she not do this, but I can't. That's only going to piss her off. Misty has a mind of her own. I need for her to come to the conclusion that this is the best option.

"My parents agree with me; I'm not cut out for motherhood."

What the fuck? I've only met her parents once. They live in Tennessee. Misty moved here to stay with her cousin, Heather, while attending college. She dropped out, but never moved back home. The one and only time I met them, they made sure to tell their daughter what a disappointment she is, as they snubbed their noses at the both of us.

I don't comment. If you don't have anything nice to say, don't say it at all. "Please, I can call the lawyer now, get the process started. I'll make sure you have anything you need."

"Evan, there will be medical bills, clothes, things for the baby. My parents, they won't help."

"I know and I got it——all of it." I hold her gaze as I say the words, willing her to keep my baby.

"If I agree to this, I'm leaving as soon as I can. I don't want this life, Evan."

I nod. "I know, and I won't stop you. As long as you've signed all the papers, you are free to go and live your life. You won't hear from me again." I wipe my sweaty palms against my thighs. She's considering it, but I have no idea which way she'll go.

"It needs to be clear in the papers that I want nothing to do with the baby. I know it sounds harsh, but I just . . . can't."

"Whatever you want. We can go to the attorney together."

She paces to the window and stares out at the green pasture, arms crossed over her chest. "Okay," she whispers.

I exhale the breath I didn't realize I'd been holding. She said okay. "Thank you, Misty. I'll call him now and get it set up. Have you been to the doctor? When is your next appointment? I want to be there for all of it."

"Yeah, I went. I'm supposed to go monthly for check-ups and then more frequently closer to time. I have an appointment this afternoon. I was going to tell them to . . . you know. I just wanted to tell you first." She turns to look at me. "I never expected this turn of events."

"Thank you for talking to me first and agreeing to this." I'm going to be a father. A single father, by choice. I'm grateful she's agreed to this, but at the same time, I want her out of my life. As soon as the words she was "taking care of it" left her mouth, I hated her.

"I want to be there for your appointments. Anything else you need, you let me know. I'm going to go call the attorney. What time do we need to leave?" I don't give her room to tell me no.

"I have to be there in an hour."

"Great, just let me make this call, and then we can go." I head to my office, leaving her alone in the living room. I just moved into this house six months ago. When I built it, I made sure it was big enough for a growing family. That was always in the back of my mind, but I never dreamed it would be this soon.

Stepping into my office, I shut the door and take a seat at the desk. Cell phone in hand, I swipe the screen, find the family attorney's number, and hit send.

My call goes to voicemail. "Mr. Fields, hi, Evan Chamberlin. Listen, I have an urgent matter that was just brought to my attention, which I will need your services for. When you get this message, please give me a call." I don't bother leaving my number; he has it. Mr. Fields has been my grandparents' attorney for years. When I took over the farm, I continued that relationship.

I find Misty still standing by the window. Being so lost in her thoughts, she doesn't hear me approach. I bite back the panic that she's changed her mind. I squeeze my cell phone a little tighter, willing it to ring. I need to get these papers drawn up and signed before she does.

"Ready?"

She startles a little from the sound of my voice. Turning to look at me, her face is void of any emotion. It's just . . . blank. "Yeah," is all she says as she grabs her purse and walks toward the door. Mutely, I follow behind, locking up. She ambles to my truck and gets in the passenger side. At least she's not trying to get out of this.

The twenty-minute drive is uneventful. We don't speak except for me asking which office she goes to. The silence is welcome. I'm still raging mad at the thought of her "taking care of it," even though I'm relieved she's agreed to sign all rights over to me.

As soon as I put the truck in park, Misty is climbing out and heading toward the door. I catch up just in time to reach around her to open it. She says nothing as we walk inside and I follow her to the receptionist's desk. I don't know if she has health insurance, but I need to make sure they know all bills should come to me.

"Good afternoon, how can I help you?" asks the chipper girl sitting behind the desk.

"Misty Newman here for my appointment with Dr. Combs." Her tone is flat.

"Great, let's see. It says here you have Medical Mutual for insurance coverage. Is that still in effect?" the receptionist inquires nicely.

"That's correct," she answers.

"Can you please make sure anything not covered by insurance is billed to me? My name is Evan Chamberlin." The overly-friendly receptionist looks to Misty for guidance, who she nods her head. I rattle off my address.

"I've got everything I need. You can have a seat and they'll be with you shortly," she chirps.

Misty doesn't acknowledge her as she turns and walks away. I smile at the receptionist, trying to cover for Misty's rudeness. Her blinding smile in return lets me know she's used to it.

I take a seat next to Misty and pull out my phone. Opening my email, I see a message from Mr. Fields. He's in court, but will call as soon as he gets a break. I reply that I will be unavailable for the next hour or so, but any time after that, no matter the time, he can call. I don't want to delay getting her signature.

"Misty," a short blonde nurse calls her name from the door leading

back to the exam rooms. As Misty strolls toward her, I follow behind like a puppy. "You can wait in exam room three while we get her weight," the nurse tells me. I nod, letting her know I understand, and take a seat in one of the empty chairs next to the exam table. Misty and the nurse join me not a minute later.

"Climb up on the exam table. I need to take your vitals." She proceeds to take Misty's blood pressure, temperature, and pulse. She then hands her a cup. "We need a urine sample. Leave the cup in the silver door behind the toilet. The doctor will be in shortly."

"I've already been here and taken a test. Why do I need another one?" Misty asks. Her voice is flat, uncaring.

"Yes, we will do this at each visit to check the levels in your urine." The nurse smiles and leaves the room, shutting the door behind her.

Misty grumbles under her breath as she, too, leaves the room. Leaning over, I rest my elbows on my knees and bury my face in my hands. My world has been flipped upside down in the last two hours. I'm going to be a father.

A single father.

Misty comes back into the room, and this time, the doctor follows her in. "You must be dad? I'm Dr. Combs." He extends his hand for me to shake.

"Yes, sir," I respond. I'm going to be a father. I swallow the lump in the back of my throat.

Dr. Combs takes a seat on a stool and opens his laptop. After a minute or so of scrolling and clicking, he looks up. "Misty, vitals look good. Weight is the same as last visit. Make sure you're eating three full meals a day. It's good to add a healthy snack in between. You're eating for two now," he grins.

Misty just stares at him.

"Right, well, you're eight weeks along and sometimes at this point we can hear the heartbeat. Lie back on the table and lift your shirt."

She does as instructed, still showing no emotion. Me, on the other hand, I feel like my heart is about to throb out of my chest. "We can really do that? We can hear the heartbeat?" I question. Even I can hear the excitement in my voice.

"Sure can. Eight weeks is sometimes a little early, so don't be alarmed if we can't. Most definitely by your next appointment," he explains.

Wiping my sweaty palms on my jeans, I don't bother looking at Misty. I know she's wearing that same bland expression, and I will not let her take this moment from me. Instead, I keep my eyes trained on Dr. Combs. I watch as he pulls out a tiny device he calls a Doppler and places one end against Misty's belly. As he gently moves it back and forth, I hold my breath, not willing to make a sound; I don't want to miss this. He moves the machine a little to the left and a whooshing sound encompassed with a steady thumping rhythm comes from the box in the physician's hand. I exhale at the sound, and the lump in my throat grows along with the well of tears in my eyes.

Hearing that sound for the first time is going down as the most amazing moment in my life to date. "Holy shit." The croaked words fall from my lips.

This causes Dr. Combs to laugh. "That's usually the reaction I get from first-time parents." He smiles at me and glances at Misty.

"It's his baby. I'm signing my rights over as soon as it's born," she blurts out.

Dr. Combs doesn't comment. He just nods in understanding as he places the Doppler back in the drawer. The room is silent as he measures her belly and asks a few questions about morning sickness and diet. "Everything looks good. We'll see you back here in a month. You can make your appointment on the way out." He then turns to look at me. "Do you have any questions?" Seems he understands all too well that Misty wants no part of this.

"Honestly, I'm too . . . overwhelmed," I say. "Maybe after I wrap my head around this; after it sinks in. I just found out a couple of hours ago."

Dr. Combs nods again, letting me know he understands. "Well, call anytime. We'll see you all in four weeks." With that, he grabs his laptop and flees the room.

The ride back to my place is silent. I have nothing to say to her that's nice, and I'm scared as hell if I piss her off she'll go back on her word. I park in front of the garage and turn off the engine. "So what can I do? Do you need clothes? Money?" I ask. I plan to hold up my end of the deal.

"Not yet. I'm good." She wrings her hands together in her lap. "I

guess I'll see you later." She reaches for the handle.

"Wait!" I grab her wrist gently. "I want to be there for all of it. You need me, you let me know. I think we should get together a couple times a week and have dinner or something. Keep in contact." I sound desperate, but I don't give a fuck. I need to stay front and center. I don't want to miss a minute of this even though we are no longer together.

"Yeah, sounds like a plan. Call me," she says as she jumps from the truck and briskly walks to her car. I stare after her, watching as she drives down the lane. My ringing cell phone startles me. Looking down, I see it's Mr. Fields on the caller ID.

Perfect.

McKinley

2

I'm officially a college graduate. I've enjoyed my reign at the University of Miami, but there's no place like home. I wanted to go away to school, see how the rest of the world lived outside the state of Kentucky. I experienced it, and I'm glad I did, but it's so damn good to be home. Aaron, my older brother by two years, is supposed to be picking me up from the airport. Our parents are in Tennessee for a cattle sale. Mom called three times offering to cancel, but I assured her it's fine. I've lived away from home for four years. I think Aaron and I can keep the house standing for a few days on our own. I am twenty-two after all.

As I'm standing in baggage claim, I pull my cell phone out of my purse and turn it on. A text comes through from Aaron.

Aaron: Hey, running a few minutes late. Got caught up in traffic.

I smile to myself. Aaron hates to be late for anything, so I know this is killing him. He's just like our father: always prepared and always on time. Both take their time and think things through, never making a rash decision. Me, I'm more like our mother. We live with our heart on our sleeves—often times volunteering and taking on too much just to help others. Not that Dad and Aaron aren't up for helping others, it's just they know when to say no. Mom and I, on the other hand, not so much. In college, I don't know how many times I'd gotten roped into helping with events around campus when I had my own projects and studying to do. Part of that could have been my roommate, Lisa's fault. She could

be very persuasive.

Tapping my foot impatiently, I watch as bags roll by, looking for mine. I only checked one, plus I have my carry-on. I shipped the rest here. I only kept what I needed to get me by the last couple of days. Lisa and I shared an apartment. She's an Alabama girl, and just like me, more than ready to go home. I'm going to miss her like crazy, but after being roommates and best friends for the past four years, I know we've formed an incredible bond and will stay in touch. It was hard to say goodbye, but then it always is.

Finally, I spot my bag and heave it off the conveyor. That's when I hear my name being yelled from behind me. Turning to search for the source, I see him. Aaron is running toward me with a big-ass grin on his face. Knowing he's about to tackle me, I release the handle of my suitcase and let my carry-on and purse drop to the floor just in time for Aaron to wrap his hulking arms around me.

"I missed you, little sister," he says as he hugs me tight.

I can't breathe, so forming words isn't possible. I wait until he releases me to respond. "I missed you too. Took you long enough." I elbow him lightly.

"Yeah, yeah," he grumbles good-naturedly.

I love teasing him; it's just too easy.

"Let's get out of here." Aaron reaches for my carry-on, hands me my purse, and then grabs my large suitcase. I don't bother to protest, as I know it won't do any good. Mom and Dad raised him right. He's going to make one hell of a husband one day, for multiple reasons. First of all, it's the truth; second, I just like to wind him up. Aaron is a thinker. He processes everything, including who he dates. He doesn't see the point in dating someone who he cannot see himself spending the rest of his life with. If he's not feeling it, he ends it. Only problem is, how is he ever going to get to know someone? Mom and I both have tried to explain this, but he's too damn stubborn. When he does fall, it's going to be hard and I'm going to enjoy every single second of watching him flounder around in unchartered seas.

I follow along behind him, expecting him to lead me to his old beat up ford. Instead, we're standing in front of a brand-new, shiny Ford F-350 four-door beast. I'm sure there is a more technical name for it, but it's freaking huge, so beast it is. "This thing is huge!"

"I know, right?" He grins at me. "Just picked it up last week. I decided to retire the other one."

"It's about time. You've been driving that same old beat-up truck since you were sixteen."

"Yeah, and with me taking over the farm, I can't depend on borrowing Dad's all the time." He shrugs. "It was time to man up and get my own. One that could actually pull the horse trailer up the hills and not take six days to do it." We both laugh at that. My brother is frugal to a fault. He's not one to need shiny new toys. He can afford it, as he's a partner in the farm with my parents, but you would never know it. He's modest and so much like our father.

"How's that going?" I ask.

"Good. Papers are drawn up. I've asked them both a million times if they're sure they are ready to pass it on, and they both agree it's time. Dad says he wants to relax and watch me sweat," he laughs.

"It's hard work, Aaron. I know you love the farm, but you've seen the long hours Dad had to put in. You sure this is what you want? No one would judge you if you didn't." I ask the question, even though I already know the answer. A resounding yes. Our family farm is in his blood, and it's always been his dream to take it over. His best friend's family owns the farm that runs parallel to ours. He and Evan have been friends for as long as I can remember and have always talked about taking over and working together.

"Yes!" he says emphatically and I grin. I know my brother.

"So what about Evan? How is he? How's his dad?"

"He's good. Adjusting. His parents moved to Alabama. There is an oncologist there who specializes in his type of cancer. The warmer climate also helps. He's always freezing." Aaron loads my bags into the truck as I climb up into the passenger seat. I actually have to climb because this thing is so big. Thank goodness for running boards.

"I can't imagine how hard that is for him. I'm sure he always pictured his dad and granddad being there when he took over," I say softly.

"Yeah, he's . . . okay, I guess. He doesn't say much. Evan just jumps in head first and gets it done, you know what I mean?"

I nod. Evan is the exact opposite of Aaron. He makes decisions on a whim and rolls with it. Senior prom is a great example. Aaron agonized

over who to ask. He didn't want his date to think it was more than that, just a date. Evan on the other hand, had accepted the first invitation he received. That's another way they differ—Aaron thought it was the man's job to ask the girl. Evan just rolled with life. That particular trait alone intensified the already massive crush I had on him. The girl who asked him to the prom, she wasn't popular, she wasn't the most beautiful, but she asked and he agreed. He didn't do it out of pity or to play games with her. Evan treated her like he would a beauty queen. He's just an all around good guy and my teenage heart couldn't help but fall for him.

"Speak of the devil." Aaron holds his phone up so I can see Evan's name lighting up the screen. "Hey, man, what's up?" he asks in greeting. I block out their conversation and stare out the window, enjoying the open land flying by. It's so good to be home.

"Earth to Kinley." Aaron waves his hand in front of my face, snapping me back to the present. "There you are."

"Sorry, just got lost in the landscape. It's so good to be back. I can't wait to ride the land and take some shots." I majored in photography and I want to start my own business. The open pastures of Kentucky have my mind racing with photo possibilities.

"I see. Listen, that was Evan, as you know. He says he needs to talk to me. Do you mind if we stop by his place. He sounded a little . . . I don't know, off."

"Sure, does he know I'm going to be with you? Maybe I should drop you off and come back to get you later," I offer. Evan may not feel comfortable talking in front of me.

"Nah, I told him I just picked you up from the airport."

"Well, all right then. It's been forever since I've seen him. When I was home for Christmas, he was in Alabama with his parents."

Aaron laughs. "That's pretty funny actually." He grins. "The path of life."

"Yes. So tell me what's been going on." Aaron spends the next twenty minutes catching me up on the ins and outs of him taking over the farm and our parents bragging about slowing down. I laugh when he tells me both Mom and Dad keep dropping hints about wanting to be grandparents.

"You are the oldest after all," I chide him.

"Yeah, yeah. Needs to be a game changer, little sister," he replies.

This is not new information to me. I just wish he would lighten up a little. I fear he'll never give himself the opportunity to open up and know someone, really know them and fall in love. Of course, that's the romantic in me.

As we pull into the long drive that leads to Evan's, we veer to the right instead of driving toward the main house. "Where are we going?"

"Evan just moved into his new place a few months ago," Aaron says.

"Oh, that's right. I'm excited to see it."

"Well, here we are." Aaron stops in front of a two-story house. It's beautiful. The front is brick, a mix of light and dark browns, with tan siding the rest. Dark green shutters adorn the windows, and a porch, which crosses the front and both sides.

"Does the porch wrap all the way around?" I ask as I take in the beautiful structure. I love this house. It's my dream house, but I would want a basement and for the porch to go all the way around.

"Yes, four bedrooms, full basement. It's massive for one guy, but you know Evan. He says this is going to be his home and he wants to be able to grow into it." He shakes his head as if he doesn't understand his best friend. Aaron is the type of guy who would need his future bride to be in the building process, discussing and analyzing every room, every fixture.

"Wow!" is all I can manage to say as I reach for the handle and climb out of the beast. I meet Aaron at the front of the truck, and he throws his arm around my shoulders as we walk up the front porch. Evan opens the door as we reach it.

"McKinley, welcome home." He wraps his arms around me and I go willingly into his embrace. Only a crazy person would pass up a heartfelt hug from Evan Chamberlin. He's tall—six foot four to be exact—with broad shoulders, and he's . . . defined. It's been a few summers since I've seen him with his shirt off, but I have a very vivid memory of the rigid planes of his stomach. It's not an image a girl is quick to forget, especially a girl with a teenage crush as big as the state of Kentucky.

"Thank you. It's good to be home," I say, stepping away. Not that I wanted to, but it's the right thing to do.

"Come on in." Evan moves back and allows us in.

"What's up, man?" Aaron gets right to it.

I watch closely as Evan pulls the ever-present Alabama hat from his head and runs his fingers through his hair before placing it back on. He's nervous. I start to panic. Did something happen to his dad?

"You might want to sit down for this," he tells us.

I do as I'm told. Kicking off my flip-flops, I curl my legs under me as I take a seat on the couch. Aaron takes a seat in the chair. Evan remains standing, staring out the window. The house is quiet as we let him gather his thoughts. Looking over his shoulder, he takes a deep breath before walking to the couch and sitting beside me. Pulling one leg up, he faces both of us. My heart is beating like a drum as we wait.

"I got some news this morning." He pauses and squeezes his eyes shut.

I tell myself not to panic, but then a slow grin tips his lips as he opens his eyes.

"It's news that shocked me, but I can't be upset about it. Well, not now anyway," he says.

"Shit, man, you're killing me here. Spit it out," Aaron complains. I'm in agreement but keep it to myself.

"Misty stopped by this morning." I remember Aaron telling me he was seeing someone. "She's pregnant."

"Wow, congratulations, man." Aaron stands to give him a man hug. Once he's seated, I lean over from my spot on the couch and hug him as well. It's quick and I fall back into my seat.

"Yeah," he says shyly. "I'm going to be a dad." His voice trails off and a haunted look falls over his eyes.

"And?" Aaron prompts.

Evan laughs humorlessly. "Let me tell you about my morning." He tells us the details of his conversation with Misty—how she'd wanted to end the pregnancy and he'd begged her not to, and her finally agreeing to sign over all rights to the baby.

As I sit and listen, I can see how much this is hurting him. How the thought of Misty doing something to harm the baby or worse, end the pregnancy sits heavy on his mind. I scoot closer to him and lay my hand over his on the couch, offering what little comfort I can as he continues to talk.

"I called our attorney. He's getting papers together as we speak. I don't want to give her time to change her mind."

"Good," Aaron replies.

"There's more. She's two months along and today she had a doctor's appointment. She was going to tell them to end it, but she wanted to tell me first. Thank the angels above she did. I was able to convince her, and then we went to her appointment." My eyes follow his every move as he leans his head back against the couch and closes his eyes. His chest gently rises and falls with each breath. Again, we wait for him to collect his thoughts. "I heard it," he says softly. Turning to the side, he opens his eyes. Big brown eyes, glassy and filled with emotion, collide with mine. "I heard my baby's heartbeat."

I can't prevent the broad smile that takes over my face. "That's amazing."

"Yeah," he says.

"Shit, man. That's intense," Aaron adds. Evan tears his eyes from mine to look at my brother.

"You have no idea. We're sitting in this exam room, tension in the air. The room is so quiet you can hear a pin drop, and then there it was, sounding through this little speaker. It was amazing."

"So what now?" Aaron asks.

"Well, hopefully, the papers will be ready in a day or so. Once she signs, I prepare to be a dad. I told Misty I want to be there for all the appointments and I would pay for anything she needs, clothes and things like that." He looks at me.

"Dude, how do you know what a baby needs?" Aaron questions. I want to smack him. I'm sure Evan is nervous enough without him adding fuel to the fire.

"It's not that hard to figure out," I say.

"Really?" Aaron asks. "Maybe not for you. It's born into women or something. For guys, it's different."

"I don't have the first clue. I know I'll need a bed, and the websites I've been on said a baby's room is called a nursery," Evan offers.

"Yes, it's called a nursery. You need a bed, changing table, dresser, and the small little baby hangers because the clothes are way too small to fit on ours," I say.

"Gram said she would help. I haven't called Mom and Dad yet. I know it's going to be hard for them, since they're in Alabama and I'm here. I'm going to be a single dad. I need to learn how to figure this shit out."

"I can help." The words fall from my lips before I realize it. Not that I mind. Evan's a great guy and Aaron's best friend, so of course I'll help him. I admire him for what he's doing. I don't know many guys, if any, who would do what he's doing.

"Really?" Evan asks with hope in his voice.

"Kinley can shop with the best of them. You're in good hands," Aaron says.

"Thank you. I can use all the help I can get."

"You're welcome."

"We better get moving." Aaron stands from the chair. "I just picked Kinley up from the airport. I want to get her home, so she can settle in."

"Sure, thanks for stopping by. I didn't want to tell you over the phone." Evan walks us to the door and the two of them make plans to get together later.

"Wow," Aaron says once we are in the truck.

"Yeah. He's a great guy. Not many would be so adamant and willing to do what he's doing."

"You know Evan. He's a stand-up guy," Aaron says defensively.

"I know that. I just mean, I really think it's great what he's doing for his unborn child."

Aaron remains quiet until we pull into our driveway. "Thanks for offering to help him. I'm sure Misty will be no help at all. His gran doesn't get around well, and with his parents living in Alabama, he's going to need a female perspective."

I just nod and smile, ending the conversation. Aaron carries both my bags up to my old room and leaves me to unpack.

EVAN

Finally, after a week of back and forth, today is the day Misty and I sign the papers at my attorney's office. Mr. Fields had them drawn up within twenty-four hours; he's compensated well. However, it took me four more days to get Misty to answer her damn phone. I drove by her place, left messages with Heather—her cousin and roommate—and still crickets. This has been the longest week of my life, fearing she'd changed her mind and gone through with, "Getting rid of it," as she'd said, without telling me.

Yesterday, she finally called. Her excuse for not getting back to me was she "was busy." Busy doing what, I have no idea. She very quickly reminded me that just because she's "giving me the kid" doesn't mean I can control what she does. These next seven months are going to be exhausting. I'll feel a little better once she's signed the papers. However, that still doesn't mean she's going to eat right and not drink alcohol. She's not even supposed to be lifting, at least that's what the book I'm reading says. How am I going to be able to relax not knowing if she's taking care of herself and the baby?

I contemplated asking her to move in. I even ran it past Aaron. He made a valid point that I have no intention of continuing my relationship with her. How could I? Having her move in may make her confuse the situation and she might try to change her mind. Yes, he has a point, but if that's what she wanted, she could have had it. No, she's not "the one," but I do . . . did care for her—I guess I still do and always will because of the baby. However, I could have made us a family. I might have moved her in and the rest would have been history, but that's not what

she wanted. The day she came to me, her mind was made up——she wanted no part of being a mother.

I knew it was a crazy thought. Aaron just helped me remember that. I'm desperate to keep my unborn child safe and it kills me that I can't be there.

Pulling into the lot of the attorney's office, I put the truck in park, but let the engine run. Picking up my phone, I check the time. I'm ten minutes early. I don't see Misty's Jeep, so I'm going to wait. I tried to convince her to let me pick her up, even told her we could grab something to eat afterward. She was adamant she could drive and she's capable of feeding herself.

Frustrating woman!

I can already see I'm going to have to fight her tooth and nail in order to be involved. I want to be there for the appointments, especially the ultrasound. I read last night that they have 4D ultrasounds. I called Misty's doctor's office and they don't have them, but they gave me the number of a place that does. The nurse made sure to tell me they are usually not covered under insurance. It's worth it. I saw a few pictures online and the detail is amazing. I'm excited and scared as hell. It's going to be a long seven months.

Twenty minutes later, Misty pulls in beside me. She's ten minutes late and I want to berate her for it, but I bite my tongue. I don't want anything to stop her from signing these damn papers.

Quickly hopping out of the truck, I jog to her door and open it for her. "Hey." I keep my voice light.

"I can open my own doors, Evan. I'm not an invalid, I'm pregnant," she smarts off.

Taking a deep breath, I reply, "I know that. I was just trying to be nice." I place my hand on the small of her back and lead her into the office. "How have you been feeling?" I ask, keeping my voice soft.

She softens a bit at my mellowed tone. It wasn't a question to make casual conversation. I really am interested.

"Good, still no signs of morning sickness." She shrugs. "I must be one of the lucky ones."

"Good. I've been reading, and for most women, it already happens so you just might be in the clear. Nine weeks right?" I ask.

She stops and stares at me. "You've been reading?"

I hold her stare as I answer. "Yes, I only have a few months to learn what I need to. I'm going to be doing this on my own and I need to be prepared. I also want to be there for you. Reading helps me understand what you're going through. I don't want to miss any of this, Misty. I know we're not together, but this baby is a part of me."

She nods once and turns to approach the reception desk. "Evan Chamberlin, we have an appointment," she tells the lady at the desk. She's casual, as if what she's about to do isn't a life-changing moment. She's signing over the rights to her baby, the one she's still growing inside her.

"Of course, Mr. Fields is expecting you." She points to the door just down the hall. "You can go on in."

I wave in greeting and follow Misty. My palms are sweaty. This day has consumed me from the minute I got her to agree to this.

"Evan, hi." Mr. Fields stands from his seat and holds out his hand. I extend mine as well and we shake.

"This is Misty Newman. Misty, this is Mr. Fields," I introduce them.

"It's nice to meet you, Ms. Newman," the lawyer says. Misty doesn't respond. Instead, she takes a seat in one of the two chairs directly across from him.

"Okay. So, Evan gave me specifics over the phone, but I first have to read through them with you so you understand what you're signing."

"I trust Evan. I don't need to read it. Just tell me where to sign," she answers.

"Ms. Newman, I highly advise against that. I need to make sure you understand what it is you're doing today."

"Trust me, I know what I'm doing. If it were any other guy, I wouldn't be sitting here. Evan wants this baby. He's a good man, so that's why I'm here. I want no part of this child's life. I don't want to be a mother." She finishes quietly.

"What about your family? Have you discussed this with them?"

Misty scoffs. "Yes, and they agree that to us, the Newman's, this child doesn't exist. He or she will be a Chamberlin and Evan will be the sole parent. I plan to move as soon as the baby is born. I've officially worn out my welcome in Kentucky."

"Misty—" I say her name, but she cuts me off.

"No, Evan! You can't change my mind. I want nothing to do with this. I meant what I said. For any other guy, I would have never agreed to this. I'm doing this for you. I know what this means to you and your parents."

My chest tightens at the mention of my parents. I called them the day after I'd found out and we'd talked on the phone for over an hour. They were both so damn excited. Mom called the next day saying she's not seen Dad in this high of spirits since his initial diagnosis. I want this for them and for me. I want him to see my children, or at least this baby.

"Ms. Newman, I'll read through this quickly. My paralegal——" he points to the corner of the room to a girl typing away, who I hadn't even seen join us "——is going to document the session. What you say could come back to haunt you later . . ."

"No, it won't. I want it documented that neither my family nor I want anything to do with this child." She points to her belly. "I want to sign over all parental rights to Evan Chamberlin."

Mr. Fields looks over at his paralegal and she nods—their unspoken acknowledgement that she did, indeed, get Misty's words recorded.

"All right, in summary, you, Misty Newman, are signing over any and all parental rights to the father, Evan Chamberlin. Evan will take financial responsibility in regards to all medical bills, clothing, and any other expenses incurred throughout the pregnancy."

"Yes, okay, where do I sign?" She sits on the edge of her seat and reaches for a pen from the holder on the desk.

Mr. Fields instructs each of us where we need to sign. As soon as she scrawls her name in all the necessary places, I feel a little of the weight lift from my shoulders.

I'm going to be a father.

I'm glad I'm sitting because there is a slight tremble in my knees. Misty passes me the pen and I see the same quiver in my hands. I'm scared out of my fucking mind, but I want this. This baby is a part of me. How could I ever not want that?

I scrawl my name on the line and push the papers back toward Mr. Fields. "Misty, what about your family?" Mr. Fields asks.

"What about them? They told me to get rid of it."

Her voice is flat, no emotion, no feeling. My gut twists at her words and my eyes fix on the papers with both of our names on them. This day could not have come fast enough.

"Just as precaution, I urge, once the baby arrives, there be a paternity test to validate Evan is the father."

Misty's head snaps up and she stares at him, processing what he just said. "I don't want to be a mother. This baby is better off without me, and vice versa. However, I didn't cheat on Evan. This is his baby. If it were anyone else's, it would be a non-issue."

Again, her words cause my stomach to churn. She's calm, her face void of any emotion. Did I ever really know her?

"Fair enough, but as reassurance to my client, it's best to do this as soon as possible. This prevents surprises years down the road after emotional bonds have been established."

"Whatever," Misty quips. "As long as it's understood I'm not, nor is anyone in my family, going to be involved, I don't care what you do."

I clench my fists. How is it possible that this is the same girl I've spent the last several months with? I want my child to have a mother, but in this moment, I have to agree my baby is better off without her.

McKinley
4

*I*t's been a week since I've been back, and Dorothy was right—there is no place like home. I spent the morning on Savannah, my horse, riding the property. I took my camera and caught the sunrise. I love being behind the lens, capturing life's little moments. My plan is to start my own photography business. My parents are on board to help me as much as possible. Last night, Dad even offered to rent me a studio in town, but I don't really think that's the angle I want to take just yet. Instead, I'm going to set up a mini studio here on the farm. We have an apartment over the garage that has an outside entrance. I'm going to clean it out and start collecting props. I'm excited to put my degree to use and start this next chapter.

I'm sitting on the front porch with my laptop, going through this morning's pictures when I hear a truck pull up. I know who it is without even looking. Evan's had that old thing since he was sixteen. It had been well used when he got it. I hear the creak of the door as he opens it, and I can't help but grin. You know you missed home when the sound of a rickety old truck door can bring a smile to your face.

I'm still looking at my computer screen, flipping through images, when his footsteps approach. I don't look up, assuming he's going to walk right past me and into the house like he always does. Only he doesn't.

Looking up, I see he's not wearing his usual dusty, worn jeans, the ones that hang just right. These jeans are more . . . I don't know, dressy, I guess you could say. It's obvious he hasn't been working today. His

flannel shirt is pressed and tucked in with the sleeves rolled to his elbows. He's sexy as hell no matter what, and it's with that thought I realize I've been staring at him. "Hey, you look fancy." I smile big, hoping to cover up my ogling.

The corner of his lips twitch in amusement, but it's not the megawatt smile I'm used to.

"Bad day?" I ask hesitantly. I know he has a lot going on with the baby and Misty. Last I heard, he was still trying to track her down to meet with his attorney and sign the custody papers.

"Yes and no." He climbs the last step and takes the seat beside me. Leaning over, he glances at my computer screen. "You're really good."

I can feel the blush coat my cheeks. "How do you know these are mine?"

He gives me that look, the one that says *I'm not an idiot.*

"Aren't they?"

I look down at the screen, averting my gaze. My face is on fire. I've displayed my work hundreds of times in college, and I've never had this kind of reaction to a compliment.

It's Evan.

"Thank you," I say, finding my voice. We're both silent and I breathe a sigh of relief as I get myself under control. Finally, I turn to look at him. "You want to talk about it?"

Closing his eyes, he rests his head back against the chair. "I just left my attorney's office. Misty signed the papers."

I wait for him to say more, but he doesn't. I can't even begin to imagine how he's feeling. He's going to be a father——a single father. This isn't how anyone plans to join the ranks of parenthood.

My eyes stay glued to him. I wish there was something I could do or say, but there's nothing. This is a bad situation all around. The only good is the miracle of a new life, his baby.

Turning his head, he opens his eyes and the brown pools stare into me. "It didn't even faze her, Kinley. She waltzed in there and made sure it was known she wants no part of this kid's life and signed on the fucking dotted line."

Instinctively, I reach over and place my hand on top of his. It's a lame attempt to comfort him.

"It's like she's not even the same person. How . . ." he stops and swallows hard. "What if I can't do this?" he asks. His voice is soft and pained. He grimaces. "What if I screw this kid up? What if I can't be what he or she needs?"

Before I can answer him, my mom opens the front door and steps out. "Oh, Evan, I didn't know you were here. It's good to see you." She takes the chair on the opposite side of me and leans forward. "How have you been?" Her eyes flash to my hand still clutching his. Reluctantly, I let go and place my hands back in my lap.

"Hey, Mom." Evan spent as much time here growing up as Aaron and I. He's always called my parents mom and dad. He looks at me to gauge if she knows. I shake my head no. Releasing a heavy sigh, he drops the bomb. "I'm good, a lot going on." He swallows hard. "I found out about a week and a half ago that I'm going to be a dad."

Mom's eyes widen and she glances back and forth between the two of us.

"Today's been a . . . bittersweet one." He goes on to explain. "Misty, she doesn't want the baby. I had to plead with her to keep it." The last part is choked out. "This morning we signed custody papers over to me. They still have to be filed with the court, but by the time the baby is here, I will be the sole custodial parent. Misty will have no rights whatsoever."

"Oh my." Mom stands and walks over to Evan. Leaning over, she places her hand on his cheek. "You're an amazing young man, Evan Chamberlin. This baby is lucky to have you." She taps his cheek and goes back to her chair.

"So, what's next?" I ask him.

"I don't know. I'm out of my element here. I mean, I'm excited about the baby. I'm scared as hell and it's not how I envisioned it, but I want it—him or her. I hate calling my baby it."

Mom chuckles. "Well, why don't you try something else like peanut?" she asks.

Evan smiles fondly at her. "Is that what you did?"

She grins. "Yep. We didn't find out with either of them. We wanted to be surprised."

I look at Evan. "Do you want to know?" I ask him.

He doesn't answer at first, and I can tell he's never really thought about it. "I don't know." Leaning his elbows on his knees, he buries his face in his hands. "I just always pictured having 'the one' by my side during all of this."

"The one?" Mom asks.

Evan turns his head to look at her. "Yeah, the one woman who makes my heart race, who consumes my thoughts. The one I spend the rest of my life with. I never pictured this scenario, and I'm at a loss," he confesses.

My heart melts and aches at the same time. Evan is such a great guy, any woman would be lucky to have him. I hate that this is happening. Not the fact he's having a baby out of wedlock, or even the fact Misty is not 'the one,' but the fact he's having to do this alone. His parents are in Alabama as his dad battles cancer for the third time and both sets of grandparents are getting up there in age.

"Well, for us, we wanted to be surprised. Of course, it was hard to shop. We had lots of yellows and greens," Mom laughs. "I assume you will be there for all her appointments?"

"Yeah, I don't want to miss any of it. I already heard the heartbeat." The dazzling smile I'm used to lights up his face.

"Well, how far along is she?" Mom asks.

"Nine weeks or so. Everything happens in weeks," he mumbles.

Mom and I chuckle at that. "Yes, certain weeks are markers. Usually, it's about halfway—so twenty weeks—when they do an ultrasound and determine the sex of the baby," Mom explains.

"Hey, what's going on out here?" my dad says as he and Aaron come walking up from the barn.

"Just enjoying the day," Mom says, not missing a beat.

Aaron and Evan bump fists, and Dad nods in greeting. "So what are you getting into?" Aaron asks Evan.

"Just got back from the attorney's office."

"She sign?" Aaron asks.

"Yeah," Evan sighs.

"Good. Give me ten to shower and we can go grab a bite to eat." Aaron doesn't wait for an answer. He races into the house and flies up the stairs.

Mom and Dad both just shake their heads and grin. Aaron and I are twenty-two and twenty-four years old, both old enough to be living on our own. Aaron loves the farm and one day in the near future it will all be his . He's in no rush to live on his own. He's content. It helps that our parents are awesome. At least I have the excuse I just graduated from college.

"Shower's calling my name too." Dad leans down and kisses Mom quickly.

"I've got a meatloaf in the oven." She stands and looks at Evan. "I'm proud of you. You need anything at all, you let me know."

Evan nods and we watch as my dad holds the door open for her and they disappear into the house.

And then there were two.

"That goes for me too," I tell him.

"Yeah?" he asks. His voice is soft and his brown eyes are watching me intently.

"Yeah." I bump my knee into his.

Aaron comes barreling out of the house, having taken the quickest shower ever, hair still wet, pulling his t-shirt over his head. "Ready?"

Evan stands but doesn't take his eyes off me. "See you around, Kinley."

I wave and watch as the two of them climb into Evan's old truck and head down the drive.

EVAN

As we drive to town, I catch Aaron up on the day's events.

"It just goes to show, you never really know someone," he says.

"I agree to an extent. But really, I can only blame myself. I didn't try to get to know Misty. We were exclusive, but it was just fun for us. We both knew that's what it was and we were okay with that."

"Yeah, you two did seem sort of an odd couple. Especially with her always saying she was leaving and this was just a detour in the road for her."

"Even though I knew that, I never would have imagined her being so indifferent toward her unborn child."

"It's all good now, my man. She signed the papers and that's what matters. You got a kid to think about now."

"Your mom and Kinley both said they would help," I tell him as we pull into the local diner.

We slide into a booth near the back and the waitress is there as soon as we sit, so we go ahead and order. We have the menu memorized.

"You know they would love to. Hell, Mom keeps telling me I need to settle down and give her some grandkids. She's going to go nuts over your baby, man."

"True. I'm going to need all the help I can get."

"Kinley too. Women just have a knack for that shit. She wouldn't have offered if she didn't want to help. She's slow right now while she

gets her studio ready. I say take her up on it."

The waitress brings our food, and just as I'm about to bite into my cheeseburger, the diner door opens and in walks Misty with Tom fucking Harris. He's bad fucking news and everyone knows that, including Misty. "Motherfucker!" I say, placing my cheeseburger back on the plate, my appetite suddenly gone.

Aaron looks over his shoulder to follow my stare. "Shit, what's she doing with that jackass?"

"I have no fucking clue." I close my eyes, willing them to be a figment of my imagination. I count slowly to ten and then open them——no such luck. Misty and Tom are being seated in a booth on the opposite side of the diner. She sits first and instead of sitting across from her, Tom slides in next to her, throwing his arm around her shoulders.

"Fuck, man, she needs to keep better company."

No shit! "Yeah, when she's carrying my baby she damn well needs to. I better not find out her ass is taking anything," I seethe.

"Is she trying to make you jealous?" Aaron asks.

I shake my head. "No, not once since she told me she was pregnant has she indicated she wants us to be together. I offered, man. She turned me down cold."

Aaron studies me, trying to see if her rejection bothers me.

It doesn't.

He's not going to find any remorse in me for her, only my unborn child she's carrying. There's a fucking cigarette behind his ear. She does not need to be around that shit. Without thinking, I'm standing and striding toward them. I reach their booth and Misty's eyes lock on mine.

"Evan," she greets me. She's not being mean or hateful. She greets me as if I'm just some guy she knows.

Indifferent.

"Misty," I repeat the gesture. I'm trying hard not to lose my shit over her choice of company. I decide to make small talk. Maybe Tom doesn't know about the baby. "When's your next appointment? I forgot to ask you earlier."

Nothing. No change in expression. "I haven't set it up yet. I'll text you."

Tom pulls the unlit cigarette from behind his ear and places it in his mouth. He lets it hang there unlit. "That's not good for the baby." I don't bother to elaborate. I know she knows what I'm talking about.

"It's not lit," she replies.

"You can't smoke around her," I tell Tom.

He laughs. "Like I'm going to listen to you."

Placing my hand on the table, I lean down, nose to nose with him. "You will. You see, Tom, Misty here is carrying my baby. Just a few short hours ago, she signed over all rights to me. In that same agreement, she signed she would not put herself in harm's way, in turn not putting my unborn child in a harmful situation." I stand back to my full height.

Misty continues to sit there unaffected.

Tom turns to her. "You carrying his kid?" he asks.

What a fucking tool.

"Yeah."

"He telling the truth? You sign those papers?"

"I did. I didn't read them. I skimmed to make sure the baby would be his full responsibility and signed."

Done with this conversation, I reach over and snatch the cigarette out of his mouth. I crush it in my hands, then dust them off on the table. I know there are more where that came from, but I want to get my point across.

"See that you follow the contract. I would hate for you to be in contempt." I stalk back to Aaron, slide in the booth, and pick up my now cold burger. I have to choke it down.

Aaron motions for the check as I make quick work of my food. He pays the bill and we leave. I feel sick at the thought of what types of situations she's getting herself into.

McKinley

I've spent the last six weeks working on my studio. I painted each of the four walls a different color. I've been picking up props at flea markets and clearance sales. It's all really starting to come together. Aaron is supposed to help me hang blinds today. Sometimes I'll need the natural light and others I won't. I'm going to get him to help me setup my green screen bar and lights when he's here as well. What are brothers for if you can't use their muscles?

Stepping back, I survey the large room. It's better than I had hoped. I have my first shoot in two days.

I can't wait!

Not wanting to lose my momentum waiting on Aaron, I drag the ladder to the far wall, gather my hooks for props, and climb up. I want the hooks high enough so the kids won't be able to get to them. I know how little ones like to explore in new places. Raising my arms to hammer in the first nail, I feel the ladder wobble. The next thing I know, I'm falling backward. Nothing but hard wood floor waits for me below. I brace myself for impact. However, it's not the hard floor I collide with—-it's strong arms.

"I got you," a deep, husky voice whispers in my ear.

Evan.

He gently places my feet on the floor while holding onto my arms to make sure I have my balance. "Thanks," I mumble.

"You're welcome. Why didn't you wait for Aaron to do this?" he

asks.

"I'm on a roll. I have my first shoot in two days and I'm excited to get everything finalized." My brain finally registers he's here. "What are you doing here? Not that I don't appreciate your impeccable timing."

"Aaron's stuck in traffic coming home from the stockyard. He called and asked if I had time to run over and help you. I believe he said, 'Kinley is chomping at the bit to get this done.'"

"I'm excited," I defend.

He chuckles. "I can see that, but we can't have you getting hurt. Now, show me what needs to be done. We can get this place whipped into shape." He reaches down and picks the hook up off the floor.

"I was . . . um . . . hanging them for those," I point to the box of hats and scarfs I've acquired for props.

Evan nods and starts to climb the ladder. "Why so high?"

"I plan to do a lot of family and kids shoots. As a matter of fact, my first shoot is with twin boys for their first birthday. Little people like to explore in new places. I wanted the props out of the way of temptation for them. Besides, there will be less of a distraction and it will be easier for me to maintain their attention." I look up at him and all I see is his ass, front and center in all its glory. Let me just tell you, Evan Chamberlin can fill out a pair of worn Levi's. My mouth waters and I feel my face flush. Damn! I quickly look down to get myself under control.

"Can you hand me the next one?" Evan asks.

Shit!

Bending down, I pick up the other hook and attempt to hand it to him without looking. "Kinley," his deep voice rumbles my name.

I get lost in the sound and forget I'm hiding my blush, which only makes me blush harder. "You good?" he asks.

Am I good? *Um, hell yes I'm good. Turn back around and let me get back to ogling your fine ass.* "Yeah," I say instead. "Why aren't you working today?" I ask to get my mind off his ass.

"Misty had her four month check-up today."

"How did it go?"

"Good. She hasn't gained much weight. The doctor told her she needs to eat more. She measured okay, but the doctor is just worried about her getting enough calories."

"What did she say about it?"

"Hmph. Nothing as usual. I offered her money for clothes and stuff and she refused. Said she didn't need anything from me. She's starting to show. I placed my hand on her belly when I saw her." He climbs down the ladder. "It's still hard for me to grasp the fact my baby's in there, you know?"

Gah! Evan is one of the sweetest guys out there and hot as hell to boot! Misty is a damn fool. "Yeah, it really is a miracle when you think about it."

"I was thinking, if we can get this all squared away, maybe you would want to go shopping with me? I've only got five months and I need . . . well, everything."

"Absolutely! I'm happy to help you." I don't bother to hide my excitement. It's hard not to get excited about a new baby, no matter whose it is.

"Thank you." I can hear the relief in his voice. "I've read a few books and looked online, but I don't have the first clue as to what this kid is going to need."

"Well, we can start with the easy stuff. You're going to need a crib, dresser, changing table," I tick each item off one by one. "Do you have a rocking chair?"

His eyes are huge as he shakes his head no. "Add that to the list."

He motions to my hand where I have my fingers raised. Instead, I hold my hand out. "Let me see your phone." Evan reaches into the back pocket of those Levi's I was just drooling over and hands it over.

"Do you have a task list?" I ask, even though I'm already searching his phone. Finding what I need, I tap the icon and make a new list. I title it "Baby Chamberlin." This brings another question. "Have you decided? Do you want to know what you're having?"

"I don't have a strong feeling either way. I just want him or her to be healthy. I can't ask for much more than that."

His honest, heartfelt confession has me swooning. Misty's an idiot, plain and simple, no other way to describe her.

I tap away on the app, adding a checklist of items I know he's going to need. When I'm finished, there are at least twenty items shining bright

on the screen as I hand it back to him. I watch as he reads through the list and finally his eyes meet mine. "You said you would help me, right?"

"Yes, but I need my studio ready beforehand."

"Let's do this. What's next?" I instruct him on the blinds and he gets to work. I would love to say I work just as diligently right along beside him, but that would be lying. Instead, I make a halfhearted effort. I spend the rest of the time stealing glances at him. I think it's a rite of passage that all little sisters have a crush on their brother's best friend. Time has been good to Evan. He's going to make some girl one hell of a husband someday. This baby is lucky to have him.

Even with my slacking, Evan and I are able to finish all of the last-minute projects in the studio. "This place looks great," Evan says as he hangs the final blind.

"Thanks. I'm fortunate to have the space. I'm excited to get started, but I didn't want a studio in town. I don't want to have structured hours. I want to be able to plan shoots on location. Next week, I'm shooting an eight-year-old's birthday party. Her parents are buying her a horse and they want me to be there to capture it all." I stop my rambling to turn and look at Evan. He's watching me with rapt attention, a grin lighting his face. "That's what I love about photography, capturing life's moments. Studio work is great and necessary for some shoots, but I don't want that to be my main focus. I want to be able to be there to capture memories for my clients."

Evan is still watching me and I can feel my face heat with embarrassment. I just rambled on and he let me.

He takes a few steps forward, and suddenly, he's standing in front of me. I have to tilt my head back to look up at him. His chocolate eyes are boring into me as he lifts his hand as if he's going to touch me, but then drops it. "Will you do that for me? Help me capture memories for my baby. I'm going to be both mom and dad, and I don't want to forget to take pictures and videos while getting wrapped up in being both parents. I'm going to need you there to help me catch it all."

I know he's talking about me taking pictures, but from the intense look on his face, it feels like something more than that—something I can't describe and don't know if I really want to. Today has been filled with simple touches and looks. Obviously, I'm attracted to him. How could I not be?

Taking a step back, I nod. "Absolutely. I would love to take pictures for you." Taking another step back, the distance eases the thickness of the air between us. "Thanks for your help today." I offer him a smile.

"You're welcome. You feel like going to the store? I don't know that I'll buy anything today, but I would like to at least look. I've never even been in the baby section. I've bought all my books online."

"Sure. Let me run in and freshen up a little. Give me ten minutes?"

Evan nods, and I turn and rush down the stairs. I don't want to keep him waiting.

EVAN

cKinley sprints out the door like her ass is on fire. Why wouldn't she? I don't know what the hell came over me? She's fucking gorgeous, but she's Aaron's little sister. Not to mention, I'm about to be a single father. She doesn't need my drama. I'm just grateful she's helping me out. I'm overwhelmed by all this.

I can't fuck that up.

Surveying the small studio, I can see her here. She's put a lot of effort into it to make it her own. After listening to her talk about photography with fire and passion in her eyes, I wanted to make sure she did that for me, captured my baby's moments. I won't deny there was an undertone to my request, something I have no business feeling or even wanting.

I lock up and decide to wait for her in my truck. As I hit the bottom step, I see her come bouncing out of the house. She's always been that way, full of life, taking each day as it comes. I used to chalk it up to her being young, but she's still that same girl. Only she's not a girl, she's all woman now.

"Ready?" she asks as she pulls open the passenger door. Her enthusiasm is contagious and I can't help but smile.

"So, where should we go?" I ask her.

"There's a Babies"R"Us in town. Let's go there first," she suggests.

"Sounds as good a place to start as any."

"So . . . have you thought about the possibility of getting rid of this old thing?" she asks as she pats her hand affectionately on the dashboard.

"What? What's wrong with my truck? This baby has been with me from day one."

Laughter escapes her lips. "Yes, I'm well aware. You and Aaron are both attached to your trucks. However, you are going to be hauling precious cargo in just a few months. It's safer for babies to be in the backseat."

Shit! I let her words sink in. "Okay, so it looks like I have something to add to the list." I hand her my phone.

"Don't look so sad," she teases, handing the phone back to me.

"It's not sadness as much as . . . apprehension. I'm doing this on my own, Kinley. That's not how I imagined this would play out."

"Maybe not, but this is your reality, Evan. Life is messy and unplanned. Very rarely do things work out exactly as we wanted them to."

"I know that. Trust me, I do, but I feel like I'm spinning out of control here. I have no idea how to take care of a baby. Gran and Gramps are not in good health. Dad is . . . not well. Besides, he and Mom need to stay in Alabama to be near his doctors. I'm fucking scared to death I can't do this." The words leave me in a rush. I feel ashamed for admitting it out loud, but it is what it is.

Reaching over, she places her hand on my arm. "Evan, from the minute you found out Misty was pregnant, you wanted this baby, right?"

With a quick glance at her, then moving my eyes back on the road, I answer, "Yes."

"That's all you need to remember. This baby is a part of you. You will love him or her unconditionally and do your best. Do you think our parents had it all figured out? Not hardly. You take each day as it comes. You face the challenges life throws at you. You make sure your child knows how much you love them. Everything else will fall into place."

"I hope you're right," I mumble the words. The rest of the drive is spent in silence. It's not awkward or uncomfortable. McKinley gives me the space I need to process what she said. Space to work through this fear I have of ruining my kid's life.

I pull into the parking lot of Babies"R"Us and kill the engine. It's full of SUV's and minivans. I can't see myself driving a minivan.

"What's wrong?"

I point to the silver van parked in front of us. "I don't think I'm a minivan dad."

Kinley throws her head back and laughs. "Of course not. You'll be the cool dad with a big four-door truck. That's the most practical for your job, you know." She winks at me and my jeans tighten just a little. Just enough that I know my body responds to her; to remind me she's Aaron's little sister and only here to help me; to bring back that my kid's mother wants nothing to do with either of us.

"Let's go, old man. We have some shopping to do."

Kinley hops out of the truck and waits for me by the tailgate. I slowly climb out and join her. Linking her arm through mine, she guides me into the store. Once inside, she stops to get a cart. "Just in case we find any deals." She grins and again I find myself under her spell.

Kinley pushes the cart, glancing up and down the aisles. I walk beside her, taking it all in. She leads us to the back of the store where a huge sign reading "Furniture" hangs from the ceiling.

"Okay, so you will need to decide what color furniture you want. I would suggest going with the color of the trim in your house. Make it all match."

"Yeah, that sounds about right," I say, pulling off my hat and running my fingers through my hair.

"There are several designs. I guess you should also decide how you're going to decorate the room."

"Umm. . . ." Decorate the room? Shit! I'm in way over my head. Kinley must notice because the look on her face is one of understanding.

"Yeah, usually there is a theme, you know—cars, planes, movie characters, things like that. Unless you go completely unisex, you should probably wait to find out what you're having before making any big decisions," she rambles on.

"Yeah, we, uh, we can find out at her next appointment. She doesn't care either way, and at first, I was on the fence. But seeing all this, I think knowing could only help me prepare better." I decide.

"I agree." A woman with a baby on her hip and too many items in her arms walks by. "Ma'am, would you like this cart? We're just looking," Kinley offers.

"Yes! Thank you. I came in for a few things . . ." She shrugs her shoulders. "You know how that goes."

"Always." Kinley offers her a kind smile and proceeds to take the items from the woman's arms, placing them in the cart.

"Thank you again." The woman waves and pushes the cart on down the aisle.

"That was nice of you."

"Yeah, she looked like she could use it more than us. Let's go check out the clothes." McKinley again links her arms through mine and pulls me to the other side of the store. She rattles on about onesies, sleepers, diapers, bottles, and a million other things that have my head spinning.

I swallow hard. "Babies need a lot of stuff."

Hearing the desperation in my voice, she stops and turns to look at me. "Yeah, but you'll have a shower. It's a little unconventional with mom not being in the picture, so maybe we should plan it for after the baby's born. Maybe a welcome home so everyone can meet the baby?"

"Nope, too many germs."

Kinley laughs. "Already sounding like a dad," she chides. "Well, I'll take care of that. I'll enlist Mom's help."

"Yeah," I say. My mind is racing; I'm overwhelmed.

"I think I've scared you enough for one day. Let's go get some food, I'm starving."

I let her lead me back out to the truck, my thoughts on everything that lies ahead in the coming months. "What sounds good?" I ask her, forcing myself out of my own head.

"I'm easy. We can just pick up a pizza if you want. I'm sure Aaron will be home by the time we get back."

I nod in agreement. Kinley pulls out her phone and orders pizza. She surprises me when she tells them to just deliver to her house. I can feel myself relax a little. Their house was my second home growing up. Aaron has been my closest friend for as long as I can remember. Their parents are my second family. With my own parents living so far away, being with them is exactly what I need.

McKinley
8

*S*itting at the kitchen table working on edits is how I've spent my day. Over the last month, I've done at least two shoots per week, which is more than I could have hoped for just starting out. They have all been referrals. Word of mouth really is the best advertisement.

"How's it going?" Mom asks as she carries in a load of laundry that was hanging out on the line. She loves the smell of fresh air-dried laundry. I have to admit I do too, which is something else I didn't even realize I'd missed until I was away at school.

"Good. Little Robbie is such a cutie. He was fun to shoot." My session earlier this week was a two-year-old. It was his birthday pictures and he was such a ham. I love photography. I only hope it never begins to feel like a job. I hope it continues to stay fun. Not many people I know can claim they have fun at work, but I can.

Mom sets the basket on the other side of the table and walks over to where I'm sitting. "Oh my. He is a handsome little devil. Look at that smirk," she laughs.

"Yeah, his parents are going to have their hands full with this one. He's already got game," I joke.

Before she can reply, Aaron comes barreling through the door. "Hey," he greets us with a smile.

"What's got you in such a good mood?" I ask him.

"Evan just called and we're going out tonight."

"Oookay, and why does that turn you into chipper 'smile so big my face could crack' Aaron?"

He ruffles the hair on top of my head. "Well, apparently Misty showed up for today's appointment after missing the one on Monday. He was able to find out the sex of the baby," he explains.

"Yay! Tell me," I demand. It's been killing us all for weeks. Not knowing is just too stressful.

"Don't know." He shrugs. "He said I had to meet him tonight at Mike's Tavern and he'll tell me then."

He turns to head for the stairs. "I can't wait that long. I need to shop," I call after him.

Stopping, he looks over his shoulder. "I'm leaving in twenty. Be ready," he says.

I glance at the time on my laptop. I've been at this all day. I could use a break. Luckily, I just need to change and add some lip gloss. My hair is in a side braid today and that is a more than appropriate style for Mike's Tavern. Saving my work, I shut down my laptop and sprint to my room. I change out my yoga pants into jean shorts and a flowing tank. Grabbing a pair of socks, I rush back downstairs. My cowboy or as I like to call them, cowgirl boots, are by the door where I left them. Just as I slide them on, Aaron's heavy footsteps get closer.

"Ready?" he asks, pulling his shirt over his head. His hair is still wet, but he'll still manage to make the girls swoon. Men, they don't know how good they have it. Lucky for me, I'm not going in the hopes of picking up a male companion. I just want to see Evan's face when he tells us what he's having. I just need to know since it's essential to my future shopping expeditions.

I follow Aaron out the door and hear Mom yell, "Be safe you two, and have fun." I can hear the laughter in her voice. Being two years apart, Aaron and I have a close relationship. Don't get me wrong, I annoyed the hell out of him and Evan when I was younger. I followed them everywhere, but when push came to shove, my big bro was always there for me. As we became older, he didn't seem to mind so much. That is unless his friends were hitting on me. Mike, the owner of Mike's Tavern, has tried many times. Aaron and Evan both made it known I was off limits. It's not that Aaron didn't want me to date; he just didn't want me to date his friends. Guys talk, and he didn't want to hear or see anything that had to do with me, his little sister, in "that kind" of a relationship. At least that was the excuse he gave me. Obviously, Evan, being his best friend, backed him up in all things.

Mike's a good looking guy. My teenage-self was interested but knew better than to push Aaron when he meant business. All he would have had to do was say the word and Dad would have shut it down anyway. Those two had some type of agreement. If Aaron approved, all was good in my world. If not, there was no use in me even attempting to date the guy. He would have Dad using his veto power. I could have rebelled, but didn't. I love them both and know Aaron was just looking out for me. To be honest, he probably saved me from a lot of heartache.

Within minutes, we are piled into his new truck and on our way. "So, I know why I'm excited to find out, but I didn't expect you to be," I say.

Aaron throws a hand over his chest, as if he clutching his heart. "Sister, you wound me. Of course I'm excited my best friend is going to be a dad," he replies.

"You've just never been one who's been much on kids."

"Well, I've not really been around many. It's not that I don't like kids, but guys are different than girls. You want to cuddle, hold, and kiss on them no matter whose kid it is. Me, I'm going to be Uncle Aaron to this kid. Of course I'm excited. I'll be the same way when you have kids."

"And what about you?" He's never mentioned really wanting kids before. I know he's waiting for "the one." He's been vocal about that. At first, I used to think it was just a cop-out to keep from getting serious with anyone, but over the years, he's convinced me to his way of thinking.

"Yeah, I mean, it's not like I'm itching for them or anything, but when the time is right."

"You know, what happened to Evan could happen to anyone. Not many would handle it the way he has." It's true. Evan has fought for his unborn child since the minute he found about him or her. Gah! I can't wait to find out what he's having. This "him or her" stuff is for the birds. Evan took to calling the baby peanut, but it seems odd for me to use the nickname and I hate when people say it. It's is a baby, people!

"You're right, it could. I don't know that there are many guys out there who would have fought as hard as he did."

"Would you?" I ask him.

I watch him as he furrows his brow. He's really considering my blunt question. "I would like to think so, yes," he finally says. "It's hard to put yourself in someone else's shoes though. Walk a thousand miles and all that jazz."

Just like that, we're in the parking lot of Mike's. My excitement simmers back to the surface; that is until Aaron turns the questioning on me.

"What about you? What if you were in Misty's shoes?" he asks.

"Never!" I say with conviction. "Never would I ever give my baby up. It might be a hard struggle if the dad didn't want to be in the picture, or my family for that matter. Not that you all would ever turn your back on me; but I can tell you with complete certainty that I would never make the choices she has. I don't know many women who would." I end the conversation by climbing out of the truck.

I stop at the front door and wait for Aaron. As soon as he reaches me, he throws his arm over my shoulder and pulls me close. "You're good people, McKinley Rae."

I can't help but chuckle as I elbow him. "Right back at ya, big brother."

EVAN

After I told my grandparents, I called my parents to give them the news. Today has been . . . life-altering. I've known Misty was pregnant for a while now, and I've seen the slight swell of her belly with my baby. However, today was an experience I will never forget as long as I live. I've heard women—my mom, both of my grandma's—talk about ultrasounds and everyone always seemed to be so excited about them. As a guy, I never really paid much attention. It didn't affect me, so why would I?

I don't have words for the onset of emotions that flooded me the minute my baby appeared on that screen. Misty kept her eyes closed and earbuds in her ears. She literally wants nothing to do with this. I still struggle with that, especially after today. Ten fingers, ten toes, and a strong heartbeat. The tech assured me the baby is healthy. Still measuring a little small, but Misty has not gained a lot of weight either. The doctor counseled her once again about eating more since she's eating for two. It took extreme effort to bite my tongue and not lash out at her. She missed her appointment this week. Took me two days to get her to call me back and get the appointment rescheduled. She doesn't look strung out, just too thin. I handed her some money today after the appointment. She tried to argue that she didn't need anything from me, but I made her take it. I meant it when I said I wanted to take care of whatever she needs.

Aaron was my next call. However, I didn't tell him. Instead, I told him he had to meet me here for a drink. It's been a long week and I could use a little downtime with my boy. Not to mention that even

though I'm ecstatic to have seen my baby, I can't help but feel like I'm missing out on something. I should be sharing this night with my significant other, you know, the one I don't have. That thought alone causes panic to build inside me. I want my baby, but I have no fucking clue what I'm getting myself into. Live and learn, they say.

I choose a booth at the back of the bar. I don't feel like fielding questions about Misty and me, or the baby for that matter. I want to kick back with my oldest friend and celebrate. I'm startled out of my thoughts when Aaron slides into the booth across from me. He's wearing a huge-ass grin. *My brother.*

"Gah! Tell me now!" I hear that sweet southern voice that can only belong to one person. *McKinley Mills.*

She slides into the booth next to me, watching me, waiting. "Evan! You're killing me here." She leans her shoulder into mine.

She and I have spent some time together since she's been home from college. She's always been a part of my life, but just recently I have learned to value her friendship as much as I do her brother's.

"Hey now, I might just make you wait until I finish this beer." I grin.

McKinley looks at the bottle sitting in front of me and smirks. Reaching over, she grabs the bottle, bringing it to her lips. I watch in fascination as she tilts her head back and drains it. Running the back of her hand over her lips, she places the bottle back in front of me. An ornery-ass grin lights up her face. "Now, spill it, Chamberlin," she demands.

Aaron throws his head back in laughter, which gives me a few seconds to adjust myself. Kinley is beautiful and her little demonstration, her lips around my bottle of beer, has my mind and cock thinking about her in ways I shouldn't.

"You win." I reach over and grab the little brown paper bag that neither one of them have noticed. She grabs it from my hands and quickly opens it, pulling out two pink cigars.

"A girl!" she shrieks and throws her arms around me. We're in the booth and it's awkward, but I return her embrace the best I can. Her response lifts my spirits.

"Hell yeah! Congrats, man. You know all her dates are going to have to meet Uncle Aaron first," Aaron jokes.

"What the hell? She's not dating until she's thirty," I laugh.

"You can't keep her locked away in some tower," Kinley argues.

"The hell I can't," Aaron and I say at the same time.

Kinley just rolls those pretty brown eyes of hers, the smile never falling from her lips.

I feel some of the stress of the week fade away. I know without a doubt that these two will be with my little girl and me every step of the way.

"McKinley, is that you?" Mike, the owner of this place and a longtime friend of mine, says as he steps up to the booth.

"Hey!" Kinley removes her arm from around my shoulder and climbs out of the booth to give him a hug.

"When did you get back in town?" he asks as his eyes devour her. I want to be pissed, but I find myself doing the same thing. She's wearing a tank top that makes her tits look incredible, a pair of short blue jean shorts, and a pair of cowboy boots. Fuck me. I knew looking was a bad idea, but I did it anyway.

Focusing my attention on Mike, I ask, "Hey, can you get us all another round?" I lift my beer bottle and give it a little shake.

"Sure, man." He points to the small stage across the room. "Live band tonight. Kinley, you need to save a dance for me." He winks at her and walks away.

I look over at Aaron and he's watching me. "You see that guy?" I ask.

"Hmm," is all he says.

Kinley takes her seat next to me in the booth. "So, now that we know you're having a little girl, we can get started on the room. That is if you still want my help."

"Definitely. I have no idea where to start," I confess.

"Well, we looked at furniture, so now you just need to decide which set you want. Are you thinking girly-girl room, or are you going to make her into a tomboy?" she laughs.

I think about her question. Fuck me, I'm at a loss here. "Honestly, I just want her happy and healthy. If she wants to be a tomboy I'm good with it. If she wants all the girly frilly stuff, I'm good with that too." I'm way out of my element.

"Awe, you got this dad stuff down already," she says.

"Tell you what. Why don't you decorate the room or nursery or whatever it's called. I'm good with whatever you decide. We can go shopping, or better yet, I can give you my credit card and you can have it delivered to the house."

"Seriously? I can do whatever I want?" she verifies.

"Yes. I trust you and I have no idea where to start. You would be doing me a favor. The only thing I want to pick out is the rocking chair. From what I've read, I'm going to be spending many nights in that thing and I want it to be comfortable."

"Done. When can I start?"

Reaching into my back pocket, I pull out my credit card and hand it to her. "Whenever you want."

"Fuck, man, you do realize you just gave my sister your credit card? She loves to shop," Aaron questions my sanity.

"Yes. I'm counting on that. Misty's at the halfway point. Twenty weeks. Five Months until my daughter arrives into the world. I have a ton to do and I trust Kinley to help me."

She sticks her tongue out at Aaron. "See, he trusts me," she says, sliding my credit card into her purse.

"Uh-huh," Aaron says.

A waitress brings our drinks and conversation of my daughter fades as Aaron and I catch Kinley up on who's with who in our home town.

I'm nursing my second beer when I hear a loud squeal. This causes the three of us to turn our heads. Kinley's best friend from high school, Olivia, who also happens to be Mike's little sister, is practically sprinting toward us. Kinley squeals almost as loud and jumps up, meeting her halfway.

"Gah! I missed you so much." She hugs her friend tight. "Why didn't you tell me you were back in town?" Kinley asks once they reach the booth. Olivia slides in next to Aaron and places a quick kiss on his cheek. She always did have a thing for him. Aaron seems to be unaffected.

"I just got in yesterday," Olivia explains. "I was going to call you tonight, but I wanted to stop by and check on my big brother. He's done well with this place."

"He really has," Kinley agrees.

Mike joins us and sets four bottles of beer on the table. "Livvy, I didn't know you were stopping by."

"Mom and Dad were hovering. So, I decided to come check the place out. You did good, big brother."

The band takes the stage and Olivia jumps from the booth. "Let's get our groove on," she says, holding her hand out for Kinley.

Kinley stands and my eyes follow her. Those short-ass shorts, long tanned legs, and cowboy boots are fucking sexy as hell.

Southern pleasure.

"You can say that again," Mike says.

His voice brings me out of my Kinley trance and I tear my eyes from her. Mike is now sitting beside me. "What?" I ask him.

"I agree, she's full-on fucking southern pleasure."

Fucking Mike! Looking across the booth, I see Aaron's not there. No wonder he's not out of his seat kicking both of our asses. My eyes scan the crowd and I catch the back of him as he walks into the bathroom.

Turning to face Mike, I see his eyes are glued to the dance floor. From the look on his face, I know it's not his little sister he's watching. My protective instincts kick in, only this time it feels different.

"Not fucking happening," I growl.

Mike slowly tears his eyes from her and faces me. The smirk on his face makes me want to hit him like a donkey kicking a barn door.

"She's a big girl, Chamberlin. She already has one big brother, she doesn't need another."

My hands, which are resting on the table, tighten into fists. I've always considered Mike a friend, but now, I just—

"Besides, aren't you the one who dubbed her southern pleasure?" he goads me.

We're sitting on the same side of the booth, which makes my next move easy enough. I grab hold of his shirt collar and bring his face mere inches from mine. "Not fucking happening," I repeat my earlier threat. "Stay the fuck away from her." I release his shirt with a shove, and his body jerks back.

"Hey, is this one mine?" Kinley's sweet voice washes over me. I'm still wound tight, my eyes never leaving Mike's.

I watch a slow smile creep across his face. "Sure is, darlin.' Don't forget you promised me a dance." He winks at her.

I clench my jaw tight to keep from making a scene.

"Yeah, I'll have to take a rain check. I have an early shoot in the morning. This is my last one." She raises her beer as she turns to face me. "Evan, do you think you could take me home? Aaron said he was going to stay for a while longer." She points over her shoulder. I see Aaron and a blonde getting friendly out on the dance floor.

"I can take you home," Mike offers.

"Uh, thanks, Mike, but Evan is going my way." She gives him a polite smile, but it's not her smile, the one that lights up her face—the smile I've come to enjoy seeing on her over the past several weeks.

Digging my wallet out of my back pocket, I throw a few bills down on the table and push on Mike's arm. Reluctantly, he stands and allows me to slide out of the booth.

I place my hand on the small of her back. Kinley leans in to give Olivia a quick hug, then turns to smile up at me.

My smile.

"Let's get you home," I say, bending down next to her ear. She nods and, with my hand guiding her, we head out to my truck.

McKinley
10

*T*his past month has been crazy. I've been busy with sessions in my studio. Business is great; I couldn't be happier. I've been shopping non-stop for the perfect room for baby girl Chamberlin. Evan says he doesn't know what he's going to name her yet. I want this little girl to have a room that dreams are made of. Even though Evan has to play mom and dad, I want to help him—-we all do. I want to make sure this little girl knows she's loved, because she is.

Evan is family, so sometimes when I think of him as something other than that, I feel guilty. I try; I really do. I try hard not to notice how amazing his body is. I try hard not to fantasize about tracing those six-pack abs with my tongue. I find myself failing in my attempts more often than not.

It's hard to prevent it when we spend so much time together. Today is a perfect example. I'm going over to his place in a few hours to start painting. I picked up the paint and all the supplies yesterday. I've been giving his credit card a workout. I've been finding bargains to save him some money, but he needs everything!

"Morning," Mom says as I walk into the kitchen.

"Morning. Something smells good."

"Waffles. You just missed your dad and Aaron. They're helping Evan with some branding today," she tells me.

Although both my father and Aaron, as well as Evan, raise and breed thoroughbred horses, they also have cattle. Branding is time consuming.

It's an all hands on deck kind of job. Evan has a small crew who works for him, but with his grandfather unable to help, my dad and Aaron have been lending him a hand the last couple of years. He does the same for them.

"Evan mentioned that last night. He called to tell me where he was going to leave the key. I'm going over after my morning session to start painting the nursery."

"You know I've been meaning to ask you. Your Dad and I want to get him something special. I know he will refuse a shower, although he shouldn't," Mom says.

"Yeah, that's a pride thing, I think. Men just don't get that a shower is all a part of having a baby. Of course, in his defense, if the baby mamma was involved, she would gladly accept a shower. He's so out of his element."

"He's been a trooper though. He really wants to do right by this baby," Mom adds.

"Yes, he does. He's a great guy."

"Hmm."

"What hmm?" I ask her.

"Nothing. So do you have any ideas of what we can get him?"

"The furniture is bought, all except for the rocking chair, but he wants to get that himself. Really clothes, bottles, everything," I laugh.

"I so wish he would let us have a shower. I was talking to Ethel at church on Sunday and she's worried about him."

"Why don't you all throw a 'grandparents' shower? It's a way around it. I know the ladies at church would understand the meaning of what you are doing. You all can shower Ethel with gifts for her new great-granddaughter."

"McKinley Rae, that's perfect! You, my daughter, are one smart cookie."

"Oh, go on," I tease her. This causes her to laugh. I love my parents; they've been there for me and Aaron every step of the way. We're lucky to have them.

"Thanks for breakfast. I have to get to the studio. My session is supposed to be here in twenty minutes." I give her a kiss on the cheek and rush out the door. I have to walk only a hundred feet to get to my studio, but I want to get the lights on and my camera set up. I guess some of Aaron's 'I don't want to be late for anything' attitude has rubbed off on me over the years.

I'm just setting up my camera when my phone alerts me to a text.

Evan: I put the spare key where we talked about. I also told Gram and Gramps you would be there. Make yourself at home.

Me: Thanks! I can't wait to get started.

Evan: I feel guilty that I won't be there to help.

Me: I got this, Chamberlin.

Evan: LOL. Okay, just be careful. No ladder's until I get there.

Me: Yeah, yeah. Don't you have cattle to brand?

Evan: On it.

Just as I'm slipping my phone back into my pocket, it rings. Glancing at the caller ID, I see it's my morning client. "Hello."

"Kinley, hi, it's Beth. Thomas woke up with a fever today, so I'm going to have to cancel our session. I'm so sorry to do this on such short notice. I got busy with calling the doctor and forgot all about it."

"Beth, it's fine. No worries. I hope Thomas feels better. Just give me a call and we can reschedule."

"Thank you so much."

I end the call and pack my camera back into the bag. Shutting down the lights, I head back to the house. Looks like I will get to start painting sooner than I thought.

In the house, I find Mom on the phone. She raises her eyebrows in question. "Session cancelled," I whisper. She nods and holds up a finger, asking me to wait.

I grab a bottle of water from the fridge and take a seat across from her at the table.

"Great, Kinley just walked in. I'll run this past her and let you know," Mom says before hanging up. "What happened?"

"Beth called and Thomas is sick. She's going to reschedule. I was just coming in to change into some old clothes before heading over to

Evan's to start painting."

"I was just talking to Mabel from church. She agrees that having a shower for Ethel is a great idea. She's starting the phone tree as we speak. We are going to plan it for a month from now after church one Sunday."

"That's a great idea! It will be good for Ethel to get out of the house and Evan can use the support for sure."

"It's all in the works. Do you need any help painting?" she asks.

"I think I'm good. Evan has the room cleared out. So I just need to lay down the tarp and tape off the trim. That will take some time. He already texted me and said I had to wait for him to edge it in."

"He's protective."

"He's been around Aaron too long when it comes to me," I reply.

"If you say so. Since you don't need any help, I think I'll head into town and look for some decorations for the shower."

"Sounds good. I'll see you later." I rush off to my room to change. I can't wait to get started on this room.

EVAN

*T*welve hours. It took us twelve hours to work through the new herd. Aaron and his dad were lifesavers. They helped instruct the crew as to what to do. No way could this have gotten done in one day without them. I'm glad to have it done, but disappointed I missed Kinley. She started on the nursery today and I was looking forward to spending time with her, but I refuse to think about what that means.

Unlocking the door, I see the glow of a light upstairs. Kinley must have forgotten to turn it off. Even though I'm dead on my feet, I rush up the stairs to see how much she got done. Sure enough, the light to the nursery is on and I'm shocked to see it's done. The walls are painted in a color that Kinley informed me is a medium lavender. To me, it just looks like a light purple.

The room looks as if a professional came in and did it. The tarp that I laid down for her is gone as are all of the painting supplies. Hard-headed as ever, it's obvious she ignored my 'wait for me for the ladder' warning I gave her. I swallow back the lump in my throat.

This is real.

In just four short months, my baby girl is going to be here. I will never be able to thank Kinley enough for everything she's done. Pulling out my phone, I swipe the screen and see it's just after nine. I helped the crew feed and water all the horses before heading home. Surely, she's still up. I decide to send her a text first.

Evan: You up?

I hear a beep of a cell phone. Did she leave her phone here? I follow the sound across the hall to my room. Opening the door, I allow the light from the nursery to light the room. That's when I see her. Kinley is curled up on my bed, phone clutched in her hands. Surveying the room, I see a floral-looking bag sitting on the floor. My eyes roam over her and I see her hair is damp. She must have brought clothes to change into. McKinley was wet and naked in my shower, in my room.

Fuck me.

Even as tired as I am, my body responds to just the thought of her wet and naked. Moving further into the room, I slowly take a seat on the edge of the bed, careful not to wake her. There's no one here to witness me lusting after my best friend's little sister, my friend. She's been a pillar of strength for me these past couple of months. I honestly don't know what I would do without her.

Her phone beeps again, reminding me of the text I sent her. I freeze, waiting to see if the sound wakes her.

It doesn't.

A loose strand of hair is hanging down in her eyes. Ever so gently, I tuck it back behind her ear. It doesn't wake her up and I'm relieved I get her like this for just a little while longer. I know I should wake her up and sitting here memorizing what she looks like in the moment, curled up in my bed, is wrong. I just can't seem to find the will to care.

Her phone dings again, and this time she stirs, causing that errant strand of hair I'd just moved to once again obstruct my view. Just as my hand goes to move it, her eyes slowly open. She recognizes me right away, and a soft smile graces her lips. "Hey," she says, her voice laced with sleep.

My hand has a mind of its own as I find myself cupping her cheek. "Hey, you wore yourself out today." It's not a question. She did a hell of a lot of work today for my daughter and me.

Her eyes light at my words. "Did you see it?" she asks.

"I did. It's perfect." *You're perfect.*

"It turned out better than I expected," she confesses.

My hand is still cupping her cheek and I know it's all kinds of wrong. I run my thumb across her cheek and reluctantly release my hold on her. I can't bring her into all this drama. She deserves nothing but the best, more than what I could give her. Not to mention, I'm sure my best friend would kick my ass if I tried to date his sister. I just need to learn to control my hormones when I'm alone with her.

"I'm glad you went with white furniture."

Sitting up, she leans against the headboard. "Yeah, with the white trim and the color of the walls, it's really going to stand out. I can't wait until you get it all put together."

I groan at the thought. "I'll start on it this weekend." I know she's itching to decorate now that the painting is done.

"Good. I'll tell Aaron he has to come help. Between the three of us, we should be able to whip it out in no time."

"You've done enough," I tell her.

"This is my project, mister. No way am I missing it."

"What time did you finish?"

Blinking, she looks down at her phone. "About an hour ago. Sorry I dozed off." I can barely see the tint of red coloring her face from the small amount of light in the room.

"Have you eaten?" My guess is she worked all day to get the room completed.

Her belly growls, not giving her time to answer. "All right then. Let me grab a quick shower and we can go grab something to eat." I stand from the bed.

"Deal." Her grin turns into a yawn as she stretches her arms above her head. The t-shirt she's wearing lifts and shows her toned stomach. I force my eyes to close and turn away from her. I busy myself with pulling clean clothes out of my dresser.

"I'll be quick."

"Good, I'm starving. I'm going to go check out my mad painting skills. I'll wait downstairs."

I hear her climb off the bed, her feet hit the floor, and the click of my bedroom door as she closes it behind her. I exhale a breath I didn't even realize I was holding.

I've got to get my shit together.

I rush through my shower and meet Kinley downstairs in less than fifteen minutes. "What are you in the mood for?" I ask, shoving my

wallet and my phone in my pocket.

"I'm open to anything; just nothing that's going to take forever."

"I think I can manage that."

The drive into town is filled with talk of furniture assembly and decorating ideas. The pressure I feel when I think about all that needs to be done before my daughter arrives lessens the more Kinley talks. She's willing to take the lead and I'm letting her. I want to be involved, but shit, I'm in over my head. I'm scared to death for my kid.

We find ourselves at Subway. "Great choice," Kinley says as she takes the first big bite of her meatball sub. She's refreshing. She's never afraid to speak her mind or be herself. Most girls order a salad and pick at it. I don't know if it's because I've known her all my life, or if it's because she's really just that girl—confident and sure. I'm going to go with the latter.

"So, I'm thinking about going to visit my parents and grandparents before the baby comes."

"That's a great idea. I'm sure you miss them. How's your dad doing?"

Misty never once asked how my father was. I never realized how disconnected we really were, until now. "Same. Mom says he started a new chemo. So far, he seems to be adjusting to it well."

"When were you thinking of going to see them?"

"In a few weeks. I have a lot to do before the baby gets here, but I need to see them, you know?"

"You should go. Family is important," she says.

"Yeah. I think I'll fly. It will give me more time with them. I don't see them coming back here any time soon. Dad really likes his oncologist."

"I'm sure it's hard to be away from them, especially with all the changes going on in your life."

I nod. She gets it—-gets me. She's so easy to talk to. I've never been one to open up, unless it was to Aaron. There's nothing he doesn't know about me. Well, there is one thing. If he knew the thoughts I'm having about his baby sister, he would kick my ass.

The flight to Alabama is uneventful. I spent the entire time running through everything that still needs to be done. I'm trying really hard not to freak the fuck out that in just a little over three months I'm going to be a daddy. I'm going to be responsible for a tiny human and all her needs. I'm a little overwhelmed.

I traveled light with just a carry-on, so I can avoid the whole baggage claim fiasco. I'm searching the crowd for my mom. She insisted she pick me up. I hear her before I see her.

"Evan!" She's already in a sprint toward me, so I stop and drop my bag to the floor, preparing for impact. When she reaches me, I wrap my arms around her and pick her up in a tight hug. "I've missed you."

"Missed you too," I say, placing her back on her feet. "How's Dad today?"

"He's feeling good. This new chemo doesn't make him as sick," she explains. "Let's get you home."

I nod my agreement and pick my bag back up. Throwing my arm over her shoulder, we leave the airport.

"How are Grandma and Grandpa?" I ask once we are on the road.

"Good, it's hard living back home with my parents after all these years." She laughs. "It's like it doesn't matter that I'm forty-eight years old, married with a child of my own. I go right back to feeling like a teenager again."

"Grandma always was a caretaker," I agree.

"Yeah, she fusses over your dad constantly and some days it drives him crazy. He just wants to be left alone. We've thought of buying a house or renting an apartment, but it just seems crazy when it's just the two of them in that big old house. Not to mention, it's nice to have the help, especially on the bad days."

We don't really talk about the "bad days." I know they are there, but they try and shelter me from it as much as possible. Like my Grandma, Mom often forgets I'm an adult she can lean on for support. Hell, I'm about to be a dad.

Mom and I spend the rest of the drive just catching up. Before I know it, we're pulling into the driveway. The first thing I see is my dad and my mom's parents sitting on the front porch waiting for us. Until this moment, I didn't realize how much I've missed them.

"Evan," my dad says as I clear the final porch step. He slowly rises

from the rocker he's sitting in and walks toward me. Reaching me, he pulls me into a hug. I notice his hold is not as tight as it used to be. He's losing his strength. I feel guilty for not coming with them to help Mom take care of things——take care of him.

"Jeff, you need to share," I hear my grandma say beside us. Dad releases me with a chuckle that quickly turns to a cough.

Grandma pulls me into a hug, with Grandpa reaching out to shake my hand. "We missed you," Grandma says.

"Congratulations, Evan," my grandpa says. He's always been a straight shooter. He's the first one to mention I'm going to be a father. I was shocked Mom didn't bring it up on the way here.

"Thank you."

"Well, I have lunch ready. Let's head inside," Grandma instructs.

Everyone heads into the kitchen. I drop my bag by the door and dig out the ultrasound pictures. Taking the empty seat across from my parents, I reach over and hand them to my mom. I watch as a slow smile forms and tears well up in her eyes.

"I can't believe I'm going to be a grandma," she says, never taking her eyes off the pictures.

I think the staff at Misty's OB office feels sorry for me. They printed out almost twenty pictures. I have one on my fridge at home. Kinley is actually the one who put it there. She, Aaron, and I were working on assembling all the furniture for the baby's room. Kinley stopped to make us a late lunch. When she called us to the kitchen, I noticed it was hanging there. I remember I pointed to it and she shrugged her shoulders, and said, "I just thought she should be here with us." I'm glad Aaron was there. If he hadn't been, I would have grabbed her and kissed the hell out of her.

"Do you have a name?" Grandma asks, pulling me out of my thoughts.

"No, not yet. I just . . . It's a big deal."

Dad laughs. "Yeah, I remember it took us seeing you before we actually decided on a name."

Mom reaches over and lays her hand on top of his. "You just looked like an Evan to us," she laughs.

I wish I had that. I wish I had a partner to stand by my side. I only have myself to blame.

"Yeah, I haven't thought about it too much. I've been busy getting everything I'll need. McKinley has been a huge help. I gave her my credit card and told her to have at it. It's overwhelming, everything a baby needs," I confess. I dig my cell phone out of my pocket and pull up my photo gallery. I bring up the recent pictures I took of the nursery after we got all the furniture assembled.

"Here's the room. Kinley's done most of it. She painted it all while I was branding cattle. She also picked out the furniture and helped Aaron and me put it all together last weekend."

Mom and Grandma talk about how pretty it is and how the white furniture really stands out with the color of the walls. All the same things Kinley had said.

"She's done a great job. I love the room," Mom says, handing my phone back to me.

"She really has. I don't know what I would do without her."

"How are they, McKinley and Aaron?" she asks.

"Good. Aaron and Jerry are still partners, although Jerry keeps saying he's ready to retire and work for Aaron," I laugh.

"I'm sure he is," Dad says. "It's hard work."

"And McKinley?" Mom prompts.

"She's great. She graduated a few months ago, so she's living at home, which I think I told you. Jerry and Sarah gave her the space above the garage and she's turned it into a studio for her photography. You should see some of her pictures. She's really good. She's been great about helping me shop and set the baby's room up. She made me a list of everything I still need to do and has even convinced me I need a new truck." I stop talking when I realize I've been gushing about her.

Looking around at my family, I see my praise didn't go unnoticed. Dad and Grandpa are smirking at me; Mom and Grandma are wearing grins that could light up the state of Alabama.

"I'm glad she's been such a help," Mom says.

I nod. "She really has." I dig into my food, hoping to end this part of the conversation.

The last five days have flown by. I've enjoyed spending time with my parents and grandparents. I don't get to see them nearly enough. Dad, Grandpa, and I went fishing. It was great to spend that time with them. I could tell it wore Dad out, but he insisted we go.

Grandma and Mom purchased the largest suitcase I've ever seen and filled it to the point of bursting at the seams with baby items. Grandma made her a quilt, while Mom went crazy with dresses and what she called onesies, socks, and a whole bunch of other stuff I have no idea about, like burp cloths.

Mom drove me to the airport and it was a tearful goodbye. I'll miss them, but once I'm boarded on the way back to Kentucky, it's Kinley who filters through my mind.

12

*E*van comes home today.

That's my first thought as I slowly open my eyes to the early morning sun. We've texted a couple of times since he's been gone, but it's not the same. I think this is the longest we've gone without seeing each other since I've been home.

I've missed him.

I know it's wrong and we're just friends, but a girl can miss her friend, right? Groaning at my thought process, I reach for my phone. I see I have a missed text from Aaron.

> **Aaron:** Morning! Text me when you roll your sleepy ass out of bed. I have a favor.

Checking the time of the message, I see it was sent at 5:55 this morning. It's now 8:02.

> **Me:** What's up?

> **Aaron:** I was supposed to pick Evan up from the airport, but one of the horses is sick. I've been in the stables since about two. Anyway, can you pick him up for me?

Today is Sunday, and I don't have anything on the books for the studio. Being a photographer, I don't have a traditional nine-to-five schedule and I love it.

> **Me:** Sure, what time is his flight?

Aaron: Lands at two.

Me: Got it.

Aaron: You're the best sister ever!

Me: LOL. Remember that when I come cashing in my IOU.

Aaron: You got it, little sister.

I smile at our banter. I love my brother. We're friends just as much as we are siblings. I wonder what he would think about the thoughts I've been having about his best friend. When I was younger, I had the biggest crush on Evan. Now, this is . . . different. I can only assume it's because we're older, but my thoughts and these feelings go deeper than my teenage crush. When I was younger, I just wanted his attention and wondered what it would be like to walk down the halls of the high school holding his hand, being his girlfriend. Now, I want to trace every inch of him with my tongue. I want to strip him naked and have my way with him. Definitely not a schoolgirl crush.

I'm excited for him to come home. Yesterday afternoon, Mom and the ladies from church had Ethel's 'great-grandmother-to-be' shower. The ladies really went overboard with the gifts. Ethel was in tears, so overwhelmed by the support. If I heard it once yesterday, I heard it a thousand times, that Evan is such a great guy and they commend him for doing this on his own. If they only knew how scared he is. I think I'm the only one who gets to see that side of him, well, besides Aaron.

Mom and I drove Ethel home with Mom's Jeep Cherokee loaded down with gifts. Ethel asked us if we would just go ahead and take them to Evan's to prevent having to transfer them today when he gets home. I agreed and used the key he told me to just keep for now. I've been in and out of his place so often helping him with the room, he said it was easier than hiding it under the rock every day.

Rolling out of bed, I grab a quick shower and throw on my signature jean shorts, tank, and cowboy boots. I'm in the kitchen toasting a bagel when Mom walks in.

"Good morning," she chirps.

"Morning."

"I still can't believe all the gifts. The ladies really outdid themselves," Mom says.

"They really did. I'm relieved because he needs everything."

"He comes home today, right?" she asks.

"Yeah, I'm actually picking him up from the airport. Aaron was supposed to, but I guess he's been up with a sick horse all night."

"Yeah, your dad's been out there too. He came in about six this morning and I packed them both a big breakfast. They were still waiting for the vet to get here."

"Which horse?"

"Morning star."

I cringe. Morning Star is a broodmare, one that is currently in foal. She was bred to a stud whose fees are fifteen thousand dollars. Not to mention, she's been with us since she was a baby——over ten or so years now. I'm sure Dad and Aaron are both worried sick about her. They both try to play tough guy, but are just as attached to the horses as Mom and I.

"Anything I can do?"

"Not that I know of."

"Well, I think I'm going to get some editing done before I leave for the airport."

"Sounds good. I'm going to pack a cooler with a few snacks and drinks to take up to the stables."

Traffic getting to the airport is terrible. When I finally make it, I have to park in the south forty. Luckily, I left to allow plenty of time. I still have thirty minutes before his flight is supposed to land. I find a seat outside of his gate and pull out my Kindle. A girl never leaves home without the necessities. It's hard to concentrate because I keep checking my watch every five seconds. I'm more excited about seeing him than I should allow myself to be. It's only been a week. I've read the same sentence fifteen times; giving up I slide my Kindle back into my purse. Instead, I pull out my phone and scroll through my Instagram feed. Olivia posted a picture of a cute new pair of boots. I comment I need to know where she got them. I'm a sucker for cowboy boots.

"Kinley?" My head pops up at the sound of his voice.

Evan is walking toward me. Without thinking, I jump from my seat

and run to him. I throw my arms around his neck and give him a tight hug. Taking a deep breath, I breathe him in. His arms are around me, resting on my waist, and he buries his face in my neck. I'm not sure how long we stand there, but reality crashes around me as to how intimate our embrace is. I pull away and put some space between us.

His chocolate eyes follow me. "Aaron?" he asks, his voice gruff.

"Morning Star's sick. He and Dad have been up most of the night with her. He asked me to pick you up," I explain.

His eyes roam over me as he begins moving toward me. My body freezes at his approach.

Leaning down, he whispers, "Thank you," against my ear as his lips brush my cheek.

My breath hitches in my throat.

Evan stands to his full height, throws his carry-on over his shoulder, and grabs a rather large suitcase. It's more than I would think he would have traveled with. "Mom and Grandma went a little overboard shopping for the baby."

I smile, because my words are still lodged in my throat.

Evan places his large hand on the small of my back. "If you don't mind, can we stop by the stables on the way back? I want to see if Aaron and your dad need any help."

"Sure," I manage to say. Evan is one of the good guys through and through. Why does he have to be my brother's best friend? I can say with 100 percent certainty that if he weren't, I would have already thrown myself at him.

I lead Evan outside and to my new SUV. "Wow, is this yours?" he asks.

"Yeah, my old Honda has seen better days. Business is good at the studio, so I thought it was time. It's kind of embarrassing pulling up to a shoot driving a beat-up old Honda Accord. This is more professional. I also have a ton of room to travel with props and equipment."

"It's nice. What made you go with a Durango?" he asks.

"I loved the way it drives, which is important, but it has a great sound system. I was thinking, for the outdoor shoots, I could use that to help whoever it is I'm photographing relax a little. It's also four-wheel drive, so I can pretty much drive it to the majority of the on-site locations.

However, I do have one up on the ridge out by Miller's place in a few weeks, so that one will be impossible to drive to."

"Miller's old place. Todd Miller?" he asks.

"Yep, he's proposing to his longtime girlfriend. He wants me hiding in the background to photograph the entire thing. The ridge is where he took her on their first date."

"Huh. You don't think she's going to be mad to find out you've been hiding in the shadows during a personal moment like that?" he asks.

"Nope. It's romantic that he wants to capture the moment. I'm going to take a few posed shots of them up on the ridge as well."

"I can see how much you love it."

"I really do. It doesn't feel like a job, and I hope it never does. I love the flexible schedule. When I'm settled down with kids, it will be even more convenient," I blurt out. I have no idea why I'm saying these things to him. I guess I feel more comfortable because he's going to be a father soon. "How are your parents? Grandparents?" I ask him, quickly changing the subject.

"Good. Dad's weak. The chemo takes a lot out of him. He, Grandpa, and I went fishing. It was nice to spend time with them. Mom and Grandma bought that big-ass suitcase and filled it with lots of pink." He laughs. "Burp cloths, was that on my list? And onesies?" he asks.

I can't help but chuckle at him. "Yeah, some use receiving blankets for burp cloths, and onesies are a very important part of a baby's wardrobe," I reply.

Evan's quiet in the seat next to me. "Hey," I say, taking a quick glance over at him. "You okay?"

I hear him release a heavy sigh. Glancing over again, I see his eyes are shut and his head is resting back against the seat. Reaching over, I lay my hand on top of his. I know this is hard for him, and I wish I had the words to make it all better.

He doesn't say a word. He just laces his fingers through mine, and that's how we drive the rest of the way to the stables.

EVAN 13

*A*fter checking to see if Aaron and Jerry need anything, McKinley drives me home. I'm surprised when she turns the engine off. Don't get me wrong, I want her here, but I'm fighting what feels like a losing battle to stay away from her. Today, just the simple things like asking about my family and reaching over to hold my hand. She's just . . . there, and I feel myself slipping more each day.

"I kind of have a surprise for you. I want to see your face when you see it," she admits with a soft blush crossing her cheeks. I want to lean over this fucking console and taste her lips. Instead, I nod and climb out of her SUV. She opens the back, so I can retrieve my luggage, and follows me up the stairs. I'm digging in my pocket for my key when she says, "I got it."

I watch her take my key, which is on her keyring, and open my front door. The act is all kinds of domestic and everything I realize I'm starting to crave with her.

McKinley steps inside and turns on the lights. I place my bags in the foyer and follow her into the living room. The room is covered in gift bags—mostly pink and all representing a baby. "What is all this?" I ask as I walk further into the room.

McKinley is sitting on the floor in the middle of all the bags, wearing a smile—-my smile. The one she saves for me. At least that's what I tell myself. I don't ever see her share it with anyone else.

"This is for you and your daughter. Mom and the ladies at the church

had a great-granddaughter shower for your Grandma Ethel."

"They didn't have to do that," I say in a low voice. I feel like a chick for how emotional this gesture is making me.

"No, they didn't. They wanted to, Evan. Having a baby is a big deal. You're going to have this little person who not only needs lots of love and attention, but a lot of other stuff too. It's a rite of passage to have a baby shower. We knew we could never convince you to let us have one for you, so we enlisted your grandma."

Kicking off my boots, I take a seat across from her on the floor. "Kinley, I don't . . ."

"I know, Evan," she says softly.

I want to kiss her. I want to lean in and capture her lips, bruise them with my kiss. This girl . . .

"So," she clears her throat, tearing me away from my inappropriate thoughts, "I was going to put it all away, but then I changed my mind. I know Misty's not in the picture and this is all so unconventional, so I was kind of thinking you and I could go through it all. That way you will know what you have, and it will be like you were at the shower, only it's just the two of us."

Just the two of us, if she only knew the images those words cause in my mind.

"I'd like that," I finally say.

"Yay!" She claps her hands and hands me a bag. We spend the next hour going through each gift. She's glowing with excitement—— excitement for me and my daughter. This girl is wrecking me.

"Now we get to pack it all upstairs." She grins at me. "Oh, maybe we should take all the tags off the clothes and blankets. I'll pick up some detergent tomorrow, and then we can wash it before we put it all away. We'll know everything in her room is good to go."

We.

She's including herself into my world; into my daughter's world. I quickly stand to keep myself under control.

"I have detergent," I say, heading to the kitchen for a pair of scissors.

"You need special detergent for babies. They have sensitive skin. You don't have to use it forever, but the first several months at least," she explains.

"And you know all of this how?" I ask her. I need to keep her talking to keep my mind off what I really want to do to her.

"It's a gift." She smiles.

After another hour of removing tags, we have two piles. One pile of laundry and one pile of everything else. "I'll grab a basket." I climb to my feet and head upstairs to the laundry room.

I find Kinley in the kitchen. The counter is now covered with bottles, what I just recently learned was a bottle brush, plates, cups, forks, and spoons—all the baby stuff that goes in the kitchen. "I wasn't sure where you wanted it, so I just left it here." She points to the counter.

"That's fine. I'll figure it out," I tell her.

"Okay, so I'm going to take the rest of it up to her room, since we can't really do the laundry without detergent."

I follow behind her like a lost puppy. The reality of the situation is I would follow her anywhere. It's wrong on so many levels, and I could never admit it to anyone but myself. If McKinley Mills ever needs anything, I'm her guy.

Once we reach the baby's room, she busies herself placing lotions and creams on the shelf below the changing table. There are a few packs of diapers and she stores them in the drawer below. She puts the handful of toys in a white basket with a liner the same color as the walls and places the lone teddy bear in the corner of the crib. I watch her as she works, letting her do her thing.

"There," she says, folding the last bag and placing it inside the other one. "Now we have a better idea of what you need for her. This will make planning a lot easier." She moves toward me.

As she shifts closer, I snake my arm around her waist and pull her into me. I want to kiss her. I want to kiss her so fucking bad, but I know when I do, I won't be able to stop. Instead, I mimic our earlier embrace at the airport and bury my face in her neck. I feel her arms wrap around my waist and it takes every ounce of willpower I have to not say, 'Fuck it.'

Realizing I'm still holding her, I reluctantly back away. She looks up at me, those brown eyes are filled with question. I gently cup her cheek and run the pad of my thumb across her lips. "Thank you for everything, McKinley. I don't know how I would have gotten this far without you."

Bringing her hand to my cheek, she mimics my actions. "I wanted to. I'm so damn proud of you, Evan Chamberlin." She stands on her tiptoes and places a soft kiss on the corner of my mouth. Before she has a chance to pull away, I wrap my arms back around her and hold her close. Just hold her.

The ringing of one of our cell phones downstairs has her pulling away. "You're going to be the best damn daddy to this little girl." She squeezes my arm as she walks around me and heads down the steps.

I stand still, missing the heat of her body against mine. I want to chase after her and beg her to stay. I wait too long, battling with my emotions. I hear the soft click of the front door and the sound of her engine starting.

She's gone.

I meant what I said, I don't know how I would be this far, be this ready for my daughter to come into this world, without her help. I need her help. I can't risk sleeping with her and fucking it all up. I would lose her and more than likely, my best friend in the process. My focus needs to be on my daughter, on making sure I have everything she will need for the day I bring her home——just me and her. As bad as I want McKinley at this moment, I know I can't have her.

I hope I didn't ruin the friendship we've built.

McKinley
14

I'm trying to edit last night's session, but I keep getting distracted thinking about Evan. Misty has a doctor's appointment today and I know Evan is nervous. He says she's not very big and the doctor has been on her about eating more, that the baby could have a low birth weight. It doesn't help matters that she's still hanging out with that Tom character. I can see how much it's hurting him, not because he loves her, but because he's afraid for his daughter. He's constantly stressing over where she is and what she's doing. What the people she has chosen to surround herself with are doing.

My phone rings and Olivia's name lights up my screen. "Hello."

"Kinley, hey girl! What do you have going on tonight?" she asks.

"Nothing really. Why, what's up?"

"Mike has a new band coming to the Tavern tonight. Come with me?"

A night out sounds perfect to me. I haven't really been out since the night Evan told us he was going to have a little girl. "I'm in," I tell her.

"Yes! Okay, do you want me to pick you up or do you just want to meet there?"

"I'll just meet you there. What time?" I ask. If I drive, I won't be stuck there all night. Olivia will more than likely drink herself into a coma and Mike will have to drive her home.

"Seven, sound okay?"

"Yeah, sounds good. I'll see you then."

As soon as I hit end, my phone alerts me to a message. It's a voicemail. Tapping on the call list, I see Evan tried to call. I wonder why it didn't alert me he was calling. I click on listen and hear his deep voice come through the speaker.

"Hey, Kinley, it's Evan. Uh, Misty showed up for the appointment, but her weight is extremely low. The baby is measuring three weeks smaller than she should be. I was just calling because I promised you I would. Talk to you soon."

My heart breaks for him. I start to call him back, but decide maybe he needs a friend right now. I quickly save my edits, grab my keys and my phone, then head out the door. It's a short drive to get to Evan's place. Parking beside his truck, I make my way to the front porch. Even though I have a key, I still knock on the door. I don't live here and Evan's not my boyfriend. I feel like I would be abusing the privilege if I just barge on in.

I raise my hand to knock and the door flies open. Evan stands still, just watching me. I don't know what to say. I can see the worry written all over his face. I wish I could throat punch Misty for the shit she's putting him through. Evan holds out his hand and without hesitation, I accept it, allowing him to pull me into the house.

As soon as the door closes, he pulls me into a tight hug. I can feel the tension in his stance. Today's visit worries him——as it should. This is his little girl we're talking about.

I wish I could make it better, take this worry off his shoulders. He's doing this alone. I hold him tight, trying to show him I'm here for him. If I had my way, I would never let go.

Evan finally pulls away from the hug, laces his fingers through mine, and leads me to the living room. He lays down on the couch and gives my hand a gentle tug, letting me know he wants me to lie down with him. No words are said as I silently nod and settle in front of him, my back to his front. He wraps his arms around me and holds tight. I cover his hands with mine, wanting that connection, to let him know I'm here, to offer him some type of comfort.

We lie there together in the silence of the room. My fingers trace the corded muscles of his arms, which are wrapped securely around me. I'm aware of every breath he takes. At first they are quick, but fade into long even breaths. This is when I let myself relax, knowing he has.

"I'm worried about my little girl," he says softly. "She's not taking care of herself, Kinley. I don't know what to do. The baby is measuring small and the doctor keeps warning her she needs to eat more. She gives him a blank stare and I just want to shake her," he says in a rush.

I don't know what to say, so I don't say anything. I don't think I've ever said I hate someone, but in this moment, I hate Misty. I hate how she wants nothing to do with Evan and this baby girl she's carrying. I hate her because she's not taking care of herself and she's putting Evan's daughter in danger. I hate her because she's the one carrying his baby.

I'm in deep.

Rolling over so we're face to face, I study him—the strong angle of his jaw and his shaggy brown hair that hangs down into his brown eyes. Unable to stop myself, I reach up and run my fingers through his hair. His eyes bore into mine, both of us refusing to look away.

Evan pulls me closer, our faces now mere inches apart. Our eyes never wander, his chocolate irises so full of despair. I want to take it away. I want to help him forget about the worry, just help him relax. Without further thought, I lean forward and press my lips to his. He doesn't respond at first, but I don't let that stop me. I softly kiss him again, running my tongue across his lips.

"McKinley." My name is a feather-soft caress falling from his lips as he presses them hard against mine.

I suddenly have no control over the situation. Evan's hand, which was resting on my back, slides up the back of my neck, holding me in place. His lips, soft yet firm, devour mine. I hear a low moan and realize it was me. I want more of him——all of him.

I allow myself to get lost in his kiss, the taste of him and the feel of him pulling me closer. I have no idea how much time passes and I don't care. I want this moment with him.

The ringing of a cell phone causes Evan to pull away. He rests his forehead against mine. My eyes are closed, but I can feel the rapid rise and fall of his chest with each breath.

A loud beep causes him to pull away. "Kinley." His voice is pained.

Looking into his eyes, filled with so many emotions—pain, desire, and maybe even regret—I place my index finger over his lips to stop him. "I'm here for you, Evan. Whatever you need. I don't regret this, being here with you, but I am going to leave. I think you need some time

to process your day. I'm going to Mike's tonight. I'm meeting Olivia there, but if you need me, call me. I will be here if you want me."

I place one final soft kiss against his lips before climbing off the couch and walking out the door. I fight the urge to look back, to see if he followed me. It takes me no time to make it back to the house. It's quiet; Mom and Dad were going out to dinner with friends and it's hard to tell where Aaron is. He might even show up at Mike's. That's where everyone usually ends up. Not much to do in this small town.

Glancing at the clock on the wall, I see I've only got a half hour before I'm supposed to meet Olivia. I'd spent more time at Evan's than I thought. Running upstairs, I freshen up, spritz a little Victoria Secret body spray, and call it good.

I pull into Mike's with two minutes to spare. As soon as I walk through the door, Olivia spots me.

"McKinley, get your ass over here, girl."

She's already well on her way to having her ass carried out of here. I'm sure Mike is thrilled.

"I didn't think you'd ever get here," she says when I reach her.

"I'm right on time." I raise my arm and show her my watch.

"Hey, McKinley, what are you drinking?" Mike asks.

"Just water for now." He raises his eyebrows, but I ignore him. Even though I'm in my hometown, I don't like to drink alone, meaning I don't have someone designated to make sure my ass gets home safely. It's a rule my roommates and I made in college and I still live by it.

Mike slides a cold bottle of water toward me. I reach out to grab it, and he pulls it back. "You still owe me a dance."

I smile and nod. I'll give him his one dance, but that's all he's getting, regardless of how charming he thinks he is.

"Let's dance," Olivia says, pulling my behind out onto the dance floor. The band is a local cover band and they're really good. Olivia and I dance for five or six songs straight, so many that I lose track. A slow one comes on and I mimic taking a drink. She nods her agreement and we make our way through the crowd back to the bar.

Mike sees us approaching and places a bottle of beer and a glass of water on the counter. I chug the water and hand it back to him to throw away. The slow song ends, but the band slips right into another. "You ready for that dance?" Mike asks me.

"Let's do this," I say in reply. I'm trying to keep our interactions as friendly as possible. I don't want him getting the wrong idea.

Mike steps out from around the bar and reaches for my hand. I place mine in his and allow him to lead me to the dance floor. He stops at the edge and pulls me against him, resting his hands on my hips. I take a step back and rest my hands on his shoulders.

"So how's the studio coming along?"

"Great actually, thanks for asking. I'm staying busy." I look around at all the people in the Tavern. "Looks like business is good," I say, making small talk.

"Yeah, I really couldn't be happier with the crowds. It took a while to get the word out, but once I started booking bands, that changed quickly."

"People do love live music," I say.

"Listen, McKinley—" he starts to say, but the song ends the lead singer starts talking to the crowd. I release a deep breath.

I once again mimic taking a drink, so we can leave the dance floor. I said one dance. When we reach the bar, Evan and Aaron are sitting there talking to Olivia.

"McKinley, thank you for the dance." Mike pulls my hand to his lips and kisses it with a wink.

EVAN 15

*S*on of a bitch!

The first thing I see when we walk into Mike's is him and Kinley dancing together. From her stance, it looks as though she's keeping her distance and they're talking. It doesn't look the least bit romantic, but it still burns my ass that he has his hands on her.

I know what it feels like to have her in my arms.

Olivia greets us with a smile and a drunken, "Hey y'all." She pulls Aaron down to her level and kisses his cheek, only offering me a wave. Not that I care. Aaron can have her. She's never hid the fact that she wants him. I have my eyes on forbidden fruit.

I focus my attention on Aaron and Olivia. They're talking about Morning Star. "She pulled through. So far, the vet comes out weekly to check her and all is well," Aaron explains.

From the corner of my eye, I see Kinley and Mike approaching us. I watch as he kisses the back of her hand, and I have the overwhelming urge to beat my fist against my chest and go all Tarzan on his ass. I'm about to do just that when he drops her hand and steps back behind the bar. I watch as Kinley wipes her hand on the back of her short-as-hell shorts. The same shorts she was wearing out at my house just a few hours ago.

I try to bite back my grin at her obvious annoyance with Mike, but it's just not possible. "What's got you all smiles?" Aaron asks.

"Nothing, man. Just nice to get out and clear my mind," I tell him. It is. Misty's appointment today really messed me up. I'm worried sick

about my unborn daughter while she's off doing God only knows what.

I tried again today to give her money, but she refused. I reminded her she's carrying my baby, and her reply was, "You don't need to keep reminding me, I know." I hate how she's not taking care of herself, and I despise it even more that I can't do anything about it. Yes, she signed the papers, but there is no real proof she's not eating. Just a suspicion I have, not to mention the doctors worry over her lack of weight gain.

The four of us stand at the bar and chat about nothing important while Mike continues to watch Kinley. He keeps offering her a beer, but she continues to refuse him. Finally, the band slows things down. Olivia pulls Aaron to the floor, leaving me along with Kinley. She's been acting like earlier didn't happen, and I don't know how I feel about that.

Leaning in close, so she can hear me over the music, I ask, "Will you dance with me?"

She doesn't answer. Instead, she reaches for my hand, laces her fingers through mine, and pulls me to the dance floor. We don't stop at the edge where she was dancing with Mike. She guides us through the crowd and stops on the opposite side where the lights are low. Placing her hands behind my neck, she gently runs her fingers through my hair.

With my hands on her hips, I pull her as close as I can get her and clasp my hands together on her lower back. I don't want her slipping away easily. Kinley leans forward and rests her head against my chest, and that simple act has my heart hammering. I watched her with Mike, and this was not how they danced; she'd kept her distance.

She wants to be close to me.

I take what feels like my first breath since she walked out of my house earlier tonight. I was sure our friendship, or whatever it is you want to call what we have, was ruined. I tried hard to regret it, but I will never regret a single fucking second I get to spend with her.

I rest my chin on the top of her head and pray the band drags this song out, or plays another slow one. Hell, they could slow it down for the rest of the night if it means I get to hold her like this. I know I shouldn't. Aaron is out here on this same dance floor and he could see me——see us. I assume that's why Kinley led us to the darkest part of the dance floor. I know I should care, but with her in my arms like this, I can't find any fucks to give.

The song comes to an end and Kinley raises her head. Instead of pulling away, she stands on her tiptoes and hugs me tight. Leaning down, I bury my face in her neck. "Please don't go out with him," I beg her.

Her lips touch my ear as she whispers, "I don't want him."

Relief.

All consuming relief washes through me. I'm still holding her and I know I have to let her go, but I don't want to. I want her like this, with me like this always.

Kinley steps out of my embrace and our bodies are no longer touching. I study her face to see how she's feeling, but she gives nothing away. Turning, she starts to walk back to the bar. It takes about two seconds for me to catch up to her. Placing my hand on the small of her back, I guide her. She may not be mine, but hopefully, all these drunk fucks won't be able to figure that out and will keep their distance.

At the bar, Mike's attitude has changed. He's no longer offering Kinley drinks and he spends the majority of his time at the other end of the bar. That means he was watching us, witnessed me holding her. I can't help but feel a little smug at the thought.

"Olivia's tanked. I told Mike we would take her home," Aaron explains.

Olivia is sitting on a barstool slumped over the bar. She was three sheets to the wind when we got here, so I'm not surprised this is the outcome. "Did you drive?" I ask Kinley.

"Yeah, I met her here."

Digging in my pocket, I pull my keys out and hand them over to Aaron. "Take my truck. I'll just have Kinley drop me off. I can get my truck tomorrow."

Aaron looks over at Kinley and she nods in agreement. "Yeah, I'm thinking she's going to need most of the bench seat in your truck. There's no keeping her up."

"Good luck, my man." I clap Aaron on the shoulder. He grumbles a reply that I can't make out, but I'm pretty sure he's calling me a dick.

Aaron lifts Olivia off the stool, nods to Mike that he has her, and heads toward the door. Kinley and I follow, me with my hand on the small of her back. Mike will be able to see us; Aaron will not. It's intimate, yet a gentlemanly gesture. I'm not doing anything wrong; at least that's what I keep telling myself.

Kinley opens the truck door, allowing Aaron to place a passed out Olivia in the seat. He buckles her in and shuts the door. "See you at the house," he says to Kinley. "I'll bring your truck by tomorrow, man," he says to me. It's not lost on me that Aaron wanted to get a drink tonight, and he had only one. He stopped drinking as soon as he saw how wasted Olivia was getting.

We watch as Aaron pulls out of the lot before heading to Kinley's Durango. She pulls the keys out of her pocket and hands them to me. "You can just drop me off and take my car. I have two sessions tomorrow in the studio, so I won't need it anytime soon." The last is said through her yawn.

I take the key from her hand and kiss the top of her head. "Let's get you home, beautiful." The words slip off my tongue as if it's something I've said to her multiple times. My reward is a sleepy smile before she climbs into the passenger seat. I make sure she's buckled in before closing her door.

When I pull up to her house, it's dark. I know Aaron mentioned his parents going out tonight. I turn off the SUV and look over to find Kinley is still sleeping soundly. Her body is angled toward mine, her soft breaths causing a gentle rise and fall of her chest. I turn so I'm facing her and rest my head against the seat. I memorize her in this moment. I don't ever want to forget how peaceful she looks.

I wish things were different. I wish, instead of driving us here, I could take her home. I could carry her up to my room and curl my body around hers. I need to find a way to block these feelings she evokes in me. I know I do, but for tonight, when it's just me watching her, I don't want to.

Glancing at my phone for the time, I see I've been sitting here way longer than what I should have. I've gone into the creeper category. There is a physical ache in my chest because I know I have to wake her up. I have to end my time with her and that pisses me off.

Raising my hand to her cheek, I softly run my fingers along her jawline. "Kinley, you're home."

Her eyes flutter, but she doesn't wake up. Leaning closer, my lips graze her ear. "Time to wake up, beautiful." That's the second time tonight the endearment has fallen from my lips, and I can only hope she's too sleepy for it to register.

Finally, her eyes leisurely open. I pull my lips away from her ear, which brings my mouth closer to hers. "Hey." Her voice is raspy and laced with sleep.

"Hey." I tuck a loose hair behind her ear. "I'm sorry to wake you." If she only knew how true that statement is.

"It's fine. Sorry I fell asleep on you."

I'm not. "You were tired." I want to kiss her.

"Yeah, I guess I was. Thank you for driving." She makes no effort to move from the car.

"Aaron will be back soon," I say. I know he will be wondering what the hell I've been doing, sitting outside with her for so long. Reluctantly, I back away and remove her keys from the ignition. "Let's get you inside."

Kinley meets me at the front of her Durango and surprises me when she places her arm through mine and leans against me. She has no idea how hard she's making it for me to leave her.

We reach the door without her losing her grip on my arm, and I manage to get it unlocked. Looking down, I see she's staring up at me. "Sweet dreams." I kiss her forehead and step back. She releases her arm from mine and walks inside. "Lock up," I say just as the door shuts, securing her safely behind it.

Locked away from me.

McKinley
16

*L*ooking at my watch, I see it's after six; no wonder I'm starving. I've been in the studio since nine and have gone non-stop until just a few minutes ago. I had five sessions today and most of them ended up taking more time than they should have. Explosive diapers, tantrums, late clients—you name it, it happened. I need to set a firm line with being late, but it was three kids, ages: sixteen, nineteen, and twenty-one. Their mom is sick and they wanted to give her a picture of all three of them. It's something she's been begging them to agree to for years. These boys came in wearing their heart on their sleeves and I couldn't turn them away.

Deciding I've had enough for the day, I pack up my camera and turn off the lights. Once in the house, I see my phone sitting on the kitchen table. I've been so busy today I didn't even realize I'd left it. I grab a cold slice of pizza, left over from last night. Aaron, Evan, and I had ordered in. Mom and Dad are at a show in Tennessee, so it was just the three of us. After I pour myself a glass of tea, I balance my drink, my cold pizza, and my phone as I settle into the couch.

It feels good to finally sit.

I take a huge bite of pizza and swipe the screen of my phone. I see I've missed multiple calls from Aaron and Evan. I assume it's just because they couldn't get a hold of me, neither are too keen on the idea. I roll my eyes as I look at my missed text messages. Olivia was supposed to text me about going to the outlet malls this weekend.

I have a text from Mom, Olivia, Aaron, and Evan. I open Mom's

first; she's just checking in. It's like they forgotten I've lived on my own for four years while in college. I open Olivia's next. She's good to go with our shopping expedition on Saturday. I type a quick reply that I'll be at her place at eight to pick her up. I open Aaron's message next.

Aaron: Where are you?

Aaron: Call me as soon as you get this.

Aaron: MCKINLEY!

Something's wrong. My hands are shaking as I try to tap the screen to read Evan's texts.

Evan: Call me

Evan: Where are you? Call me as soon as you get this.

Evan: I need you.

Reading his last text slays me. With hands shaking even worse than before, I pull up my favorites list and hit Evan's name. When I bring the phone to my ear, I feel the tears I was unaware were falling. The shrill ring of his phone and then the sound of his voicemail picking up—*"This is Evan. Leave a message."*—causes a sob to break from my chest.

Hitting end, I tap Aaron's name and hold my breath, waiting for him to answer.

"Kinley." His voice is gruff.

"What's wrong?"

"Where are you?" he asks.

"I'm at home. I left my phone in the house. I had a full day in the studio. What's wrong?" My voice breaks on another sob as I ask the question again.

"I'm almost there. I was coming to look for you. We were worried."

"Evan, where is he?"

"I'll explain when I get there. Be ready to leave. I just pulled onto our road."

I hang up, not caring if he has more to say. Cold pizza and hunger forgotten, I grab my purse, phone, and keys. Locking the door behind me, I walk out to the driveway and pace back and forth.

Waiting.

Wondering.

I hear Aaron's diesel truck before I see him. He pulls up beside me and I wrench the door open and climb inside. "Talk!" I demand as I fight back another round of tears.

"Hey." Aaron reaches over and grabs my hand. "Take a deep breath. What's got you so upset?"

"Something's wrong. The text messages . . ." My voice trails off as I bite down hard on my bottom lip to control the tears.

"Okay, but I need you to stay calm. Misty had an appointment today. During her exam, the doctor noticed the baby's heartbeat was low. Too low." He takes a minute to let that sink in. "Evan had to rush her to the hospital where they are monitoring her and the baby. If there is no improvement, they're going to have to take the baby," Aaron calmly explains.

"She's too small," I cry. "She's not due for another two weeks and she's already measuring tiny. It's too early," I argue.

Squeezing my hand, he says, "Yes, you are right on all counts. The doctors are giving Misty shots of steroids to help strengthen the baby's lungs, just in case they do have to deliver early."

"How is he?" I force the words out. I know how he is. His last text message flashes through my mind. *"I need you."* I can't imagine what he's feeling right now.

Aaron is quiet the rest of the drive, allowing me to get lost in my thoughts, my worry for Evan. As soon as he parks the truck, I'm jumping out with him hot on my heels. "I'll take you there," he says, falling into step beside me.

We enter the hospital and Aaron leads us to the elevators. He hits the button, which one I have no idea. I don't need to know. I just need to get to him. When the elevator doors open, Aaron motions for me to exit, letting me know this is our stop. As soon as I step out, we are in a waiting room and what I see breaks my heart. Evan is sitting all alone, elbows resting on his knees, face buried in his hands. I don't even think as I move toward him. He must hear my heavy footsteps. Lifting his head, his eyes find me and he stands just in time for me to crash into him. We wrap our arms around each other, and I hold onto him telling him without words that I'm here.

"Kinley." His voice cracks and, I swear, so does my heart. Neither

one of us move. We stand there in the quiet waiting room of the maternity ward and hold on as tight as we can.

Eventually, he pulls away. His eyes are red and filled with moisture. "Are you okay?" he asks me. I can hear the concern in his voice.

This man.

He's going through hell, the worry for his daughter evident, yet he takes the time to ask and worry about me.

"I'm good. I left my phone at the house. I've been busy in the studio all day," I explain.

Evan nods as he laces his fingers through mine. I've completely forgotten Aaron was with me when I got here, until he clears his throat. We both turn to face him. I try to pry my hand from Evan's, but he's not having it.

"Any word?" Aaron asks. I can see the question in his eyes, but he doesn't voice it.

"No change. We're waiting for the doctor. I actually need to get back in there. I just needed . . ." He trails off and silently squeezes my hand. He needed to know I was okay.

"We'll be here, go. You don't want to miss what the doctor has to say," I tell him.

"She's right. We're not leaving. You'll find us here when you need us, man. Don't leave the decisions up to Misty." Aaron says her name with disdain.

Evan nods. "Thanks, man." He releases my hand. Leaning down, he places a kiss on the top of my head, then squeezes Aaron's shoulder and walks away.

"What was that?" Aaron asks.

"He's emotional, Aaron. His daughter's life is at risk," I say defensively.

"Yeah, I get that, but I've been standing here the whole time. He was worried about you," he points out.

"Well, yeah, I'm like a little sister to him. We've spent a lot of time together the last few months. I've been his shoulder through all this."

"McKinley Rae," he warns.

"Look, there's nothing going on between us. Am I happy about that?

No, not really. Can I change it? No. Evan is a great guy, you know that. He has too much going on in his life to notice his best friend's little sister."

"He looked like he noticed to me," he retorts.

"He's hanging on by a thread, Aaron. Misty hasn't been taking care of herself and his biggest fear is possibly about to become a reality. His daughter is in danger. His parents don't live here and his grandparents are not in good health. They can't sit here with him, so he needs someone. That someone is me."

Aaron's quiet for a few minutes before he finally says, "I get that, Kinley. I do. He's my best friend and I'm glad you've been there for him. Hell, I even encouraged him to let you help him. What worries me is your feelings are more than just helping out my best friend. I don't want to see you get hurt."

"I won't. You have nothing to worry about, Aaron. He needs us right now more than ever."

He puts his arm around my shoulder and pulls me into him. "You're right. I just worry about you. About both of you, really."

"You don't have to. I'm a big girl. I just . . . my heart breaks for him, Aaron."

He doesn't say anything. Instead, he guides me to one of the chairs along the walls and we settle in, waiting to hear from Evan.

EVAN 17

he's here. She's okay. I keep repeating those words on my way back to Misty's room. I needed her, and when I couldn't reach her, I about lost my shit. My daughter's life is in danger and McKinley was missing. It was almost too much for me to process. The rational side of my brain realizes she wasn't missing, but the stressed, over emotional side put up a strong fight.

Knowing she's here, it helps. I wish I could say I'm focusing on my daughter and make it better, but I can't. It all comes down to hurry up and wait. Wait to see if Misty's body can give her what she needs. Wait to see if my little girl's heartbeat resumes to a normal, healthy rhythm. Wait for the doctors to tell me if I'm going to meet my little girl two weeks earlier than what I thought.

I fucking hate waiting.

When I enter Misty's room, she's resting. I don't know if she's really sleeping or just has her eyes closed. I don't care either way. I have no plans to talk to her. I blame her for this. She refused to take care of herself, to take care of my baby, and now I could lose her. The doctor said the shots they are giving Misty will help the baby's lungs fully develop faster and two weeks is minor in comparison to some early deliveries. Regardless, she did this. I will never forgive her.

Light filters through the room as the doctor comes in. "Evan, there's no change and I'm not willing to risk waiting any longer. We're going to take Misty in to do an emergency cesarean. You can scrub in and be in the room. I'm going to go prep. I'll send the nurses in to get her ready." He walks closer to the bed and to her. "Misty," he says, turning the light

on above the bed. She opens her eyes.

"I heard you," she says, no emotion whatsoever in her voice.

The doctor nods his head. "Evan, if you'll come with me, you can stop and update your family and then let the nurses know you need to scrub in."

I wait for him to leave the room before I address Misty. "I'll see you in there."

She nods and rolls to her side, putting her back to me. Not able to be alone with her for one more second, I leave the room in search of my family—Aaron and McKinley. I find them where I left them in the waiting room. McKinley has her head on Aaron's shoulder and they are watching whatever mindless show is on television. As soon as she spots me, she lifts her head and sits on the edge of her seat.

"Hey," I say, stopping in front of them. They both stand and I want nothing more than to pull her into me and hold her, pull comfort from her. Instead, I clench my hands into fists to prevent it.

"So, uh . . ." I clear my throat. "There's no change in the baby. Her heart rate is still too low and the doctor doesn't want to wait any longer. They're prepping Misty for an emergency delivery," I explain.

Tears fall from McKinley's eyes. Tears for me and my daughter. The woman who has carried her for over eight months shows no emotion, but this girl, she's broken over it.

I clench my fist tighter.

"I have to go too. To scrub in so I can be there when she's born." My voice cracks. I'm trying really hard to keep my shit in check, but I'm scared to death for my daughter.

"Evan, man, she's going to be okay. You're going to have a healthy little girl here really soon. A little girl who we are going to spoil rotten and whose dates we are going to scare away." Aaron tries to break some of the tension.

It works. I offer him a watery smile. He's my best friend. He's been there for me through it all and I could not be happier to have him here to help me welcome my daughter into the world.

"I can't wait to meet her," Kinley says, displaying her own watery smile. I watch as tears stream down her cheeks.

No longer able to resist, I cup her face with my hands and wipe her tears away with my thumbs. "Thank you for everything," I say, then kiss her forehead.

I then turn to Aaron and pull him into a hug. "Thanks for being here, brother."

I feel him nod. With that, I spin around and walk away from them. Stopping at the nurses' station, I ask them where I need to be. Following their directions, I head toward the surgery department.

"Evan Chamberlin," I tell the girl at the desk.

"Yes, sir. Right this way." She leads me behind the doors that read *Authorized Personnel Only*. Reaching into a cabinet, she hands me a pair of scrubs. "Slip these on over your clothes and these go over your shoes. Once you're done, go through those doors," she points behind her, "and give them your name."

I do as I'm told, slipping the blue scrubs over my clothes and the covers on my feet. When I make it through the double doors and give the nurse there my name, she instructs me to follow her to the sink where she proceeds to scrub my hands. After drying them, she sheaths them with rubber gloves. She hands me a mask for my face and opens a door, telling me to go on in.

The room is sterile. The smell that lingers in all hospitals is stronger here than I've ever smelled before. Misty is laying on a table with a blanket hanging at right about her chest. I assume it's to keep her from seeing what's about to happen. She's staring up at the ceiling.

"Mr. Chamberlin, come on in. There's a chair." The nurse points to a stool that is up close to Misty's head.

I mumble a half-assed, "Thank you," and take my spot on the stool, thankful for the chance to sit. My legs are shaking. Hell, my entire body is trembling. The doctor comes in followed by a team of people dressed just like me.

"This is your team. Baby girl Chamberlin will be in good hands," he says, stopping beside us. "Misty, do you have any questions?" he asks her.

"No," she replies. Still showing no emotion, she answers just as she would if someone was asking if she wanted fries with her burger.

"Evan?" he asks.

"I don't . . . I don't know," I tell him honestly.

"Once we take the baby, if all is well, which I'm optimistic about and is the reason I didn't want to wait any longer, we will allow you to see her, but the staff behind me will take her, run some tests, and clean her up. Once she's been assessed, you will be able to hold your daughter," he explains.

"Okay," I say because what else do you say to that? At least they are going to let me see her before they take her away.

The doctor nods, and just like that, a flurry of activity happens around us. Even though I blame her, I'm sure she's scared as hell. At least I am. Reaching over, I take Misty's hand in mine. She doesn't speak, but she does turn to look at me. I hold her stare until she squeezes her eyes closed and points her head back toward the ceiling. Still nothing. I wish I knew what she was thinking. I wish I knew how she could be so indifferent to everything that's happening.

I continue to hold her hand, offering her silent support. At least I tell myself it's for her. In reality, it's just as much for me. I hear the doctor ask for a scalpel and my chest tightens. I focus on trying to suck in deep, even breaths, waiting for them to tell me she's okay.

There's no semblance of time as I wait for them, just trying like hell to keep breathing. That is until I hear it, hear her. The moment I hear my little girl cry, I release a heavy breath at the same time the doctor announces, "It's a girl," to everyone in the room.

She's here. My daughter. My little girl.

A nurse walks around the curtain and holds her up so we can see her. I don't bother checking to see if Misty is paying attention. I know she's not. Instead, I take her in as tears begin to fall.

My daughter is testing out her lungs as she screams, apparently not impressed with her arrival into the world. I don't care. In this moment, her cries are the sweetest sound I've ever heard. She's here and I love her more than I ever thought possible.

This is real.

"We need to take her for some tests, but you can wait for her in the nursery if you want." I nod, not bothering with the tears as they fall.

I'm a father.

I watch as the team places her under a light and wheels her out of the room. Once she's out of sight, I turn to face Misty. "Misty," I say her name, but she doesn't bother looking at me.

"I know you can hear me. I just want to say thank you. Thank you for giving me my daughter." I don't waste time waiting for a reply I know will not come. Instead, I rush out the door in hot pursuit of the nursery.

Quickly stripping out the blue getup, I toss it in the trash and make my way back to the maternity department. Aaron and McKinley are there, waiting for me, just like I knew they would be.

"Well?" Aaron asks.

"She's here. She's got a set of lungs on her," I laugh. "They took her for testing, but said I could wait for her in the nursery. Will you guys come with me?"

I need them there.

"Does a cat have climbing gear?" Aaron asks, causing me to throw my head back and laugh. I know she's not out of the woods until they run all the tests, but her lungs are strong and I have faith my little girl is a fighter.

"Have you called your family?" Kinley asks.

"Shit, no. I just . . . I came straight to you guys from the operating room."

"Do you want me to call them?" she asks.

I run my fingers through my hair, torn. "Yeah, I don't even know how much she weighs or anything. Can you just let them know she's here and doing well and I will call them when I get to finally hold her?" I ask.

"Sure. You guys go on. I'll make the calls and catch up with you," Kinley suggests.

I hesitate, because out of everyone, I want her there with me. She's been there for me more than anyone else and I want to share this with her.

She picks up on my hesitation and she says, "I'll hurry. Now go, both of you. You better get your time in because I can't wait to hold her." Her eyes mist with tears. Reaching out, I give her hand a gentle squeeze and mouth, "Thank you," before turning to Aaron. "Ready?"

"Let's do this," he says, handing me a pink cigar.

Aaron and I stand outside the glass of the nursery, peering in at all the babies. One of the nurses notices us and comes to the door. "Who are you looking for?" She smiles.

"My daughter, um, Chamberlin. Baby girl Chamberlin," I say.

"Oh, she's a cutie that one. We just finished with all her tests. Do you want me to bring her to your room?"

My room. Shit, I didn't think about that. Normal couples would be in the room together, but Misty wants nothing to do with my little girl. "Uh, her mom, she doesn't———" She holds up her hand to stop me.

"We are well aware of your situation, Mr. Chamberlin. We've moved you to a room at the end of the hall. It's one of the small rooms that we hardly ever use. It will be yours while you're here. I'll send her in with the doctor. It's room 612."

Aaron and I make our way to the room and wait. *More waiting.* "You nervous?" he asks me.

"You have no fucking idea," I admit.

The door opens and in strolls a nurse pushing a bassinet of sorts with a little bundle wearing a pink hat, the doctor right behind them.

"Evan, everything looks good. Her lungs are strong and she passed all her tests. You have a healthy little girl. I've instructed the staff that no one is to be left with her except for you. Misty is on the opposite end of the hall and has made it clear she wants to be discharged as soon as possible. As for you two, she will be able to go home in the morning. We just need you to fill out some paperwork, give this little one a name, and you will be all set. We ask that you follow-up with your pediatrician within three to four days of discharge due to her low birth weight."

"H-how much did she weigh?"

"Six pounds one ounce and she's nineteen inches long. Congratulations, Dad," he says.

I can't speak, so I nod. The nurse scoops her up and brings her to me. "Would you like to hold your daughter?"

What is it that Aaron said? Does a cat having climbing gear? What kind of question is that? Hell yes, I want to hold her. "Yes," I croak out. I'm an emotional fucking basket case. I'm nervous as hell. My hands are shaking and my palms are sweaty. What if I drop her? I'm excited to meet her. To be able to hold her after wondering all these months what she would look like.

I finally get to meet my little girl.

The nurse hands her to me, explaining that I need to always support her head. My nervousness must be showing.

"Why is she wrapped up so tight?" She looks like a little white and pink burrito.

The nurse smiles. "Babies like to be swaddled. It makes them feel secure. She was in her momma for all this time, not a lot of space in there," she patiently explains. Everyone here has been amazing.

"Can I unwrap her? I need to count fingers and toes." When I was in Alabama visiting my parents and grandparents, Dad made the comment that when he held me for the first time he had to count all my fingers and toes. I remember thinking about how I would feel in this moment; nothing could have prepared me for this.

Nothing.

"Of course you can," she says.

With shaky hands, I slowly remove the blanket. "She's so tiny." I touch her little hand and she clutches onto my finger, onto my heart. I love this little girl with everything in me. I have no fucking clue how to raise her, but I vow in this moment to be the best father and best stand-in mother she's ever had.

McKinley
18

I feel like I've been on the phone forever. I called Evan's parents and his mom continued to pepper me with questions I don't have the answers to. After promising her multiple times that I would call as soon as I knew more, I was finally able to hang up.

My next call was to his grandparents here in Kentucky. Ethel ran me through the same stage of questions multiple times, until I too had to convince her I would call as soon as I knew more.

The last call was to my parents. Mom didn't ask near as many questions, understanding I didn't have the answers yet. However, she too insisted I call when I had them.

I get it. They all love him and even though they've never met that little girl, they love her too. I feel bad for his family in Alabama, unable to travel to see her and living so far away. I'll be sure to take lots of pictures to send to them.

Stopping at the nurses' station, I ask, "Evan Chamberlin, baby girl Chamberlin." I'm directed to the room all the way at the end of the hall. I quicken my step to get to them.

Slowly pushing open the door, I step into the room. I stop in my tracks as a take in the scene before me. Evan is holding his daughter, her tiny finger tightly gripping his. Aaron is sitting in a chair next to him and they're both looking down at her like she's . . . everything.

I wish I had my damn camera. Deciding this moment cannot go without being captured, I reach in my back pocket and pull out my

phone. I tap the screen. The shutter sound that the photographer in me refuses to turn off alerts them to my presence.

Evan and Aaron lift their heads to look at me, both wearing grins that light up the room. I can see from my spot just inside the door that Evan has watery eyes and if I'm not mistaken, Aaron does too. These "tough guys" are brought to their knees by this precious baby girl.

"Kinley," Evan breathes my name, grabbing a hold of my heart.

Walking further into the room, I stop in front of Evan and bend down. He adjusts his hold on her, so I can get a better look. I reach out and touch her tiny hands and she latches onto my finger. My eyes find Evan's and I can't describe the look in his eyes. My heart is racing and I'm overwhelmed by what's happening. This little girl brought us together. Our friendship grew because of her. Now, here, on the day we finally get to meet her, she's still bringing us together.

"Evan, she's beautiful," I say as tears begin to fall. "Is she okay? How much does she weigh? What did the doctor say?" I fire off some of the questions I just fielded with our families. "Can I hold her?" I blurt out.

Evan chuckles. "Yeah, I just need to wrap her back up."

A nurse, who I hadn't notice was in the corner, speaks up. "Let me show you. Lay her down on the bed."

I step back, allowing Evan room to stand and do as she has instructed. The three of us listen intently as the nurse shows us the proper way to swaddle her. When she's once again snug in her blanket, Evan ever so gently lifts her back into his arms and motions his head toward the chair he was just in. "Sit," he tells me.

Without hesitation, I do as I'm told and hold my arms out for her. The sound of Aaron's ringing cell phone startles her and she jumps. "Shhh, I got you," I say, gently rocking her.

"It's Mom. I'm going to step out and take this." Aaron keeps his voice low and quietly steps out of the room. I told Mom he was here; apparently, she's not as patient as I thought. Of course that could be because I was a little snippy with her.

I'm so lost in this little angel in my arms I don't notice Evan is now kneeling before me, observing me just as I had him only minutes ago. "Evan, she's so precious."

Nodding his head, he lifts his hand to my face and wipes my tears with his thumbs. His big brown eyes so full of happiness and love, they're sparkling with it. I'm just about to comment that I hope she has his eyes——I love his eyes——when he leans in and softly presses his lips to mine.

"There is no one I would want to share this with more than you. You've helped me so damn much, Kinley. I just—"

"Does she have a name?" I interrupt him before his over emotional brain says something he won't be able to take back, something that my sentimental brain will never be able to forget.

"Yeah, well, no, but I've been thinking a lot about it. I was thinking about Lexington. It's Mom's maiden name," he says. "I want to call her Lexi."

"Lexington Chamberlin. Lexi." I love it. I beam at him. "Good call, Daddy," I say with a wink.

I see a slight blush creep over his cheeks. Damn, I really wish I had my camera to capture this moment. "So does Miss Lexi have a middle name?" I ask, focusing my attention back to the little angel sleeping peacefully in my arms.

"Rae," he says softly.

It takes a few seconds for my brain to register what he said. When it finally hits me, I jerk my head up to find him staring at me. "W-what did you say?"

"Rae, her name is Lexington Rae Chamberlin." He pauses to let the fact he's naming his daughter after me sink in. "Lexi Rae," he says as an afterthought.

Tears, big fat crocodile tears, are rolling down my cheeks. "Evan . . . I . . . you can't . . ."

Both his hands hold my face and he softly wipes them away——at least he tries to. My eyes are like a damn faucet. "You, McKinley Rae Mills, are an amazing woman. Every step of the way you've been there for me and for my daughter. You've helped me prepare for her, when I otherwise would have been on my own. I love Aaron, but he's not much help in the baby department." He smiles. "I owe you so much, and if my daughter grows up to be anything like you . . . well, I couldn't ask for more. Hell, I hope she does. I pray you continue to be a part of my life, of both of our lives, and she will grow up learning how to be a remarkable person just from watching you."

"I'm honored and I promise to always be there for both of you," I choke out as the waterworks continue.

Aaron chooses this moment to walk back in the room. "Uh . . . everything okay?" he asks. His eyes dart between Evan, me, and baby Lexi.

Evan stands and takes a seat on the bed. "Yeah, man, everything's good. I was just telling Kinley her name." He smiles.

"Let's hear it," he says. "No, wait. I need my turn, baby hog."

Reluctantly, I allow Evan to take her from me and hand her over to Aaron, who is now sitting in the chair beside me.

"Uncle Aaron says no dating until you're thirty," he coos to her. "All right, so what are we calling this little beauty?" he asks.

"Lexington. It's Mom's maiden name. I'm going to call her Lexi," Evan says.

"That's a kick-ass name, man. Does Miss Lexi have a middle name?"

"Rae. Lexington Rae Chamberlin." Evan's voice is strong with conviction that this is what he wants, to name his daughter after his mother's family and me.

Aaron studies him then turns his gaze toward me. Our conversation about me being careful is running through his mind; I know it is. I smile broadly to let him know I'm good with this. He doesn't say anything, but nods his acceptance.

Leaning his head down, he whispers, "It's nice to meet you, Lexi Rae."

EVAN 19

*T*oday's the day I get to bring my little girl home. I'm not gonna lie, I'm scared as hell. This little angel depends on me for everything, me alone. I don't want to fail her. Last night, I kept her with me in the room they gave me. I'm surprised they gave Misty and me both a room, and when I mentioned it to the nurse, they said that census was low and it wasn't an issue. Lucky for me, I was able to keep Lexi with me all night. McKinley and Aaron offered to stay, but I told them to go. Lexi is my daughter, and I'm not going to have them there when we get home. I need to get used to this.

I also needed some . . . distance from McKinley. The more time I spend with her, the more the lines blur. It's a constant struggle to keep it to myself. Those lips—full, soft and so damn sweet—I can't help but think about the kisses we've shared. Apparently, we're friends who kiss. Friends, who kiss and don't talk about it. I'm not sure how I feel about that. Not the kissing——that's hot as hell. I'm not sure how I feel about not talking about it. On one hand, it's a relief she's not reading more into it. On the other hand, it kind of pisses me off that she's not. Like she thinks those moments with her don't mean something to me.

I'm a fucking mess.

Lexi whines from her bed and even though she barely slept last night, I can't prevent the smile I know I'm sporting right now. Her being awake, again, means I get to hold her. The nurses said I'm going to spoil her. Of course I am, she's my little angel.

"Come here, sweet girl," I whisper as I lift her from her bed. She

immediately goes quiet and closes her eyes. I take a seat back on the bed and lay her against my chest. My little girl wants her daddy. It's a heady feeling, one that has twisted my heart around her chubby little fingers.

I wake up to the sound of soft voices. "He's held her most of the night." I open my eyes to see who's talking. McKinley is here, talking to one of the nurses.

"Hey, sleepyhead." She smiles softly—my smile, the one that makes her eyes sparkle. I could get used to waking up to that smile.

"Hi." I kiss Lexi on top of the head and slowly sit up.

"Can I?" Kinley asks, her eyes never leaving my daughter.

I nod. My throat is tight with too much emotion from her simple request. My daughter's mother wants nothing to do with her, yet this amazing girl can't seem to get enough of her.

"Hello, sweet girl," she whispers as she pulls her close and breathes her in. "I brought her some clothes," she says, her voice soft and low. "I also brought the car seat, but we're leaving it in my car. No way are we taking Miss Lexi home in your truck. I thought you were going to get a new one?" she asks.

"She kind of surprised me," I chuckle and point to Lexi. "But, yes, I had planned on a new truck before she arrived. Thank you for the clothes for her and the car seat."

"There's a bag for you too." She nods toward the chair across the room. I see Lexi's manly diaper bag that Kinley picked out, as well as a bag for me.

"Thank you for taking care of us."

"It was nothing. Now go shower and let me have my Lexi time." She grins.

Standing from the bed, I lean down and kiss Lexi on top of her tiny little head then do the same with Kinley. I hear her intake a breath and have to make myself stand and walk into the bathroom to freshen up.

I rush through a shower. It does wonders to wake me up. I'm packing my dirty clothes back into the bag when I hear someone singing. Careful to not make a sound, I move toward the door and quietly turn the handle. McKinley is sitting in the chair singing to Lexi. I can't tell if she's got her rapt attention or if Lexi is sound asleep. Regardless, I'm captivated.

I push open the door, alerting her that I'm done with my shower. I watch as a blush creeps over her cheeks. "Oops, looks like Daddy caught us."

Daddy. I'm a daddy.

"What are you girls up to?" I ask like I didn't just catch her.

"Just having some girl time, right, Lexi?" she asks.

"Uh-huh. Thanks again for the clothes. That shower felt so damn good."

"You're welcome. I'm sure you smell better." She finally looks up at me, and she's grinning like a fool.

"Har har."

This causes her to chuckle, a sound I've grown rather fond of over the last several months.

"So what time does she get released?"

"Soon. The doctor said babies usually stay until the mom is discharged, but due to our situation, Lexi is doing well, eating good, so we can go home. I have to make an appointment with her pediatrician in three to four days just to make sure she's gaining weight and all is well," I explain.

"I bet you'll be glad to have her home. Get settled into a routine?"

"Yeah, it's surreal really." I don't tell her I'm scared as hell. That being here with the nurses checking up on me gave me confidence. Who's going to check up on me at home? Gran and Gramps are up there in age; neither one of them get around all that well. Mom, Dad, Grandma, and Grandpa won't be able to make the trip from Alabama. It's just me and Lexi.

"I brought her a cute outfit for her hospital pictures and there's a gift for you in the diaper bag."

"Kinley—" I start to protest.

"Oh hush! Just say, 'Thank you, Kinley,' and open the bag," she scolds me.

"Thank you, Kinley," I say, my voice sugary sweet. Although, I'm mocking her, I do as I'm told and dig into the diaper bag. Inside is a small black point and shoot camera. At least that's what the box says.

"I know you don't have a camera, other than your cell phone. I didn't

want you to miss out on capturing a moment of this little one's life."

It takes everything in me, all the willpower I possess, to not stalk across the room and crush my lips to hers. This girl . . . she's nothing if not amazing. I'm so damn lucky to have her in my life, to have her in Lexi's life. I hope that's something that never changes.

McKinley

20

I've spent the morning at the hospital with Evan and Lexi. I taught him how to use his camera and he's already taken a gazillion pictures. I know he's worried. I can see it in his eyes, but he has nothing to be worried about. Less than twenty-four hours and he's already the best daddy. You can see how much he loves her.

"All right, baby girl. Let's get you home," Evan says, placing Lexi in her car seat. He went down and got it when the hospital told him he had to prove he knew how to work it. They also have to watch him putting her in the car before he can leave. Who knew?

I insisted he take my Durango and I would drive his truck. He complained, but not as much as I would have thought. I think his only complaint is he was not okay with me driving his rust bucket either. I waved off his concern. It's not that the truck is dangerous, it's just . . . not reliable. I would feel much better knowing he wasn't stranded on the road with her.

"Really, Kinley, I can't thank you enough for all you've done," he says as he straps Lexi into her seat.

"It's nothing. You can keep my car until you get a new one. I've got nothing going on the next few days, and even if I did, I could take your truck," I tell him.

"No, that's not—"

"Evan, I'm not taking no for an answer," I interrupt him.

"Fine, I'll rectify the situation as soon as possible. Thank you."

"You're welcome. Do you need anything?" I ask him.

"No, I don't think so. The hospital gave me a ton of formula and thanks to you, her room is ready for her."

"Okay, well, call me if you need anything. Aaron said he would stop by later tonight."

"Sounds good. Thanks again," he says.

I nod, pick up his bag of clothes, and follow him out of the room. The nurse follows us down to the parking lot and watches as Evan straps Lexi into the seat.

"Take care, Mr. Chamberlin," she says after he passes the test.

"She's so tiny," he says, looking at Lexi snuggled in her seat. "She's riding back there all alone."

I was thinking the same thing but didn't want to say anything. "I can ride back with you and have Mom bring me back to get your truck," I offer.

"I can't ask you—"

"You didn't." I squeeze past him and slide into the backseat beside Lexi. "Hey, sweet girl, you want some company?" I ask her. I don't look at Evan, even though I know he's watching me. Instead, I focus on Lexi. Eventually, he closes the door and slides in behind the wheel.

He adjusts the seat and the mirrors. "You girls ready to go home?" he asks. His eyes find mine in the rearview.

"Yes, she's ready to see her new room."

"Oh, she is, is she?" Evan chuckles.

"Yep. Girl talk, buddy, get used to it," I tease him.

"Got it," he says through his laughter.

The drive to his place doesn't take long. Of course, that could be because I spent the entire ride watching a slumbering Lexi on her first car ride. I even pulled out the camera and snapped a few pictures for Evan.

"Do you mind going to see Gran and Gramps with me? I know they're dying to see her."

"Sure."

He parks in front of the old farm house and hops out of the driver's seat. Instead of opening the door on his side of the Durango, he walks around and opens mine. I climb out, pulling the diaper bag with me, as he leans in and releases Lexi's seat.

I lead the way up the steps. "Just knock and go on in," Evan says from behind me. I do as he says and hold the door open for him.

Evan heads down the hall and turns left into a room that I assume is the living room. "Surprise!" he says.

His gran clutches her chest. I'm thinking that was not the best way to announce our arrival.

"Sorry, Gran," Evan says sheepishly. "Would you like to meet your great-granddaughter?" he asks them.

"What kind of question is that, boy?" his grandfather's hoarse voice says. "Bring that girl here so we can get a better look." They're both sitting on the couch.

Evan sets Lexi's seat down, carefully removes the straps, and cradles her in his arms. "Gram, Gramps, I would like to introduce you to Lexington Rae Chamberlin," he says proudly, handing her over to his grandmother.

I watch as tears well in her eyes as she takes in baby Lexi. I catch Gramps swiping at the corner of his eye. I feel like I'm intruding on a precious family moment. Stepping back, I plan to escape to the Durango to give them some time when Evan turns to me. "Kinley, would you mind taking a few pictures for us?"

"Absolutely," I say, happy to have a reason to be here. I reach into the diaper bag and pull out the camera. I snap a few shots; well, maybe more than a few. You can never have enough pictures.

"All right, I need to get this little one home. It's almost time for her to eat." Evan takes her from his gramps and kisses the top of her little head before placing her back in her seat.

We say our goodbyes and load back up to drive just a few hundred feet to Evan's place. I text Mom on the short trip, asking her to come pick me up. I'm sure Evan doesn't want me hanging around his first day home with his daughter.

"Mom's on her way," I tell him once we have carried everything inside.

"I can't thank you enough, Kinley."

"You're welcome, and I wanted to."

The sound of tires crunching gravel gets both of our attention. "I hope you're ready to give her up, at least for a few minutes. Mom's going to want to love on her."

Evan smiles. "Yeah, I figured she would." He looks down at the little pink bundle in his arms. "You ready for some Grandma Mills loving?" he asks her.

At first, I'm surprised he referred to my mom as grandma, but I shouldn't be. Evan has practically grown up at our house and has always referred to my parents as his "second set."

I make my way to the door and pull it open before she even has time to knock. "Is she sleeping?" Mom asks as she passes me to walk into the house. I can hear Evan chuckle in the other room. He obviously heard her.

I point toward the living room and Mom doesn't waste any time as she heads that way. "Oh, Evan." Her voice cracks. "Can I hold her?"

When I join them, Mom is sitting on the couch, Lexi in her arms as she unwraps her from her swaddle. "Ten fingers and ten toes, you're such a cutie. Your daddy's going to have his hands full with the boys when it comes to you," she tells the baby.

Evan groans. "She's not allowed to date."

Mom laughs. "Oh, Evan, she's going to date and you're going to have to learn to deal with it. All you can do is give her the values and make sure she respects herself enough to make good decisions."

"Or," Evan says with a grin, "she can not date until she's at least thirty."

Mom focuses her attention back on Lexi. She offers the baby her finger and Lexi latches on. "You're just going to have to wrap Daddy and Uncle Aaron around your finger. Don't worry, Kinley and I will be there to guide you." She laughs.

"Hey now." Evan grins.

We spend the next half hour talking while Mom loves on Lexi. It's me who finally suggests we head home. "Mom, you about ready to go?" I ask. She insisted she feed Lexi to give Evan a "break."

"Oh, I guess we should let these two settle in." She stands and hands Lexi back to Evan. "You call if you need anything," she tells him with a pat to his cheek.

"Yes, ma'am. Kinley, I can't thank you enough for all that you've done for us."

"I'm happy to help. Call me if you need anything. Oh, and I bought an adorable outfit for her newborn pictures. Mine will be way better than the hospital's. Maybe I can stop by tomorrow sometime?" I ask.

"We'll be here," he says with a smile.

Mom and I say our goodbyes then leave father and daughter alone for the first time.

EVAN 21

"*I*t's just you and me, kid," I say to my daughter, who's sleeping soundly in my arms. She doesn't have a care in the world. If I get my way, she never will. I want to give her the world. Instead of putting her in her room, I place her in what Kinley calls a pack-n-play. She said I would need it if I take Lexi places with me, so she has a safe place to sleep. She also mentioned I would probably want her close when I first brought her home. Once again, she nailed it. I owe her so much.

Once I have Lexi settled, I unpack the bag Kinley brought to the hospital for me and start a load of laundry. I busy myself unpacking the formula samples the hospital gave me and then call my foreman, letting him know Lexi came a few weeks early and I'm going to need him to handle the crew and, well . . . everything for a few days. He and I had already talked about this, so the only surprise is that it's a few weeks sooner than we discussed.

I do a few more things around the house as quiet as I can and she's still

sleeping. I'm glad I read all those books or I would be freaked out that something was wrong. Babies sleep a lot. Deciding I should try to catch a quick catnap, I stretch out on the couch and close my eyes. Just as I'm about to drift off, I feel my pocket vibrate.

Pulling out my phone, I see I have a text from Aaron.

Aaron: I'm at the door.

I pull my tired ass off the couch and go greet my best friend.

"Hey," Aaron whispers when I open the door. "I didn't wake her, did I? Kinley said she was probably sleeping."

"Nah, she's sleeping, but it's all good. Come on in." I step back to let him pass.

"I bet you're glad to be home."

"You have no idea," I say, following him into the living room.

Aaron stops by the pack-n-play to peek in on my daughter. My daughter . . . it's surreal she's here.

"She's a cutie, man. We're going to have our hands full." He softly chuckles.

That's my best friend. Always there no matter what the situation. He automatically includes himself in the future of warding off horny boys from my baby girl. "I don't even want to think about that yet."

This causes Aaron to laugh and the sound startles Lexi. "Shit, man, I'm sorry," he says before placing his hand over his mouth.

"Don't be. I read that you need to not keep everything quiet so they will learn to sleep through everyday household noises. It didn't wake her, so we're all good."

"Do you need anything?" he asks.

"Nah, I'm good."

"Kinley told me she refused to let you bring her home in your truck. She said you were going to be getting a new one. Any ideas of what you might get?"

"Honestly, man, I don't know. I haven't thought much about it. I know I need something more reliable. I might check out Dodge. I really like Kinley's Durango."

"Yeah, it's sweet. I looked at Dodge before I bought mine, but decided I needed to stay a Ford man."

"Yeah, I need to get that taken care of soon. I can't keep Kinley's Durango forever."

"She's in no rush. She works at home most of the time and I already told her if something comes up she can take my truck. I spend most of my days in the stables anyway."

"Yeah, but it's something I've been planning on. It would have been easier to do it without taking a newborn with me, but it is what it is."

"Yeah. Have you heard from her? From Misty?"

"No. I don't really think I will. It's all on me, and I don't regret it. I love that little girl, I can't even express what it felt like to hear her cry for the first time."

"That's heavy stuff, bro. I'm happy as hell for you. I know nothing about babies or how to raise them, but I'm in your corner. Anything you need, I'm there."

"Thanks, man. I'm not sure how truck shopping is going to go with a newborn, but I'm about to find out."

"I'm sure Mom or Kinley would be happy to keep her."

My chest tightens ares the thought of being away from her. I just got her after months of worrying about Misty taking care of herself and praying my baby girl arrived healthy. Can I leave her?

"What's that face?" Aaron chuckles. Fucker, he knows damn well what I'm thinking.

"Maybe I could convince Kinley to come with me," I say. She could help me with Lexi and I wouldn't have to leave her yet, although I know I'm going to need to eventually. Speaking of that, I need to arrange childcare too. I thought I had a few more weeks to get that all squared away. Yeah, I'm the boss, but I work the horses and cattle with the rest of the crew, so not helping isn't an option. I need to be out there with them, keeping my finger on the pulse of the operation.

Aaron laughs. "You know she will. All she and Mom talked about when Dad and I got in today was baby Lexi."

"Yeah, they were both here for a while. Your mom fed her. She's going to be after you to settle down, man," I laugh.

"Not opposed to it, just need to find her."

Aaron has always said he's holding out for the one. He doesn't do relationships. If he's not feeling it within a few hours of meeting her, he's one and done. I don't know how many times I've heard Kinley preach to him about not being able to really get to know someone if he doesn't give them a chance. His theory is it should be instant. Not sure I agree with him, not after all the time I spent with Kinley. My feelings toward her have changed; so much, I fight them anytime I'm near her.

"What do you have going on the rest of the night?" I change the subject. No way do I need to be thinking about Kinley with Aaron sitting here.

"Nothing, man. I thought about going into town to get something to eat. Mom and Dad went out and Kinley is editing, so she will be glued to her computer for hours. You hungry? How about I go pick us up a pizza or something?"

"Starving! Now that I think about it, I haven't eaten all day." I was too nervous about bringing my daughter home to worry about food. My stomach is finally protesting.

"I'm all over it. I'll be back in a bit," Aaron says, standing from the couch. "Do you need anything for this one?" He points to where Lexi is sleeping peacefully.

"No, your sister is a lifesaver. She made sure I was all set." He studies me for a few long seconds and my palms start to sweat. Can he see it? Can he tell she's more than just his little sister to me? That she's more than just the friend who has helped me over the past few months?

Finally, he looks away and heads toward the front door. "Be back in a few," he says over his shoulder and then he's gone.

McKinley

22

he sun blaring through my bedroom window causes me to groan in frustration. It's was after one this morning before I finally let sleep claim me. I lost track of time while editing, but at least I'm all caught up. Today, I don't have anything scheduled in the studio, so I plan to take my camera and the outfit I bought to Evan's and get some, hopefully, adorable newborn pictures of Lexi. However, I first need a shower and food, since I skipped dinner last night.

After rushing through a shower, I head downstairs and find Mom pulling a casserole dish out of the oven. It smells amazing. Looking at the clock, I see it's only nine-thirty. "That smells great," I tell her.

"Thank you. I made lasagna for Evan. It's something he can eat on for a few days and it's easy to reheat. Do you think you could drop it off for me?" she asks. I'm surprised she doesn't want to herself.

"Sure, I'm headed there anyway. I'm going to take some newborn pictures of Lexi. I can't wait to see her in the Alabama outfit I bought off of Etsy."

"Those ears are just too cute," Mom says. I purchased a gray crocheted hat with elephant ears and a matching diaper cover in gray with a red "A" right on the bottom. I can't wait to take these pictures. Evan is a hardcore Alabama fan.

"They really are. I was going to surprise him, but I don't know if I can get him to leave her long enough. He's smitten."

"Hmm, that he is. I'm sure for you he would be agreeable," Mom

replies.

"What do you mean for me?"

"He just seems to trust you. You two have gotten closer since you've been home." She goes back to packing up the lasagna in her carrier. I study her to see if she can tell, for him, I would be agreeable to anything. It's not Evan; it's me. Now that Lexi's here, it's just going to be harder to resist him——them. She is the sweetest baby.

"Yeah, he needed help. That's what friends do." I try to sound nonchalant. Mom doesn't call me out on it and I'm grateful. I don't want to talk about how I'm falling harder every day for my brother's best friend, for my best friend. Evan and I have become really close, and I feel guilty that I want him, but I just . . . his kisses are hard to forget.

After scarfing down a bagel, I run to the studio and grab the outfit and a few other props I use for newborn shoots. Once I have everything I need, including Mom's lasagna, loaded into Evan's truck, I'm on my way. The drive takes mere minutes from our place to his. I park and grab the lasagna. I can come back to get everything else. I'm hoping I can convince him to get out of the house for a little while so I can surprise him with the pictures.

I knock softly, not wanting to wake the baby if she's sleeping. I wait, but no answer. Maybe they're both sleeping. Using my key, I slide it into the lock and slowly push the door open. I hear a soft whimper coming from the living room and the sound of Evan's voice as he tries to soothe her.

I take the lasagna to the kitchen, kick off my shoes, and make my way to the living room. I find Evan pacing back and forth with Lexi in his arms, begging her to sleep. "Rough night?" I ask. The sound of my voice startles him. When he turns to face me, I can see the dark circles under his eyes. He's exhausted.

"You could say that. She's hardly slept," he says, defeated.

With a few steps, I'm standing beside him. I place my hand on Lexi's back and gently rub. "Let me take her. You go get some rest."

With glassy eyes, which I'm sure have more to do with emotion than exhaustion, he says, "Kinley, what if I can't do this? I love her, but what if I'm not what she needs?"

Reaching out, I take Lexi from him and cradle her in my arms, gently rocking her from side to side. "Evan, you are what she needs for the simple fact that you do love her. You have to remember, most of the time, there are two parents, two people to take shifts until this little one gets her days and nights on the right schedule. It takes time, and you are trying to do it on your own."

"I just—"

"You're just tired. Have you eaten?"

"Yeah, Aaron came over last night and brought pizza."

"Today, Evan? Mom made you a lasagna, not exactly breakfast, but it's still warm and it smelled amazing when she was making it. I set it on the counter in the kitchen. Go make yourself a plate, then go upstairs and sleep. I have nothing planned today. I'll take care of this one." I look down at Lexi. "You, little one, have worn Daddy out. You and I are going to spend some time together while he gets some rest." I talk to her like she understands me. I'm sure I look like a crazy person, but Evan's so tired he probably doesn't even notice.

"Kinley, I—"

"Evan, go. I got this. We will be here the entire time. She needs you rested. Now go get some food and then sleep."

He's too tired to protest further. He nods and leaves the room. Lexi is no longer whimpering; she's passed out in my arms. Babies can feel tension and I'm sure this little one was feeding off his exhaustion. Not wanting to move her just yet, I reach for my purse and pull out my Kindle. I settle down on the couch with this precious baby girl to read. I need Evan to see I'm good with this so he won't feel guilty.

A few minutes later, he joins me with a heaping plate of lasagna and a glass of sweet tea. I pull my feet up, so he can sit on the opposite end of the couch. "She's out," he observes.

"Yeah, I think the two of you were keeping each other up." He doesn't say anything; instead, he digs into his lasagna. I open my Kindle and start reading, letting him eat.

"I can't take care of my own kid," he says, setting the now empty plate on the coffee table.

"Evan, every parent needs help. You can't expect to do it all alone. Let me help. Go crash for a few hours. I got her. I'm going to make sure she's in a deep sleep before I lay her down. I have my Kindle." I hold it up for him.

He runs his hands over his face and releases a heavy sigh. Finally, he stands and carries his plate to the kitchen. When he comes back, he sits on the edge of the couch close to me, tracing a finger down Lexi's cheek. "I love her so fucking much, and it kills me to think I can't take care of her," he confesses.

"You can take care of her. You're exhausted, Evan. Go get some rest," I say softly.

Leaning in, he cups my face with his hand and runs his thumb across my cheek. "What would I do without you?" he whispers the question. I assume it's a rhetorical question, so I don't answer. "You're amazing, Kinley." Leaning in a little further, his lips press against mine. "Thank you," he says, pulling away. He watches me for a reaction, which he's not going to get. I can't let him see how he affects me. I would rather have stolen kisses we don't talk about than have him pull away when he finds out those kisses make my heart full.

Standing, he says, "She ate about two hours ago, so she will be hungry soon."

"Okay, I promise to wake you if we need anything. Now go get some rest. We'll be right here when you wake up."

Evan nods and heads upstairs.

Not twenty minutes later, Lexi begins to stir. Closing my Kindle, I change her diaper and make her a bottle. She drinks greedily and gets mad when I make her stop so I can burp her. She sucks the rest down and her eyes are once again closed. I rub her back and gently pat until she burps again and sighs, making me smile. She's got a full belly and is sound asleep. Placing her in the pack-n-play, I pick up the bottles Evan left sitting on the table from last night and quietly load the dishwasher. After wiping off the counters, I decide to go ahead and sweep the kitchen floor. After that's all done, I slip outside and grab my camera and props. Little Miss Lexi doesn't need to sleep all day. Maybe if I keep her up, Evan will get some rest tonight.

Another hour passes and I decide it's time to wake her. When I pick her up, she stretches her little arms and legs. I swear she's the cutest kid ever, but then again, look who her daddy is. I strip her out of her clothes, place the diaper cover on her, and secure the elephant ear hat to her head. She sleeps through it all; it doesn't even faze her.

I take way too many pictures. It's going to be hard to choose my favorite. I can't wait to surprise Evan. I slip the outfit back into my bag and put her back into her sleeper, and just like that, Daddy has no idea. After making sure she's settled back in the pack-n-play, I take a few pictures of her sleeping and then run my equipment back out to the truck.

EVAN 23

I wake with a startle. I hear Lexi downstairs and I panic. Jumping from my bed, I rush down the hall. It's not until I hear Kinley's voice that I stop to take a breath and proceed down the steps at a normal pace.

Kinley has Lexi on the couch changing her diaper. My little angel is not impressed with this. "I know, sweet girl. It's almost over," Kinley coos to her. "It's okay, Lex, as soon as we get you in some dry clothes, we'll get you a bottle."

"She giving you trouble?" I ask.

Kinley jumps. "You scared the crap out of me." She finishes changing Lexi and as soon as she picks her up, her cries turn to a low whimper. "Nah, she's just not happy with the fact that we had to change her clothes and diaper before bottle. She soaked through." She stands with Lexi in one arm, dirty diaper and clothes in the other.

"I can take her," I say, walking toward her.

"I got it. Just relax," she says, carrying a now pacified Lexi into the kitchen. I look around and see she cleaned up.

"Kinley, you didn't have to clean," I tell her as I follow her into the kitchen. It too is spotless.

"I know I didn't have to. I wanted to. How you feeling?" she asks.

"Better. I feel human again."

"Good. You only slept about three hours."

"Three hours of sleep, after what I've had total the last two days

makes it feel more like twelve," I laugh. Kinley is completely comfortable in my home, making a bottle for my daughter. She doesn't mention the kiss, and I don't either. I can't. If I ignore it, I can pretend I did it because I was exhausted and thankful for her. That was only part of it. The other part? I blame those sweet lips of hers.

Okay. I need to stop thinking about it. "So, I was thinking. I really need to go get a truck. I was wondering if you would want to come with me. I don't know that I can handle a newborn in a car lot for hours."

"Sure, but you can go and I can stay with her if you want. I don't mind at all, or Mom would be happy to watch her."

"Yeah, Aaron said the same thing. At first, I wasn't real thrilled with the idea of leaving her just yet. . . ." I stop there and wait for her reply.

"I'm good either way. I don't have anything in the studio for the next three days. So, anytime you want to go, I'm your girl." She smiles.

'I'm your girl?' I wish like hell she was.

"Great, thank you. I just would feel better to have someone else with me. I know I need to get over leaving her; hell, I need to find childcare."

"I think you should talk to Mom. She would love to do it. I'm happy to help too on days I don't have a shoot. Right now, that's about two to three days a week. I can book them on the same days. The only time that wouldn't work is when I have to go to them. More often than not, that's on weekends for birthday parties and events, so it could work."

"You really think she would be willing?" I ask.

"Hell yes, she would. She's always telling Aaron to settle down and give her grandbabies, you know this. Besides, it wouldn't be every day with me helping out. I'll talk to her and see what she thinks," she tells me.

"That would be . . . perfect! I don't like the thought of people I don't know keeping her. She's so tiny."

"Well, I know I would love to spend a few days a week with her." I watch as she kisses Lexi's cheek. "All right, little one, let's get you fed." She passes by me to go back into the living room.

"You sure you don't want me to take her?"

"No way. This is my Lexi time." She grins. "Is there anything you need to do? Go check in at the stables? We're good here."

Yeah, I need to kiss the hell out of you. "That's all taken care of. The stables are in good hands."

"Well, just kick back and relax, Dad. We got this."

"In that case, I'm going to go shower. Maybe we can go to the car lot after she eats? Is it okay to take her out this young?" I have no clue what the rules are for this kind of thing, or even if there are any.

"We'll keep her bundled up and no one gets to touch her. They need to keep their germy hands off. Other than that, yeah, we can take her."

Just like with everything else this girl has said and done, her protectiveness for Lexi causes these . . . feelings I have for her to grow. I'm in deep trouble with this one. Even knowing that, it's impossible for me to keep my distance.

I rush up the stairs to shower and change. By the time I make it back downstairs, Kinley has Lexi in her car seat and is shoving items into the diaper bag. "Better safe than sorry," she says.

"I agree. This is a first venturing out with a newborn baby; hell, we can take half the house if you think we might need it."

This causes her to throw her head back and laugh. I'm not trying to be funny; I'm being serious. "Let's go, funnyman." Kinley grabs the diaper bag, leaving Lexi for me.

* * *

"Two hours, not bad," I say to Kinley as we load Lexi up in my new truck.

"Nope, not bad. I had the same experience when I bought my Durango from Todd. He doesn't push and makes the process so much less painful."

"So, how about we grab something to eat?" I ask her.

"Yeah, or if you want to get this one home, I can stop and pick us up something," she offers.

"How about some of your mom's lasagna?"

"Perfect. I'm going to run by the house real quick, but I'll meet you there. You two good?" she asks.

I look at my daughter so tiny in the backseat of my new Dodge one-ton truck. "Yeah, we're good. See you soon." I fight the urge to pull her in for a kiss. That seems to be our thing, kissing. Instead, I watch her climb into her Durango and drive away.

I take my seat and adjust the mirror so I can see in the backseat. Kinley said I have a mirror at the house that I can hang on the back of the seat so I will be able to see Lexi while I'm driving. That must be installed pronto. Lexi whimpers and I know it's getting close to time for her to eat again. "Let's get you home, baby girl."

McKinley
24

I didn't tell Evan why I needed to stop by the house first, and he didn't question me. I plan to pack a change of clothes and stay with him and Lexi tonight. He needs help until they get into a routine. I have nothing going on tomorrow, or for the next few days actually. It's the perfect time for me to help him. I also want to talk to Mom, if she's there, to see if she is interested in watching Lexi for him on the days I have a full schedule. I'm positive she's going to be over the moon excited, but I want to ask her just the same.

"Just the lady I need to talk to," I say when I see her sitting at the kitchen table.

"Well, that's a warm welcome. How are Evan and Lexi doing today?" she asks.

"Good. When I got there today, Evan was exhausted and frustrated. I guess Miss Lexi was up most of the night and he was running on no sleep since the night she was born."

"That boy, he should have called us."

"Yeah, he had almost convinced himself he can't do this—-that he can't be a dad to her. I made him eat some of your lasagna, which he inhaled by the way, and take a nap. I took care of Lexi, snuck in some shots with her little Alabama outfit, and cleaned up while they were both sleeping."

"I can't wait to see them. Evan didn't catch you?" she asks.

"Nope, he slept through it all, so did Lexi," I laugh. "Anyway, I'm

going to grab a few things and stay over there tonight. He didn't ask me to, but I don't think he will. He's too busy trying to prove he can do this. I feel bad for him because most people have a spouse or significant other to share in the duties. Evan is adjusting to all of this on his own," I explain.

"That's very nice of you, dear. I think Aaron is planning on stopping over in a little while also."

"Even better. I can nap while he's there and then take the last shift with Lexi. That will help Evan be available for her tomorrow during the day, so he can start to get a routine down. Maybe once he gets the daytime routine without being exhausted, the nights will fall into place."

"How did you get so smart?" she teases.

"Hey, Evan's looking for someone to watch Lexi during the day. You know of anyone?" I ask her. I don't even get to count to ten before she's volunteering her services.

"Me. He can bring that sweet girl to me. I would love to watch her. I know Carla would do the same thing if I wasn't able to do it for you or Aaron." Mom and Carla are best friends. She was heartbroken when they moved to Alabama, but that's what was best for Jeff and his treatments.

"I had a feeling you might feel that way. I'm good with helping too."

"You make sure you tell him I would be honored to watch that little angel."

"Will do. I'm going to go gather a few things and head over there. When Aaron gets there, I'll sleep." I dash up the stairs, throw some clothes into a bag, grab my toothbrush, and call it good. It's not like I'm trying to impress him. I'm just trying to keep the guy from being dead on his feet, so he can take care of his daughter.

When I get back to Evan's, I don't bother knocking. I just walk on in. "Kinley?" Evan yells from what sounds like upstairs.

"Yeah, it's me," I call back. I can hear Lexi crying.

"Could you come up here please?" he yells back. His voice sounds funny. I drop my bag in the living room and make my way up the steps. "Where are you?" I ask. Her cries are getting louder as I reach the top of the steps.

"In the master bathroom," he replies.

I slowly push open his bedroom door and Lexi's cries are coming at me in surround sound. "Kinley," Evan yells for me.

"Yeah, I'm here. What's wrong?" I ask, pushing open the bathroom door. What I find has me biting my tongue, trying not to laugh. Evan has a naked Lexi, holding her high over the bathroom sink, and she's covered in, well, shit. "Oh, my God, what happened?" I manage to ask. The look on his face is just too damn funny.

"What does it look like happened? My little angel made all this," he says, nodding to her. "I'm in over my head here, Kinley," he admits.

"Where is her bathtub?"

"Uh, I don't know. In her room, I guess," he breathes out. I rush out of the room and into Lexi's in search of her bathtub. Sure enough, I find it in the bottom of her closet. I grab the caddy, which has all the baby wash, and snag one of her washcloths and towels before I dash back to Evan's room.

"Give me just a second," I say to Evan as I race back into the bathroom. I set the baby tub inside the big tub and turn the water on, throwing in the little rubber ducky that tells you if the water is too hot. Once the temperature is good, I stand and reach for the messy baby. "Let me have her."

Evan hands her over, and I place her into her baby tub. The screams get even louder. "Looks like Miss Lexi doesn't like bath time. It's okay, sweet girl," I coo to her.

"Is she hurt?" Evan asks. I don't take my eyes of Lexi, but I can hear the strain in his voice.

"No, she's not hurt. She's just not happy. She's got shit up her back and, apparently, she's not a fan of bath time. This is all new to her too. We just have to give her some time. She can sense you're tense, Evan," I tell him.

"Hell yeah, I am. I had no idea what to do. If you hadn't come back when you did, I don't know. . . ." He trails off.

"Let me get her cleaned up. Why don't you go get me a fresh diaper and some clean clothes?"

Evan doesn't say anything else, but I hear the door close, so I know he's gone. "All right, little miss, you need to calm down. We just need to get you clean, and then we'll get you all snuggled back up." I begin to

sing "Girl Crush" by Little Big Town. It's the song that was playing on the radio when I got here and the first thing that popped into my head. Regardless of the words, it soothes her, and her wailing cries turn to a soft whimper. I keep singing, and by the time I have her all cleaned up, she's quiet as a mouse, except for some leftover hiccups from getting herself so worked up.

Picking her up, I lay her against my chest as I slip the hooded towel over her head. I'm soaked, but she's clean, so that's all that matters. I wrap the towel around her and stand. Opening the bathroom door, I find Evan sitting on his bed, a pile of clothes and a diaper beside him.

"Kinley, I panicked," he says softly. "What would I have done if you hadn't shown up?"

"Evan, you have to remember Lexi takes her cues from you. She can tell if you're stressed or worked up about something. You have to stay calm for her. This is not going to be the last time this type of thing happens."

He lies back on the bed and throws his arm over his eyes. I give him time to process what I just said and tend to Lexi. "All right, Miss Lexi, now that you're all clean, let's get you dressed." I lay her on the bed and unwrap the towel from her body. I make quick work of getting the diaper on her to avoid another accident. Next is her onesie, and finally, the little purple sleeper.

"Look at me, Daddy," I say, holding her up in my arms.

Evan sits up and takes her in. "Good as new," I say with a smile. "Now, you two head downstairs while I clean up the mess in the bathroom. If it's okay with you, I'm going to go ahead and put her tub in the spare bathroom and make sure all of her bath stuff is moved in there as well. I don't know why I didn't already have that done."

"I can do that," Evan says.

"Nope, I got it. You two go relax," I say as I hand Lexi over to him.

Evan holds her close. I watch as he breathes her in. When he realizes he's busted, he just winks at me and walks out of the bedroom.

EVAN 25

I'm sitting on the couch holding my little girl and she's happy, clean and content. "I'm sorry I freaked out on you. Daddy's new to all this and it's going to take me some time." She just watches me like I'm the most fascinating thing she's ever seen.

The feeling's mutual.

"Come in," I yell when there's a knock on the door.

"Uncle Aaron's here," Aaron says as he comes into the room. "What's going on, man?"

"Oh, you know, this little cutie just had a massive explosion in her diaper. I freaked the hell out. Luckily, Kinley came in and saved the day."

"Ouch! Where is my little sister?" he asks, looking toward the kitchen.

"She's upstairs. She said she was going to clean up the bathroom. I offered, but she gave me strict instructions to come down here and relax. Apparently, the baby can tell when I'm stressed and that's why I couldn't get her to calm down," I explain.

"Sounds like a logical reason. Listen, don't beat yourself up about it. You're learning as you go. You're going to nail this daddy gig." He grins.

"Now you sound like Kinley."

"Who sounds like me?"

I look up to see her enter the room and my mouth goes dry. Kinley is standing at the bottom of the steps, wearing what looks like one of my t-shirts and nothing else.

"What are you wearing?" Aaron questions her.

"Oh, my clothes were soaked from Lex's bath. I hope you don't mind, Evan. I grabbed one of your shirts out of your closet."

Mind? Hell no, I don't mind. She looks hot as hell in my shirt. "Evan?" she says my name again and I realize I'm still staring at her.

"Yeah, no of course. That's fine." My voice cracks. Shit, nothing like giving myself away.

"Aaron, I'm glad you're here. I'm going to go upstairs and lay down for a few hours, so Evan can get a good night's sleep," she says.

Wait? What? "McKinley, you don't have to do that."

"I know I don't *have* to do that. I *want* to do that. This way you will be rested tomorrow and can get little miss in her daily routine. I don't have anything in the studio for the next few days, so this is the perfect time. You need the help, Evan. Say, 'Thank you, Kinley.'" She smiles.

She had to go and throw my smile out there, didn't she? Damn girl, I swear she's trying to get me killed. "Thank you, Kinley."

"You're welcome. Now I'll be upstairs taking a nap if you need me." Just like that, she's back up the stairs in my shirt. That's when it hits me that my room is the only room with a bed. She's going to be sleeping in my bed, in my shirt. Holy shit, she is trying to kill me.

"You know how she is when she sets her mind to something. You might as well give in," Aaron says.

"Yeah," is pretty much all I can say at this point. McKinley is upstairs in my bed. I need to stop thinking about it, need to change the subject. "So, did you see the new wheels out front?"

"Hell yeah. I meant to tell you I liked your choice. The black looks sick."

"Yeah, it's got coolers in the backseat in the floorboard. Thought with this little one that feature might come in handy someday."

Aaron laughs. "I'm sure it will. So you going to hog my niece all night or can I hold her?" he asks.

"Where were you a half hour ago?"

"That's my uncle psychic abilities showing through. I know when she's clean, fed, and a happy girl." He says that last part in a high voice as he talks to Lexi. She's wide-awake as she watches him.

"Your mom made a big-ass pan of lasagna, you hungry?"

"Always," he says, keeping his attention on Lexi.

I stand to go make us both a plate. I wish Kinley would've eaten before she went to sleep. "You good?"

"We got this, Daddy," Aaron says in a girly voice, moving Lexi's arm, telling me to go away.

I fight the urge to run upstairs and see if Kinley has fallen asleep yet. I can't go to her while Aaron is here. I know for a fact I don't have the kind of willpower needed to not steal another kiss or a simple touch, not when she's curled up in my bed, her long brown hair spread out on my pillow. Nope, definitely not going upstairs.

Aaron eats his plate of lasagna with one hand, refusing to put Lexi down. She's still wide-awake. "I think this is the longest she's been awake at one time."

"You know why, don't you?"

"Enlighten me, old wise one."

Aaron tsks like I should know the answer. "She refuses to miss out on any Uncle Aaron time, duh," he says.

I don't bother to argue with him, because to be honest, I have no clue. He could be right. Could be that my little girl already knows her Uncle Aaron is going to be a big part of her life. Kinley said babies are perceptive.

"I think it's time to give her back," Aaron says, scrunching up his nose.

"Again? How can you have anything left, kid?" I ask my daughter as I take her from Aaron.

"I got to get up early anyway. Looks like you are on your own until Kinley wakes up. She's a bear when you wake her up, so I would not advise it if I were you." He laughs his way out the door.

After getting Lexi changed, I make her a bottle. She went longer this time between feedings. By the time she's finished, she's sound asleep. I carry her up to her room and ease her into her bed. Reaching over, I turn on the baby monitor. Leaving the door open so I can hear her, I head to my room. Kinley is curled in a ball, my t-shirt riding high on her thighs. Careful to not make any noise, I set the baby monitor down on the opposite side of the bed and turn it on high. No way do I want to miss hearing Lexi wake up. I'm a little nervous with her being in the

other room, but she's just right across the hall. I refuse to let her sleep with me after all the horror stories I've read. Slipping out of my jeans, I place my cell phone on the nightstand and pull my shirt over my head. Without a second of hesitation, I slide into bed, pulling the covers up and over both of us. I lay there, stiff as a rail, staring at the ceiling. I'm tired beyond words, but can't seem to let sleep claim me when I'm lying here next to Kinley.

Finally, after staring at the shadows on the ceiling, wasting away precious hours of rest I could be getting while Lexi is sleeping, I start to drift off. It's also in this exact moment that Kinley decides to roll over. And by roll over, I don't mean just to face me. No, she rolls over and pushes her tight little body next to mine. On instinct, I wrap my arm around her and pull her close.

Suddenly, I'm once again wide-awake.

I tell myself I'm just going to hold her. That I'm going to enjoy having her this close to me. That gets shot all to hell when I run my hand through her silky hair. It's so damn soft, not to mention the simple movement causes Kinley to burrow further into me. Stroking her hair leads to my fingers trailing ever so softly up and down her back. My heart is pounding in my chest just from this simple act. That shows me right there how much she affects me. Never before has this happened.

Only McKinley.

There are a million reasons why what I'm doing is wrong. There is only one that tells me it's right, and that's the way my heart is racing. I block out all the questions running through my mind, all of them but one. How soft is her skin. Without further thought, I slide my hand up underneath her t-shirt—my t-shirt. I run my bare hands up and down her back until my hand connects with silk.

Silk fucking panties.

That's it.

Silk panties and my shirt are all that cover this gorgeous girl.

Fuck me!

McKinley
26

I wake to the feeling warm hands softly caressing my back. Keeping my eyes closed, I focus on even breathing. I don't want to give him a reason to stop touching me. I know when I wake up, this will all be over.

I'm not ready for it to be over.

My wish is short-lived when Evan's hand suddenly stills on the small of my back. He doesn't move and neither do I, at least not until he moves his hand.

"Don't stop," I whisper into the darkness.

I hold my breath while I wait to see what he'll do. Is he going to stop? Push me away? It only takes about thirty seconds for me to get my answer when I feel the heat of his hand connect once again with my skin.

I exhale at his touch. My hand, which rests on his rock-hard abs, begins its own journey. Evan Chamberlin is a work of art. His body looks as though it has been chiseled to perfection. His is not your average six pack. He has actual peaks and valleys that my fingers slowly trail over. He pulls me closer, if that's even possible. The fact that he wants me next to him has me placing a featherlight kiss on his chest. As soon as my lips make contact, I hear him suck in a breath.

"McKinley." My name falls from his lips.

Lifting my head, I peer up at him. His hand still under my shirt, it slides up and circles the back of my neck. His chest rapidly rises and

falls, its rhythm matching my own. Lifting myself further, with the guidance of his hand, our lips meet. He kisses me, soft and leisurely at first; that is until I trace his bottom lip with my tongue. Evan growls deep in his throat and pulls me so I'm lying on top of him. Reaching up, I run my fingers through his hair, grabbing a hold as he deepens the kiss.

This kiss is different than any of the others we've shared over the past few weeks. This one holds more fire, more passion, as my tongue meets his stroke for stroke. Resting my legs on either side of his waist, I'm now straddling him. We both moan the minute our bodies connect. He's hard and I'm soaked, nothing but his boxer briefs and my silk panties separating us.

I rotate my hips against him just as there is a loud cry, which comes through the baby monitor. We both freeze, waiting to see what happens next. Seconds later, Lexi is screaming into the night. I rest my forehead against Evan's, not ready to move.

"She's probably hungry. She's slept for four hours straight," he whispers.

"I'll get her. You get some rest," I say, preparing to dismount him. I feel embarrassment wash over me.

"Hey." Evan once again slides his hand around the back of my neck and guides me closer to him. "Don't second-guess this."

I nod, not able to find my voice, and he releases me. "I can get her," he says, sitting up.

"No, it's fine. I'm rested. You get some sleep. I'll take care of your girl." I offer him a shy smile before racing out of the room to tend to a hungry Lexi.

"Hey, sweet girl," I coo to her. She's still crying, but the sound softens a little at my voice. I remember how she responded to my singing to her earlier, so I begin to sing "Just a Kiss" by Lady Antebellum. It's fitting and not only calms her, but me as well.

It only take a few seconds of me singing for her to quiet down. I continue to softly sing the lyrics that speak so much of what I'm feeling inside. Once her diaper is changed, I lift her from the changing table and her cries stop all together.

"You're so good with her," Evan says from behind me.

I take a deep breath before turning to face him. "So are you. You're still nervous, but Miss Lexi is the first baby you've ever been around. I have years of babysitting under my belt."

"It's more than that," he says, handing me a bottle.

I take it from him and settle into the rocking chair so I can feed her. I watch as her little eyes close and she starts to eat. "Maybe," I say into the quiet room. "Aren't you supposed to be sleeping?" I ask, never taking my eyes of Lexi.

"I'm where I want to be," he says as he takes a seat on the floor, resting his back against the wall. He's still wearing nothing but his boxer briefs, his rock hard body on display. The same rock hard body I'd trailed my fingers over just minutes ago.

I don't argue with him. He should be getting some rest, that's why I'm here, but after our little tryst in his bedroom, I wouldn't be able to sleep either. Realizing it's time to burp, I carefully pull the bottle from her mouth and lift her to my shoulder. She's not impressed and starts to cry. I begin to sing "Just a Kiss" again, and as soon as I do, I realize my mistake. Evan's hearing every word. Lexi instantly calms, so I continue to sing until she finally burps and I'm able to continue feeding her.

Nothing like just throwing it out there.

Evan and I are quiet as we both watch his precious little girl eat. She finishes quickly and her little body sighs with satisfaction this time when I remove the bottle from her mouth. Placing her on my shoulder, I rub her back. Evan stands and grabs the bottle from the table and disappears.

After about five minutes of rubbing her back, she gives me what I'm waiting for. I settle her back in her bed and whisper, "Sweet dreams." Evan is standing in the doorway, arms and legs crossed, shoulder leaning against the frame. His eyes capture mine as I move toward him. When I reach him, he stands to his full height and holds out his hand. I slip mine in his and allow him to lead me back to his room. A protest is on the tip of my tongue, because that's what I think I should do, not what I want.

He stops when we reach his bed, pulls back the covers, and looks at me. "McKinley." My name falls from his lips, sounding like a plea. I know what he wants, and it scares me how much I want it too. I climb into bed and settle on the opposite side, the same side I slept on earlier. Evan climbs in behind me, pressing his front to my back, and pulls me into his arms.

My body instantly relaxes into his hold.

I don't move or speak. I'm too busy memorizing what it feels like to be here with him, like this.

Our breathing slows to a matched, even rhythm and, surprisingly, sleep starts to claim me. That is until I hear his whispered words, "It was more than just a kiss."

I want to ask him what he means. What was it to him? Why is he holding me? What are we doing? Instead, I lie there in his arms, his soft breaths against my neck, and drift off to dream of more than just a kiss.

EVAN 27

$\mathcal{S}$he's more than just a kiss. I want more than anything to tell her how my feelings for her have changed. Tell her how I think about her all the damn time and how, anytime something happens, she's the first person I want to tell. I want to bare my soul to her, but I won't. She needs more than what I can offer her. I'm a single dad who is barely hanging on. Without her, I fear I would fail at this daddy gig I have going on. I can't risk us not working out and losing both of my best friends, just to feel what it's like to be inside of her.

I lie awake far longer than I should, enjoying the feel of her in my arms. I let my mind wander to what Aaron would think if he knew what I was doing right this minute. If he knew I was holding her tight in my arms. If he knew what I was thinking, I'm sure he would kick my ass. She's his little sister and my other best friend, and . . . more. I want her to be a hell of a lot more.

If only things were different.

I place a kiss on her shoulder and allow sleep to claim me, enjoying this moment of falling asleep with her tucked close.

If feels like only minutes pass, when I'm woken by the soft whimpers of my baby girl. Reluctantly, I release the hold I have on Kinley to reach over and turn off the monitor, making a mental note to turn it back on later. I don't want it to wake her. Slowly, I climb out of bed and make my way toward Lexi. I stop when I reach the door and turn back to look at my bed. McKinley is so peaceful, so fucking beautiful it makes my

chest ache, and she's in my bed. I want to memorize this moment. I want to store it away for all the nights to come when she won't be here. My feet move on their own accord and, before I know it, I'm standing beside the bed——her side of the bed. Only one night and I'm already giving her claim. With a feather-soft touch, I remove the hair from her eyes. This image of her in this moment will forever be one of the most beautiful things I've ever seen.

A louder whimper from Lexi tells me she's about to get serious with her cries. My baby girl is hungry. I give a mental fist bump that I can tell what kind of cry it is. She's the only person who could pull me from the beautiful slumbering McKinley.

By the time I reach her, Lexi is angry. As soon as I pick her up, she settles down. "Hey, baby girl. Daddy's here," I coo to her. It sounds foreign to me to refer to myself as daddy, but that's who I am to her. She's a part of me.

After a quick diaper change, which I'm getting better at each time, we head downstairs to the kitchen. The process of making her bottle is . . . messy. I spill the powdered formula all over the counter. I'm still learning to do this with one hand. Miss Lexi is not impressed when I try to lay her down. McKinley makes it look so damn easy.

I settle on the couch and my little piglet begins to eat her breakfast. "I didn't hear her wake up," Kinley's sleepy voice greets me.

Looking up, I see her standing at the bottom of the stairs. My rumpled t-shirt is now covered with one of my flannel shirts hanging past her knees. Her hair is in disarray and that smile——my smile——lights up her face. She's every man's wet dream and she was in my bed last night. More than anything, I wish I could keep her there.

"Yeah, I turned off the monitor. I didn't want to wake you."

"Evan," she says, walking further into the room. "That's why I stayed last night, so you could get some rest and try to get on a normal schedule. You've been burning the candle at both ends."

"I'm good," I tell her. I'm fucking fantastic. I got only a couple of hours of sleep at best, but I feel like I slept for days. Having her here feels right. Although, I'm not sure she feels the same way, considering she's acting as though last night never happened.

It was more than just a kiss, damn it.

"Hey, Lexi has her first doctor's appointment today. I was hoping you might come with me. I'm still nervous about taking her out on my own," I confess. Talk of the doctor's appointment gets me out of my own head. She's not mine. I can't think like she could be or even will be.

McKinley walks into the room and sits on the couch beside me. Reaching out, she offers her finger to Lexi, who grips it tight. "Sure," she says softly.

I relax with the knowledge she's going to be there. I'm a grown-ass man and the thought of taking my daughter out alone terrifies me. I don't have to say it out loud. Kinley gets it.

"What time is her appointment?"

"Ten." I glance over my shoulder at the clock; it's six now.

"Are you hungry?" she asks, standing from the couch.

"Uh, yeah, I guess." I'm not sure why she's asking. I watch as she leans over and kisses Lexi on the cheek then stands. "I'll make us some breakfast." I watch her walk away, her long tan legs wearing nothing but my shirt. Do you know how perverted it feels to have a raging hard-on when you're trying to feed your newborn daughter? It's damn uncomfortable.

"That's smells amazing," I tell McKinley when I enter the kitchen. I take the bottle to the sink and rinse it out. "She fell right back to sleep."

"She's such a good baby, Evan."

"She is. That little girl owns me."

Her lips turn up at the corners. "She's not even a week old and has you wrapped around her little finger."

I don't respond, because she's right. My baby girl may terrify me, because I have no idea how to take care of her, but I love her with everything in me.

"I can't wait to see how you react when she starts to date."

"Fuck that! She's not dating until she's at least thirty."

McKinley throws her head back and laughs, her long slender neck on display. I want nothing more than to press my lips there, right against her pulse, and taste her.

And my hard-on makes another appearance. Just like that. All she has to do is laugh and I'm hard as steel.

"Breakfast is ready," she says as she carries two plates filled with bacon and eggs to the table.

Like a magnet, I follow her and settle into the chair right beside her. I can't have her, but I'm sure as hell going to take full advantage of being close to her when I can. I dig into my plate and we enjoy a quiet breakfast together. Kinley talks about her studio and informs me, between her and her mom, Lexi will be in good hands while I work. I feel a weight lifted from my shoulders. It's a relief to know people I trust will be taking care of her during the day. Just one more reason why McKinley and I can't happen.

McKinley

28

"Evan, go, we got this," I tell him for the third time.

"I know. It's just the first time I've left her. I didn't know it would be this hard," he says, running his hands through his hair.

"Oh, honey, it gets easier. Why don't you plan on eating lunch here today? I'll have it ready at noon. This way you get to see this little one and ease you into it," Mom suggests.

Evan seems to brighten a little at her suggestion. Bending down, he pushes the handle down on Lex's car seat. I watch him as he releases the straps and removes her, just like an old pro. Two weeks and he has come such a long way. "Daddy loves you, sweet girl. You be good for Kinley and her momma. I'll see you in a few hours."

"All right, Daddy, time to go," I say, holding my arms out for Lexi. Evan kisses her forehead and places her in my arms.

"McKinley, I can't even tell you how much this means to me." He turns to look at Mom. "You too, Momma Mills." He grins, using the name he's called her all his life. "I can't thank you enough for watching her for me. I don't know if I could have left her with anyone else."

"She's my granddaughter. Of course I'm going to watch her," Mom says, like he should already know this.

"And we share a middle name; we're best friends," I say with a grin.

Evan's brown eyes lock on mine. I hear Mom say something about laundry and her footsteps as she leaves the room. Evan takes a step

forward, aligning our bodies. He places one hand on Lexi's back and the other caresses my cheek. He doesn't say a word, just keeps his eyes trained on mine. When he leans in closer, my heart stutters in my chest. Evan's lips softly press against mine for mere seconds before he pulls away and kisses the back of Lexi's head. "I'll see you soon," he whispers, before turning and walking away. I watch him through the glass as he climbs in his truck and drives away.

"Oh, Lex, your daddy, he has no idea what he does to me," I confess to her.

"Evan gone?" Mom asks, startling me. How long has she been there? What did she see?

"Yeah, he'll be back at lunch time. This little one has her hooks in him."

"Um hmm," Mom says.

Shit! "What do you mean um hmm?" I ask her.

"Just agreeing with you, dear."

Double shit! "Let's watch some cartoons, Lex." I leave her car seat and pick up the diaper bag. Whatever Mom thinks she's seen, or happened to see, is not what it looks like. Evan and I, we're not . . . we're just not.

Lexi falls asleep not ten minutes into our cartoon date. I know I should put her down and let her sleep, but she's just too sweet and I love to cuddle her.

"You're going to spoil her," Mom says, taking a seat on the couch beside me.

"I know, but . . ."

"But nothing. If we hold her all day, Evan is never going to get sleep at night. She's going to get used to it and refuse to sleep without someone holding her."

Knowing she's right, I stand and place Lexi in the pack-n-play I bought yesterday. I figured it would be easier if we had our own, less for Evan to take back and forth. I got a good deal on it at Target.

"You want to talk about it?" Mom asks.

"Talk about what?" Damn it, she did see him kiss me.

"McKinley, I'm your mother. I know when something is bothering you."

"Your radar must be off. Everything's fine," I lie. Evan's kiss still has me reeling.

"Fine, I'll talk, you listen." She turns sideways, pulling both legs up on the couch. Looks like this is going to be a long listening session.

"The chemistry between the two of you sucks the air out of the room. The way he looks at you, follows you with his eyes—I've watched it for months, but what I saw today," she shakes her head. "That boy's fighting what he feels for you," she says matter-of-fact.

"Mom, he's grateful for all the help I've given him. He had no clue how to prepare for Lex, and I felt bad for the guy," I lie right through my teeth to her face. I'm a terrible liar.

"If that helps you deal with what's happening, you can pretend all you want."

"He's Aaron's best friend."

"And yours too," she fires back.

"Exactly. Listen, yes, he's gorgeous and he's a great guy, but there is nothing between us. He's close to me now, leaning on me as he learns his way. That's all this is. You're mistaking appreciation for attraction." I turn to look at Lexi sleeping soundly. I can feel Mom's gaze on me.

"How did the pictures turn out?" Her question surprises me. It's not like her to give up when she feels so strongly about something. Maybe she was just trying to feel me out, get me to confess. She really doesn't think our chemistry sucks the air out of the room as she put it.

It does. It so does, but maybe, just maybe, she's oblivious and I can keep living in the land of pretend.

Turning to face her, I find she's smirking. Shit. No such luck. She's giving me this, letting me tell myself there is nothing there. I need to be more careful.

"The pictures turned out so great. Lexi looks adorable. I sent them off for print. I bought a ton and blew a few of them up for Evan as well."

"He's going to be surprised. That boy has always been an Alabama fan. That's a nice thing you did."

I shrug. "Guys don't think about things like that. I did it for Lexi just as much as Evan. She doesn't have a mom to dress her up and make sure she gets her picture taken. A mom to make sure she will have those

pictures and memories to look back on when she's older. Evan's learning his way. He's not thinking about making sure he documents her milestones. He's too focused on learning how to keep her alive—his words, not mine," I chuckle.

"They're both lucky to have you. I can't wait to see the pictures."

"Don't worry, Grandma, I got you a few copies as well. I want them to be a surprise or else I would grab my laptop and show you."

"I can handle that. So, you have anything in the studio today?"

"No, I kept it open. I knew Evan was going back to work today." I stop there, afraid if I say more I'll reveal what I'm trying so hard to deny.

EVAN 29

wo months today. It's hard for me to believe I've had her for eight whole weeks. It still seems like yesterday. She's growing and changing every day, and she no longer sleeps all day long. Kinley and her mom are great about keeping her up during the day and our nights have gotten better. It's hard as hell doing this on my own. Well, I'm not alone; Kinley has been there every step of the way, as have Aaron and their parents. My parents have been going crazy with wanting to see her. I'm going to have to make a trip to see them soon. Dad's too weak to travel. I've been putting it off because I don't think I can do it alone. I've been trying to find a way to ask Kinley to go with me. I hate to take her from the studio, but I need her.

Speaking of Kinley . . .

Me:	Hey, I'll be there to pick you girls up at three for Lexi's appointment.
Kinley:	Okay, but, Evan, you got this.
Me:	Are you bailing on me, Mills?
Kinley:	Never! But you got this daddy thing down.
Me:	At home, but out, not so much.

What if we're out and she needs something, or something happens that I can't handle. What if the doctor asks a question I can't answer about my own daughter? Kinley went with me on her first appointment. I asked her to go again on the second, and for this one, I didn't ask, just told her the day and time and made sure she knew we, as in the three of

us, needed to be there.

  Kinley: We'll be ready.

  Me: Thank you.

I shove my phone back in my pocket and go back to the paperwork surrounding me. I love the business, working with the horses, even the cattle, but the accounting part not so much. It's a necessary evil.

Glancing at the clock, I have three hours before I have to pick up the girls, and I still have to meet with the staff about some new horses coming in this week. With a heavy sigh, I dig into the pile of receipts, no longer able to put it off.

"Let's get dinner," I suggest to McKinley once we are back in the truck. Lexi passed her two-month check-up with flying colors. She had to get vaccines this time. That was so fucking hard. She wailed and I wanted to push that damn nurse away from her. Instead, I scooped her up in my arms as soon as she was done. Her cries turned to a whimper, and when McKinley started talking to her, she stopped all together. It appears that not only am I enamored with Kinley, but my daughter is as well.

"Sure. You sure you're ready for this?" she laughs.

"Yeah, you're with me. I wouldn't do it by myself, not yet anyway."

She just shakes her head at me. "Evan, you know what you're doing, and I know for a fact you would rather cut off a limb than hurt that little girl." She points in the backseat.

I don't say anything, because she's right. "What sounds good?" I ask instead.

"Well, we need to go somewhere family friendly."

"Pizza?"

"Perfect."

It's always easy between us, just something else to add to my ever-growing list of how amazing she is. Like I need that list to grow.

"I'll grab a high chair for her seat," Lexi says, holding the door open for me. She has her purse and the diaper bag slung over her shoulder, while I carry the car seat. I stand and watch in fascination as she talks to one of the waitresses, who nods her head. "She's going to bring it over," she says, smiling as she stops to stand in front of me. "She said we could sit anywhere. I say away from the door. We don't want all that cold wind on Lex." She turns to walk toward the back of the restaurant.

All I can do is follow her.

"Here you go," the perky young waitress says. Kinley sets the car seat on the chair and it fits snug. Huh, I would have never known to do that. "Your daughter is adorable," she says to Kinley.

"She's not . . . thank you," she says softly.

The waitress hands us menus and tells us she'll be back. "I'm sorry," Kinley says immediately.

Looking across the booth, I see her face is red with embarrassment.

"Sorry for what?"

"I let her think Lexi is mine. I shouldn't have done that. I just . . . It was easier than explaining that we're friends. Shit, I should have just said she's my niece."

Reaching across the table, I clasp her hands in mine. "McKinley, look at me." My thumb traces her knuckles as I wait for her to look at me. "Please," I give her hands a gentle squeeze.

She looks at me from under her lashes.

"You didn't do anything wrong. You are the closest thing to a mother this little girl has ever known. Fuck, Kinley, we could only be so lucky if you held that role for her, for both of us." I clamp my mouth shut, already saying too much.

"Evan." My name falls from her lips.

"No," I cut her off. "Forget it. You did nothing wrong. It's no one's business."

"This is a small town," she counters.

"Yeah, and I don't really have two fucks to give any of them. You, McKinley, have been there for us——" I point to a sleeping Lexi in her car seat "——from the minute I found out about her. Let them say and think what they want."

"Y'all ready to order?" the young waitress asks.

We order a pepperoni to share and water to drink. I wait for the waitress to leave before I lighten the mood. "So how are things in the studio?"

"It's going really well. I'm beyond thrilled with my clientele. Word of mouth seems to be the best advertisement."

"You do good work; that speaks volumes." I'm not just blowing smoke up her ass. She really is phenomenal at what she does. A slight blush tints her cheeks and I know I've distracted her from our earlier conversation.

The rest of dinner is easygoing. We're both relaxed and talk about our week so far. Lexi wakes and I feed her a bottle while I listen to Kinley talk about getting her website up and running.

"Thanks for today, for letting me pull you from your work to go to her appointment with me, and for dinner. It was nice to get out, and Miss Lexi did great."

"You're welcome. It's not a hardship to spend time with either of you," she says.

I want to pull her across this seat and kiss the hell out of her. I want her to come home with me and curl up beside me in my bed, on her side of the bed. Yes, I still refer to it as her side. I'm truly fucked when it comes to this girl. My attraction only grows stronger each day. How am I going to continue to fight this?

"I'll let you two get home." She climbs out of the truck and opens the back door. The truck is so tall she has to climb into the backseat, but she does it without complaint. "I'll see you tomorrow, Miss Lexi. You be good for Daddy." I watch in the rearview as she kisses two fingers and places them on Lexi's cheek.

Like I said, truly fucked!

Once I get home, I get Lexi settled on the floor on a blanket underneath her baby gym—that's what Kinley calls it—while I sit on the couch and go through my mail. When I get to the envelope from an attorney in Tennessee, I'm confused. Ripping it open, I read the words three times just to make sure I'm comprehending what this lone piece of paper is saying.

They want my daughter.

What. The. Fuck!

Lexi coo's on her blanket and I have to fight back the tears threatening to fall—tears of anger and worry because they want to take my baby girl. Reaching for my phone, I swipe the screen and hit the first number on my favorites list.

"Yo, what's up, bro? You were just here, you should have come in to say hello," Aaron says.

"They want to take her." My voice is hoarse.

"What? Wants to take who? What the hell's going on, man?" he asks. I can tell he's worried, as he should be. He can hear the pain in my voice.

"Lexington," I whisper her name.

"Are you home?" he barks into the phone.

"Yeah."

"I'm on my way." The line goes dead. I drop my phone and fall to my knees. I scoop my baby girl up in my arms and hold her close. She coos, making her sweet baby noises, and the emotion that's been threatening to bubble to the surface since I read that fucking letter the first time, falls from my eyes.

"Evan!" I hear Kinley yell.

Kinley!

Turning at the sound of her voice, I watch her run into the living room. She stops when she sees me, and tears begin to fall from her eyes, matching mine. I stand to greet her. She loves my little girl as much as I do. "Evan," she breathes my name. I have Lexi cradled in one arm, and I hold the other one out to Kinley, an open invitation to come to me.

I need her.

She wraps her arms around my waist and I do the same, holding her tight against my chest—my girls, both of them.

"Fuck, bro, what the hell is going on?" Aaron asks.

Kinley steps back, and I want to stop her, but I don't. "Got home today and was going through the mail, got that letter." I point to the letter now lying on the floor.

Aaron bends to pick it up, and I watch his face as he reads the words. "Holy shit. Can they do that? Misty's gone?"

"Apparently."

"Can who do what? What do you mean Misty's gone?" Kinley looks up to me, searching for answers.

Reaching out, I run my thumb under one eye then the other, wiping her tears. "Misty died in a car accident almost a month ago. Her parents

are suing me for full custody of Lexi," I explain.

"What? No, they can't do that." She turns to look at Aaron. "Can they do that?"

Aaron holds up the letter. "Says here they are claiming Evan can't give Lexi what they can."

"Of course he can. He loves her," Kinley fires back.

"I know." Aaron holds the letter up. "This states they feel they can provide the guidance she needs with both a father and mother figure in the household."

"Bullshit!" I seethe.

"She signed her rights away," Kinley sobs. "She gave her up. This sweet, beautiful little girl, she just gave her away. She didn't love her. They have no right."

"I don't really know much about the laws, but I know there are grandparent rights and all that. Not sure how that works if the parent signs away their legal rights to the kid," Aaron says, worry in his voice.

"Fuck!" I yell, the sound startles Lexi and she starts to cry. Kinley steps close to me once again and starts to sing as she rubs her back. Lexi calms instantly.

"It's my guess this is a farfetched attempt. They can't claim you are unfit, so they are claiming that psychologically she will be better off with a mother and father figure—ironically enough, the relationship their own daughter refused to provide to her," Aaron says.

Now that I've calmed down, I call bullshit too. "Yeah, I was pissed off and scared as hell at first, but now that you're here and broke it down, I agree."

"We need to get married," McKinley blurts out.

"Say again?" Aaron says.

McKinley looks up at me. "We have to get married, Evan. You'll have a wife and Lexi will have a mother. They will no longer have an excuse to take her from us."

From us. This girl.

"Kinley," Aaron says softly. I can see this is tearing her up.

"No, Aaron. You know I'm right. If Evan gets married, they have no fight. I'm the best choice. I won't hold him to the marriage after all this shit blows over, and it would be believable. I've been there since he found out. I was there when she was born. Hell, Mom and I watch her," she ticks off items one by one, raising her fingers as she does.

"McKinley, I can't let you do that. There has to be a way to fight this." Those are the words that come out of my mouth. Inside, I'm screaming *YES!*

"I've been to all her doctor appointments. I've been there, Evan. This will work. I know it will. We can't let them take her." She breaks on a sob.

"It's crazy as hell, but she has a point, man. This would kill their only concern and the reason for the suit," Aaron agrees with her.

What the hell?

"Evan, can I . . . can I hold her, please?" McKinley asks, her voice small. As bad as I want Lexi in my arms, I can see the real fear in Kinley's eyes as well. She needs this just as much as I do. I give my baby girl a kiss on the top of her head before passing her to Kinley.

I watch Kinley as she holds her close; she loves Lexi. Never in a million years did I ever imagine this is how things would be; never thought I would be contemplating marrying my best friend's little sister. Hell, she's my best friend too.

Can we do this? Will this work to stop the lawsuit? Can I marry her and then let her walk away when this all blows over? Regardless of the fact I will want to hold on tight, I'll have to let her go. We'll have to live under the same roof, share every aspect of my life with her, and then let her go because that's the right thing to do. She's offering me a way to fight them to keep my baby girl. I won't hold her back when this is over.

"McKinley, you're amazing for offering, and I can never thank you enough, but this is a big deal."

"You're right, it is. They want to take her from us, Evan. We can't let them do that. We have to do whatever it takes to make that happen. You can trust me. I won't hold you to the marriage once we get them to drop the suit."

"What happens after you divorce, once this all blows over and they start the suit up again?" Aaron asks.

She shrugs. "I'll still be around, be in her life. We can play it off that I'm still her mother figure. I would be honored to play that role for this little girl." She pulls Lexi in a little closer to her chest.

"That could work, man," Aaron agrees.

"McKinley, I can't let you do this." My plea is weak at best. My head is telling me it's the right thing to say. My heart is telling me to drag her to the courthouse right this second. That maybe there won't be an end once we have a beginning.

"You're not *letting* me do anything. I want to do this."

"Your parents?" I say meekly.

"They'll get it, man. Don't worry about our parents. I think she's right. This is the best way. You won't be strapped to some stranger or some girl who will try to take your ass to the cleaners when this is over. Kinley has been here from the moment you found out. You all have spent a lot of time together. She has a point about the doctor's appointments and all that stuff. This will work, man. Take her up on it. Save your little girl from those monsters," Aaron tries to persuade me.

I'm convinced. I just needed to appear to put up a fight and make sure she understands what she's volunteering to do.

"McKinley, look at me."

Her eyes snap to mine. I step into her, closing off the space between us. "I need you to look me in the eye and tell me you are really okay with this. You will be putting your life on hold for me——for us."

"Yes." No hesitation, her voice never wavers. "It was my idea, Evan. I promise you I will have no regrets. We can't let them take her."

"We should probably go talk to your parents first."

"No, we shouldn't. I'm an adult, Evan. I don't need their blessing or their permission."

I raise my hand to her cheek and she leans into my touch. "I know that, but I do. You're going to be my wife, McKinley. I need them to know I will respect you always. I want to make sure they understand the complexity of this situation, but that I will never do anything to hurt you. They're my second family. I need them on board with this before we can go through with it."

I watch as her eyes soften with my words. She's knows I'm right.

"I'll call them, have them come over. No need in taking Lexi back out when they can come here," Aaron offers.

I feel like I'm in a bubble watching this all unfold. He's on board with this plan; he's okay with me marrying his little sister. I can't imagine their parents will be so understanding.

"Call them."

McKinley
30

I settle on the couch with Lexi in my arms. She's wide-awake and making all of her cute baby noises. I block Evan and Aaron out, while she and I have some girl time. I love her. I don't think I could love her more if she were my own. The thought of Misty's parents taking her, causes my heart to crack wide open.

Evan and Aaron know I'm right. Getting married will fix this. Anyone who hears about it will believe it; we're always together. This is the only way. Evan insists my parents know, but honestly, I couldn't care less what they think. I'm going to do whatever it takes to keep Lexi with Evan. By doing so, I keep her with me.

"I'll let them in," Aaron says when we hear my dad's truck pull up.

Evan paces the floor in front of me. Mom and Dad follow Aaron into the room, both wearing looks of concern. "Why don't you two go ahead and have a seat," Aaron suggests.

"Is everything all right?" Mom asks, worried. Dad guides her to the loveseat and they both sit. Aaron takes his spot in the recliner, leaving me and Lex on the couch and Evan pacing.

"No, but it will be," Aaron tells her. "Evan?" Evan raises his eyes and gives Aaron a tight nod. "Evan got a letter today from an attorney in Tennessee. The letter was informing him that Misty was killed in a car accident a few weeks ago. Her parents are now suing Evan for custody of Lexi, stating he can't give her what she needs—a mother and a father role model in her life," Aaron explains.

"I call bullshit!" Dad seethes.

"You're right, it is; we all know that. However, none of us knows the laws or the legal rights. Misty signed away her rights, but does that void grandparent rights as well? None of us know. What we do know is they have enough money and connections, at least from what Evan knows from Misty, to fight this battle."

"There has to be something we can do," Mom states.

"There is," I speak up for the first time. "I have the solution, but he," I point across the room at Evan, "insisted the two of you agree to it."

"Well, let's hear it," this from my dad.

"Evan and I need to get married. Lexi would have a mom." I go on to explain, listing the same reasons as I did earlier with Evan and Aaron. "Once this all blows over, we can have the marriage annulled. I'll still be in her life as her 'mother' figure and this will all go away."

Evan stops pacing, his attention on me. "I can't let you do this."

I sigh in frustration. "I thought we worked through this? You're not *letting* me do anything, Evan. They can't take her. I won't let them. This is the only way."

"I think you might be right," Mom says, shocking the hell out of us all. Dad watches her, something seems to pass between them.

"If it's any consolation, I agree. At first, I didn't think so, but after McKinley listed all of the reasons it would be believable between them, I agree this will work," Aaron adds.

"Evan," Dad says his name, causing him to give my father his full attention. Dad doesn't say anything just gives him a tight nod. Mom places her hand over Dad's resting on her leg.

"Have you talked to your parents? I'm sure they want to be there," Mom says.

"I . . . um . . . n-no I haven't talked to them. They don't know about the letter."

"Mom, it's not a real wedding," I tell her.

"We need to make it look real, Kinley. If you are going to go through with this, we need to make sure it looks real. There will be no room for anyone to doubt it."

"Dad can't travel," Evan says.

"Well, looks like we're taking a road trip," Mom says. "You call them and let them know what going on. Then I'll call your mom and we will take care of the details."

Evan joins me on the couch, and I'm once again the center of his attention. "McKinley, I need you to be sure about this."

"Positive."

"I don't know how I will ever be able to thank you for what you're doing for us."

"You don't have to thank me, Evan. I want to do this. They can't have her."

He tucks a stray piece of hair behind my ear. "Thank you."

"All right, well, we're heading home. I've got some planning to start. Evan, you let me know once you've talked to your parents and I'll take care of the rest. You have enough to worry about. Your mom was just saying how she can't wait to meet her granddaughter. Looks like she's going to get that wish." They say their goodbyes with the promise this is all going to work out.

"You about ready, Kinley?" Aaron asks.

Am I ready? No, I don't want to leave her. "I . . . not really," I admit.

"You can stay tonight. I might need backup with Mom and Dad. Mom will want to talk to you to make sure you're okay with all of this," Evan tells me.

"Yeah, there are probably a lot of things we need to discuss about this . . . arrangement."

"All right, well, you all know where to find me if you need anything. Kinley, I can come back for you later," Aaron offers.

"I'll bring her home in the morning. I would have been dropping Lexi off anyway. I think she needs this time with my little girl as much as I do," Evan tells him.

"Yeah," Aaron says. "You guys call if you need anything."

I stand and hand Lexi off to Evan. "I'll walk out with you."

Aaron says his goodbyes and we head outside.

"Aaron, I know this has to be weird for you, but I have to do this," I lay it out there for him. I refuse to ask his permission; I don't need it.

"I get it. I'm also not blind, Kinley. I can see the way you look at each

other. I'm worried one or both of you are going to come out of this crushed, but I understand this is the only way to keep them away from her."

"He's a great guy, and he's been through enough."

"What about you? Can you keep your heart out of this?"

"It's too late, Aaron," I tell him honestly.

He pulls me into his arms and hugs me tight. "You're not the only one, little sister. I can read Evan like a book. He's been fighting this."

"Regardless, we both know we have to do this. When it's over, the fact that we saved that little girl from those people will heal the pain I'll feel from no longer being a part of their family."

"You'll always be a part of their family, McKinley." His voice is scolding.

"You're right, but not the way I long to be. I know that, and I accept it."

Aaron nods, he gets it. "Call me if you need anything. I'll see you tomorrow."

With one last hug—the kind only my big brother can give—he's gone. I watch his truck until I can no longer see his tail lights before heading back inside.

EVAN 31

*L*exi is just finishing her bottle when Kinley finally comes back into the house. "Let me lay her down and we'll call my parents."

"Can I come with you?" she asks.

"Of course you can."

She follows me up the stairs and into Lexi's room. "Goodnight, baby girl. Daddy loves you," I say softly, kissing her on the forehead.

I step back, letting Kinley say goodnight as well. "Sweet dreams, Lex. I love you," she says so softly I almost don't hear her.

I grab her hand and lead her to my room. Without hesitation, Kinley sits on her side of the bed and pulls her knees to her chest. Taking my cell out of my pocket, I dial my parents. I sit on the edge of the bed beside her and lay my hand on her knee. She covers mine with hers and we wait for them to answer.

"Hey, Mom, can we talk?" I say. She gets Dad on the other line and I proceed to tell them about the letter and about Kinley's offer to marry me. Her selfless offer to ensure I keep my baby girl.

"Is she there with you?" Mom asks.

"Yeah, she's sitting right next to me." Where I've longed for her to be since the night I held her.

"Can I talk to her?"

I hand Kinley the phone. "Mom wants to talk to you."

"Hello," she says quietly. She listens intently as my mom talks. "Yes,

I know what I'm doing. It was my idea. I refuse to let them take her," she says with conviction.

They talk a few more minutes before Kinley passes the phone back to me.

"Evan, you okay with this?" Mom asks.

"More than I should be," I say honestly.

"Okay, I'll call Sarah in the morning and we will take care of it all. I'm so excited to meet my granddaughter."

I can't help but laugh at her excitement. "Night, Mom, love you. Tell Dad too," I add. He got off the call when Mom wanted to talk to McKinley.

"Will do, honey. Take care of your girls," she says before hanging up.

My girls.

"What did she say?"

"She told me to take care of my girls. She's going to call your mom and start planning."

"Good."

"Should we——" she cuts me off.

"Nothing to talk about. We're getting married. We're going to prevent those heartless people from getting their hands on that precious little girl. When it all blows over, we'll annul the marriage and your life can go back to normal. Until then, we're two best friends doing what we need to do to save your little girl."

"All right, we should get some sleep." I go to my dresser and pull out a t-shirt. "You can sleep in this." I hand it to her.

"Thank you." She takes the shirt into the bathroom to change. I strip down to my boxers, turn off the light, and climb into bed. I'm more excited than I should be that she's going to be in my bed again, at least I hope she is. We didn't talk about it, but after tonight, I just need to hold her. Besides, she's going to be my wife. How in the hell am I going to stay away from her now? We should talk about it, about living and sleeping arrangements, but that's not what we do. We share kisses and sleep in the same bed and pretend it doesn't happen. I'm just going to let the cards fall where they may.

I watch the shadows dance across the ceiling, willing my racing heart to slow its rhythm as I wait for her to finish in the bathroom. When the door opens, she turns off the light and walks toward the bed. There is just enough moonlight to lighten her features. I lift the covers, inviting her to join me. Her step doesn't falter as she climbs in. Dragging the covers up over both of us, I pull her into my arms and hold her close for several minutes before I finally whisper, "Thank you," into her ear.

She rolls over so she's now facing me, our bodies aligned. I place my arm around her, resting it on her back, and move her as close as I can get her. "We're really doing this?"

Her hand rests against my cheek. "Yeah, we really are."

I open my mouth to speak, but I can't find the words. Instead, I lean in and press my lips to hers. The kiss starts soft, as I trace her bottom lip with my tongue. She opens for me, and the minute my tongue slides past her lips, I lose all train of thought. I have a single purpose—to have more of her. I need more. I need to taste her for hours, everywhere I want to trace her soft skin with my tongue and to be buried so far inside of her that we both forget our own names.

I want her.

I can no longer fight it. I don't know if it's the thought of her being my wife or just because it's her.

More than likely, it's both.

She throws her leg over mine and presses her body closer. My cock pulses against her belly. "Evan," she moans my name. *Moans my fucking name!*

Breaking our kiss, my lips find her neck. My hand slips under her shirt and I'm once again treated to the silky smooth feel of her skin against mine. I guide them up her spine and she shudders in my arms.

She's so fucking sexy.

"Evan." This time, my name on her lips is a pant.

"Tell me, McKinley. Tell me what you need." I'll fucking give her anything she wants. I just need to know she wants this. Her actions tell me she does, but this is a turning point for us. I need to hear her say it.

Instead of telling me, she sits up and pulls my shirt over her head, throwing it across the room, and then lies back down.

"You," she whispers.

Fuck me!

I close my eyes and will myself to slow down. I want her and this will change us, but we're getting married. We're going to change regardless.

With my index finger, I trace the contour of her face down to her neck. I continue my journey until I reach her full breasts, tracing each pert nipple with my finger. No longer able to hold back, I bend my head and take one, then the other, in my mouth. Giving them both equal attention with my tongue and a gentle tug of my fingers.

"Evan," she moans again and the sound goes straight to my dick. I'm now painfully hard with want for her.

Never moving my mouth from her breasts, my hand skims her flat belly, touching every single part of her I can. When I reach the hem of her silk panties, I don't even hesitate to slide my hand underneath.

I gently run the tip of my thumb over her. This causes her to raise her hips from the bed. Exploring further, my hand is coated with her. I want to bury my face between her legs and feast, but I can't seem to tear my mouth from her chest, from the tight, perky nipples, I've not had my fill of.

My hand is going to have to do for now.

McKinley
32

I'm naked except for my barely there panties. Evan sucks a nipple into his mouth and it sends fire through me. His hands on me—this is something I've thought about more than I care to admit. He's holding back; I don't want him to hold back.

"Evan." His name falls from my lips. He doesn't lift his head, just continues to suck and nip at my breasts, driving me insane with lust for him. His finger is softly tracing my folds, so I know he knows what his touch does to me. But he doesn't make a move to take this further. It's almost as if he's just enjoying the feel of his hand covered in . . . me.

I need more.

I know he's in his head. He's thinking this is wrong and, honestly, it might be, but I don't give a damn. Nothing that feels this good can be wrong. We're adults. Adults who agreed, just hours ago, we should get married.

Deciding he needs a little encouragement, I keep one hand in his hair, holding him to my breasts. The other follows the same path he just covered until my hands slips underneath the hem of my panties. I place my hand over his and push. I need him to touch me. I need . . . him.

"McKinley." His mouth falls from my breast. I watch as he squeezes his eyes closed and bites down on his lip. It's a heady feeling, having him fighting his control.

"Touch me," I whisper, raising up to capture his lips. He moans deep in the back of his throat and deepens the kiss. His hand still under mine,

I begin to move his fingers where I want them. It takes seconds for him to give in to whatever he was fighting and slip inside.

Turning my head, I break our kiss. His hands . . . finally . . . he's driving me crazy.

"I got you, baby. Just feel," he whispers in my ear. It's with those words that I let the pleasure roll through me and fall off the blissful cliff that is Evan.

My body slumps against the bed, sated and relaxed. Evan kisses my neck, then my lips. Guiding me to lay on my side, he wraps me in his arms. I know I should repay the favor, but I'm putty at the moment. Instead, I allow him to pull my body close, and he buries his face in my neck. "Fucking amazing," he mumbles. My heart swells at his words. I refuse to let my worry over, well . . . everything take this moment. I focus on what it feels like to be skin to skin with him and drift off to sleep.

EVAN 33

The sunlight shines through the curtains and I fight the fact it's time to get up. I just want to curl my body around Kinley's and hold her a little longer. The thought of Kinley has me reaching for her. When I find cold sheets, I force my eyes open. I'm in bed alone. Damn, I really wanted to wake up to her.

After a quick stop in the bathroom, I throw on a pair of shorts and head out to find my girls. Kinley's laughter travels from downstairs, and I take my time with each step while enjoying the sound. When I reach the bottom, I see Kinley lying on her side beside Lexi on the floor. Lexi is under the baby gym, kicking her feet and flapping her arms. Her baby jabber is a mile a minute.

"Is that so?" Kinley asks her. I couldn't prevent my grin if I tried. "Well, okay then," she laughs, continuing on like Lexi has something important to say.

This girl.

"Morning, ladies," I say, taking the spot on the other side of Lexi on the floor. She turns at the sound of my voice, and I maneuver my way through the gym to kiss her cheek. Then, leaning over, I do the same to Kinley. She tries unsuccessfully to hide her shocked expression.

"You girls had breakfast yet?"

"Miss Lexi just finished hers and was telling me how good it was." She taps the end of Lexi's nose, which causes her legs to move even faster.

"If you've got her, I'll fix us something."

"Yeah, we're good, aren't we, Lex?"

I leave them to play and head for the kitchen. Kinley is always taking care of me, so I like the fact that I get to make her breakfast. Too bad it's not in bed, preferably with her naked. She didn't mention last night, and I won't either. That's not what we do.

I'm not exactly the best cook, but I can make a mean bagel—toasted with bacon, egg, and cheese, melts in your mouth. It's also quick. I make two plates, grab two bottles of water and a couple of napkins, and head back into the living room.

"Your breakfast, my lady." I hand Kinley her plate and settle back on the other side of Lexi before giving her the water and placing the napkins out of reach of little fingers. Lexi has a firm grip for such a little thing.

"Do you have her today or does your mom?"

"Me. I had a message this morning saying the shoot I'd blocked most of the day for cancelled. Triplets who are sick."

"Does that happen a lot?"

"When it comes to the little ones, yeah. It's hard enough to get a three-year-old to sit still for pictures, add in the fact they don't feel well, and it's . . . a long day," she laughs.

"I'm such a bad dad. I haven't taken any 'professional' pictures of Lexi yet."

"Pshh," she waves her hand in the air, "I'm all over that. I took newborn, one month, and two month. We are almost ready for month three, aren't we, Lex?" She speaks to her like she's a little adult. I think it's adorable. I know I sound like a lovesick fool, but it just can't be helped.

"Thank you, McKinley. For everything."

"I love her, Evan. I can't let those people take her. They told Misty to . . . not have her. Now they want her? Not on my watch."

Reaching over, I run my fingers through her hair. "I have some errands today, but it won't take me long. I'll try to get back early, so you can get some editing done."

"No rush. Lex and I play, and then I edit while she sleeps. I've even done a shoot with her."

"Really? How did you manage that?"

"I used the swaddler. I picked it up at Target. I put it over my head then place her in it, and she rests tight against me. I had both hands free to do the shoot. She was fussy that day and Mom couldn't calm her, but when I held her, she was pacified. I decided to try it out and she seemed to love it."

"You already had this carrier thing?" I ask her.

"Yeah, I kind of always make a trip through the baby section when I'm at Target. I found it on sale and thought it might be useful for you to get stuff done, being on your own and all. I just kept forgetting to give it to you. It worked out." She grins.

All I can do is grin back at her. She's so carefree. I expected her to be consumed with this marriage we both agreed to. I expected her to be . . . different, I guess, about last night, but I should have known better. This is McKinley. She's tough as nails.

"I think I need to see this . . . contraption," I tease her.

"Hey, Lex loves it."

"Uh-huh." I stand and pick up our dishes. "I'll clean the kitchen real fast and grab a quick shower."

"And we," she lifts Lexi from the floor, "will go pack your bag, little miss."

McKinley
34

$\mathcal{T}$oday, Evan, Lexi, and I leave for Alabama. We decided to drive since little miss requires so much gear. It's an eight-hour drive, so here we are at five in the morning, piling into the car. My family, as well as Evan's grandparents, will be flying out this weekend for the wedding. We've decided to keep things as simple as possible, but all the family needs to be there for appearance's sake. His grandparents don't get around all that well, but insisted they be there. Evan tried to tell them we understood, but like I said, they insisted.

Evan loaded the Durango last night, and I spent the night here; it was just easier. Not to mention, when we come back from Alabama, this is where I will be living. I will continue to use my studio at my parents' and Mom is still going to help out with Lexi on the days I cannot be with her. Everything's falling into place.

"Okay, I think I have everything. I loaded the last of our bags with toiletries. You girls ready to hit the road?" he asks.

"She's oblivious," I laugh. Lexi is now three months old and sleeping through the night. When Evan got her out of bed this morning, she just stretched and fell right back to sleep after her diaper change. She'll be ready to eat around seven, which will be the perfect time for us to stop and eat breakfast as well.

"Let's do this." Evan swoops down and picks up the car seat before holding the door open for me. Just like that, we're on the road to Alabama to be married.

I'm marrying Evan Chamberlin!

"Can you believe Aaron got ordained?" Evan laughs.

"I know! I mean it makes sense, keeping it all in the family, but it's going to be weird, right?"

Evan reaches across the console and rests his hand on my knee. "It's going to be fine," he says with confidence.

During the past few weeks, we've kissed a lot. There's been more a few times, but not much. Neither one of us talk about it. We slip into his room late at night, and then the next day, it's like it never happened.

Except it does.

My heart knows it and so does my body. I ache for his touch and long to be in his arms each night. After this trip, we'll be sleeping under the same roof every night. So far, it's just been the occasional evening when he has to work late, so I watch Lexi and end up staying instead of driving home. It's a weak excuse, considering my parents' house is not a five-minute drive from his.

"So, depending on how she does, we should be there tonight. We're in no rush, so if you decide you want to stop somewhere and spend the night, we can."

"Sounds good. Everyone else will be there on Friday. I'm glad you'll have a few days to spend with your parents and grandparents with Lexi before everyone arrives."

"And you," he says.

"Me?"

"Yeah, they get to spend that time with the three of us."

He's been doing that a lot lately—including me in the small group that is made up of him and Lexi.

"The way our mothers are acting, you would think we've been dating for years."

Evan chuckles. "I know. I mean, our families have been intertwined for as long as I can remember, but they know, you know what I mean?"

I know what he means. This isn't a real marriage. We're not madly in love and suddenly going to live happily ever after. We care about each other and I love his little girl. We're doing this for her.

"Yeah," I finally say.

"You can catch some more sleep if you want. I'm going to drive until she decides to wake up. No sense in waking her."

"I think I might. I can drive whenever you want."

"I'm good, babe."

That's new too. He's been calling me babe more often than my name, no matter who's around. When it's just us, he calls me baby and I love it. I shouldn't—I'm only setting myself up for more heartbreak when this "arrangement" is over—but I can't help it. You try having a sexy as hell, shirtless, abs on display Evan call you baby and see if you're not wet in zero point two seconds.

It's not possible!

I close my eyes and get comfortable in the seat. I'm not all that tired, but it's easier to think about the way I feel about him when he can't read my eyes. He's too damn perceptive when it comes to me.

Instead, I'll pretend to be asleep while he draws lazy circles on my thigh, driving me mad with want. I should have ridden in the back with Lexi.

EVAN 55

My girls and I are on the road to Alabama. In just five short days, McKinley will be my wife. I have to keep reminding myself it's not real, that she's not really going to be mine, but then again, she is. The problem is it feels real—every smile, every touch, and every simple gesture. When her body is pressed tight against mine as we sleep, it's all real.

I've been driving for about three hours, one hand on the wheel and one on Kinley. I can't seem to help myself. If she's near, I need to touch her. It was a desire before, but after we decided that getting married was our course of action and since the night I first tasted more than her lips, it's turned into a need.

Lexi starts to babble and I know she's in need of a diaper change and a bottle. Pulling into a small bakery, I turn off the engine and look over at Kinley. She's facing toward me, looking so damn beautiful. She hasn't been asleep as long as she would like for me to think. She was faking, or hiding—however you want to look at it. Eventually, the ride with her eyes closed lulled her to sleep.

Leaning over the console, I kiss her forehead. "Time to wake up, babe." I slide my hand behind her neck, my thumb trailing back and forth. Her skin is so damn soft. "Kinley," I whisper against her ear.

Her eyes flutter open and a soft smile graces her lips. "Hi."

"Time to stretch your legs, beautiful. Lexi—" Before I can say anymore, Lexi shrieks. It's not an 'I'm starving' or 'Get me the hell out of this seat' shriek; no, this is a 'I just learned I can do this' shriek. She

started it a few days ago.

We both laugh. "—is awake," Kinley finishes for me.

"Yeah." Not able to resist her lips being so close, I give her a quick, chaste kiss and pull away. "I'll get Lex. You mind grabbing the diaper bag?" I ask.

We take a small table in the back and I remove Lexi from her seat. She's all smiles this morning.

"Oh, your little girl is so cute," the waitress says.

"Thank you, do you have a restroom?" I ask.

"Yeah, we actually have a changing table in the women's. I keep telling my manager we need to get one for the men's, but he won't listen," she rambles on.

"Looks like it's you and me, Lex." Kinley reaches for her and slings the diaper bag over her shoulder, and off they go.

"I'll be back in a few," the waitress says, and then she's gone.

I'm looking at the menu when I get a text.

> **Aaron:** You all get on the road okay?
>
> **Me:** Yeah. Lexi just woke up, so we stopped to feed her and get some food ourselves.
>
> **Aaron:** Good. Have a safe trip.
>
> **Me:** Will do.

I'm sliding my phone back into my pocket when the girls make it back to the table. "All better," Kinley says, sliding into the booth with Lexi on her lap. "I thought I would just hold her while we eat. Give her a break from that seat."

"I can take her," I offer.

"I don't mind." She grins at Lexi as she sits on the table. She's loving the attention. The waitress comes back and we order. I make Lexi a bottle at the same time and push it across the table to Kinley. My little girl, who is all crazy arms and legs with excitement, immediately settles down once she starts to eat.

Kinley eats one-handed. I offer to take Lexi, but she just smiles and says she's fine. We hang out for about twenty minutes after we're all finished eating, letting Lexi get a break from the seat. When she starts to get restless, we know it's time to move on.

"Want me to drive?"

"I'm good, babe." We are already three hours into our total eight-hour drive time. Five hours to go. Depending on how Lexi does will determine how many stops we'll need in the future. So far, my girl travels like a champ.

"Aaron texted me," I say once we are loaded back up and on our way. "He just wanted to make sure we got on the road okay and to say have a safe trip."

"He's surprisingly doing really well with all this."

"Yeah, I mean, I'm sure it has to be weird his best friend marrying his little sister and with the circumstances and all," I admit.

"He knows this is what's best."

My phone rings before I can answer. I see it's my attorney, Mr. Fields. "Hello."

"Evan, I've been doing some research. My paralegal has it documented Misty insisted, on the record, her parents never have anything to do with Lexi. This should help your case."

"That's good, but I told you they don't have a leg to stand on. I'm getting married this weekend, so their claim that she doesn't have a mother is null and void."

"But you don't have to get married. I think this is the piece we need."

"I know I don't have to. I want to." It's true. I want to marry Kinley. Not just so I can keep my daughter, but for reasons I cannot allow myself to think about. I know she'll be leaving once this all blows over, and I'll need to be able to let her walk away, but the thought already causes panic to set in. I don't know how I'm going to do that.

"Oh, I just assumed—"

"Yeah, well, you shouldn't," I fire back. I didn't tell him we were doing this for Lexi. The less people who know the truth, the better.

"Did you think about that pre-nup?" he asks.

"No, no pre-nup. We've talked about this. I'm driving us there now. Anything else you need to tell me?"

"Evan, I wish you would reconsider."

"No," I practically growl.

"Fine, have a safe trip." I don't wait for him to say anything else before ending the call.

"You know I'll sign anything you want, Evan."

I drop my phone in the cup holder and place my hand on her thigh. I always have to be touching her. "That's the thing, babe. There is nothing I want you to sign except for the marriage license." No truer words have ever left my mouth.

McKinley
36

*W*e made it. We only had to stop one other time for lunch. We changed and fed Lexi, ate, and then went to the mall. We walked around for a bit, stretching our legs. They had a play area that was not busy at all considering it's Monday. I laid out a blanket on the couch in the center of the mall and let Lexi stretch and play. She loved it. After that, we loaded up and drove the rest of the way. So here we are. I'm nervous as hell. Our parents are close, so I've known Evan's parents my whole life, but seeing them this time is different. Now I'm not just McKinley, their son's best friend's sister and their friends' daughter. I'm here to marry their son.

Evan pulls into the drive and shuts off the car. Before we have a chance to get out, his mom is rushing toward us. "Prepare yourself, Lex. Grandma is about to unleash some major hugs and kisses," he chuckles.

Sure enough, his mom goes straight to the back door of the Durango and rips it open, tears streaming down her face. "Oh, Evan, she's beautiful."

I feel like I'm invading on a family moment, so I climb out of the car and go stand at the back, giving them time. Not a minute later, Evan is rounding the back with a concerned look on his face.

"What are you doing?"

"I just felt like it was a private moment for the three of you. I didn't want to take away from that, so I was giving you time."

He steps in close, his hands resting on my hips. "Baby, look at me."

I tilt my head up and the look in his eyes tells me, whatever he's about to say, he means every word.

"I don't want time away from you, McKinley. You're going to be my wife. I take that very seriously. It may not be a traditional marriage in the sense of why we decided to do it, but it will be a real marriage. I won't hide things from you and I won't keep you separated from anything in my life."

"I . . . I wasn't sure, and I wanted to give you time," I try to excuse my actions.

"I don't need time, baby. You're a part of this. I'm always going to want you wherever I am, just remember that. I always want you."

His words cause my heart to race. I will it to slow down, reminding myself he's just being nice. He's appreciative of what I'm doing to help him keep his daughter. He feels obligated to have me there. He's blurring the lines and I have to hold strong. I can't let myself fall any deeper than I already have, or I fear I won't recover from it when it's all over.

I should have thought this through a little better. Regardless, I would not have changed my mind. All that matters is keeping Lexi with Evan. This is for Lex.

"McKinley, oh, give me a hug. It's been too long," Carol says. She's got Lexi in her arms.

"Hey, Carol," I say, giving her a one-armed hug. As soon as Lexi sees me, she grins big and holds her hand out. It's almost like she's reaching for me, but I know she's not. When I step back from the hug, Lexi begins to whimper.

"It's okay, sweet girl. Grandma's got you," I say, stepping close to her and placing my hand on her back. She again holds her arm out and I want to take her, like I know she wants, but I can't. Carol needs time to bond with her as well.

Evan steps close and places his hand on the small of my back. "She loves you," he whispers in my ear. I fight to not break out in tears. I love her too, so much more than I ever thought possible.

Lexi is still fussing and just like me, Evan can't handle it. He reaches out and takes her from his mom. "She just needs time to warm up to this," he says gently.

"Oh, by bedtime I'll have her used to me." Carol grins. "Let's get you inside. Everyone is dying to meet her and see both of you." I don't miss how she includes me.

With Lexi in his arms and his hand on the small of my back, Evan guides us to follow his mom into the house. Carol leads us into the living room where his grandparents are both sitting in matching recliners and his dad is sitting on the couch looking more frail than I've ever seen him, his feet propped up on a pillow on the table.

"Is that my granddaughter?" he asks. His voice is husky.

"Hey Dad. Yeah, this is Lexi." I expect him to drop his hand, but instead, he guides me to the couch. The three of us are now standing in front of his father. "Have a seat, babe," he says to me.

I sit next to his dad and gently touch his arm. "Good to see you, Jeff."

"McKinley, girl, it's been ages," he says, patting my hand.

Evan kneels in front of us. "Dad, this is Lexi. Lex, this is your grandpa." Lexi is watching Evan's dad just as she did Carol. She doesn't crack a smile, her tiny face so serious. Evan sits her in his dad's lap and leans back on his heels. I can see what this moment means to him. He's worried about his dad, the cancer eating away at him. I know he was scared this moment would never happen, worried his children—Lexi—would not get to meet his dad. Evan confessed that before the "wedding" talk started, he was trying to work up the nerve to ask me to take this trip with him.

Lexi holds her arm out for me and I slip my finger into her tiny hand. "Who's got you, Lex?" She babbles at me, telling me all about it. I keep talking to her, letting her hear my voice. Once Evan see's she's going to be okay with his dad, he takes the seat next to me on the couch. His arm goes around the back and he angles his body toward us, so he can talk to his father and take in the sight of him holding his little girl.

"She's a beaut, Evan," his dad comments.

"Yeah, she is. I told Kinley she's not dating until she's thirty," he laughs.

"Oh hush, you," his mom joins the conversation.

"Don't be hogging all the loving, son," Evan's Grandpa Lexington chimes in. "I need to meet the angel who carries on the family name."

Just as he says the words, Lexi lets out a shriek and leans into me. Instinctively, I grab her and pull her into my arms. Her chubby little

hands grab at my face as she smiles and shrieks again. Evan rubs her back as he chuckles, and to anyone watching us, we look like the happily little family we're about to be, but for how long?

EVAN 37

onight has been . . . overwhelming. I never thought I would be an emotional sap seeing my parents with my daughter. When Mom held her, I got choked up, but when Dad held her, yeah, I had to bite my damn tongue to keep the tears at bay. Mom made dinner, and the rest of the night was spent passing Lex from one person to the next. That is up until about ten minutes ago when she decided she was done. I took her from Mom, who hasn't stopped smiling since we pulled in the drive.

"I'll make her a bottle," Kinley offers and scurries off to the kitchen. I watch her go, because, well . . . she's gorgeous.

"You're smitten," Mom calls me out.

You have no idea. "She's been there from the beginning. I owe her everything." I try to deter the conversation.

Dad laughs. "Evan, you look at her like I still look at your mother. You sure this is a good idea?" he says hesitantly.

Is this a good idea? Hell if I know. Do I want to marry her? Yes, without question. Is it just to keep my daughter with me? No, it's not. Can I confess that to them? I've always been close to them, but this . . . "No reservations," I tell them.

"Does she know?" Mom asks.

I look at the door leading to the kitchen, watching for her. I don't want her to hear this and make what we're about to do awkward. "No." I pretty much just lay it all out for them in that simple word. My parents are smart and can read between the lines. This is more for me.

I'm fucked!

They don't get the chance to say more as Kinley walks back into the room. Lexi is snuggled up on my chest, eyes wide as she watches my parents. At the sound of Kinley's voice, she lifts her head. "Here you go, baby girl." Kinley hands the bottle to me.

I settle Lexi into the crook of my arm and she begins to eat. Her arm reaches out and Kinley doesn't hesitate to offer her finger for Lexi to hold on to. Lexi goes back to eating, never letting go of Kinley. Her other hand is grabbing at my chin, so I offer her my finger as well. She locks on tight and settles. Kinley's eyes find mine and she smiles my smile.

My girls.

Just as Lexi finishes her bottle, Kinley yawns, which causes me to yawn as well. It's been a long-ass day, and I'm ready for bed. "I'm going to lay her down," I say to Kinley.

"I'll help you set up the pack-n-play." She stands from the couch and I follow her upstairs. My grandparents' house has four bedrooms, so Mom made up both rooms, one for me and Lexi and the other for Kinley. She pulled me off to the side earlier and said she wasn't sure if we wanted to share a room, so she got the other ready just in case.

Kinley sets up the pack-n-play while I change Lexi's diaper and get her into her pajamas. She sleeps through it all. She's been such a good girl today and travels so well.

"She's out," I say as I lay her down.

"Yeah, she's had a big day." Kinley kisses the tips of her fingers and presses them to Lexi's forehead. "I guess I'll see you in the morning," she says and looks back at Lexi one last time before walking away.

I reach out and grab her arm. She stops and looks over her shoulder at me. "Stay," I whisper my request, scared as hell she'll turn me down. I've slept a handful of nights with her beside me and as far as I'm concerned, it needs to be that way from now on. She's going to be my wife after all.

"Your parents," she offers a meek excuse.

"We're adults," I counter. *Adults who will be married in just five days.* "It's been a long day, McKinley. I just want to hold you." What is she doing to me? "I'm going to go downstairs to rinse out her bottle and tell everyone goodnight. I'll be back in a few." I don't give her time to argue. Instead, I kiss the top of her head and leave the room, hoping like hell she's in my bed when I get back.

My grandparents went to bed hours ago, and I can tell that Dad has reached his limit as well. I find them in the living room and pick up Lexi's bottle. "We're all going to bed. It's been a long day."

"Did you all find everything in your rooms?" Mom asks. I know she's hinting to see what our sleeping arrangements are.

"We're good, Mom. I'm just going to rinse this out and then head back upstairs. I'll see you guys in the morning."

In the kitchen, I wash the bottle and place it in the strainer. I hear my parents as they head to their room. There are two bedrooms upstairs and two downstairs. Dad's weak all the time, so they occupy the second "in-laws" suite, as it's called. I wait until I hear their bedroom door close and take the stairs two at a time.

I enter my room and release the breath I didn't even realize I was holding. Kinley's standing in the middle of the room in nothing but a pair of panties. She's digging through my luggage with nothing but the light from her cell phone, I assume for something to sleep in. Closing the door and turning the lock, I reach back, grab the neck of my shirt, and pull it over my head, all the while walking toward her.

The room is dark, but I can hear her with each rapid breath she pulls in. Reaching out, I snake my arms around her waist, her bare back now flush with my chest. Resting my chin on top of her head, I hold her. Her head rests against my heart and I know she can feel it as it thunders inside my chest. It's all different with her. Every touch is . . . more.

"Arms up," I say, releasing her. She complies and I slide the shirt I just removed over her head. As soon as she drops her arms back to her sides, I'm hauling her back against me. Everything is different with her, it's . . . more.

"Let's get some sleep." I pull back the covers and wait for her to climb in, following right behind her. As soon as I drag the covers up over us, she backs into me and I wrap her in my arms, just like I have each night we've shared a bed.

"Night, Evan."

I hold her a little closer. "Goodnight, baby."

McKinley
38

The week has flown by. Evan and Lexi have gotten to spend a lot of time with his parents and grandparents. Lexi warmed up to them by the end of day two. Now it's like she's been around them since birth. Tonight is our last night with them before my family and Jeff's parents arrive. Day after tomorrow, we're getting married.

"Mom, yes, I'm sure he hasn't seen it. It's not like this is going to be a real marriage. Why are you so worried?"

I'm currently up in our room, or Evan's room, talking to my mom. "Honey, it's a real wedding and your first, so, of course, I want this to be perfect."

I fight the urge to roll my eyes. "Carol showed it to me the day it was delivered. Evan was outside with his dad and grandfather. She has it in her room."

"Good. I just talked to her too, and the flowers will be delivered early Saturday." She rambles on about the wedding.

It's hard not to get caught up in the excitement of it all, especially when I fall asleep with his arms around me each night. He always finds little ways to touch me—hand on the small of my back or on my knee, arm around the back of my chair. It's endless.

He calls me babe in front of everyone and doesn't care who hears him. He even slipped up and called me baby last night when he asked me if I was ready for bed. His mom heard him; I could tell by the smirk on her face. Evan didn't seem to notice or care. He just said his

goodnights, picked Lexi up, and guided me up the steps.

This sweet, caring, charming, sexy-as-hell man is going to be my husband day after tomorrow. Yeah, it's hard as hell not to get caught up in that. He makes it all feel real.

"So either Evan or I will be at the airport to pick you up. I don't know that both of us will come, so there will be enough room in the Durango for your luggage."

"Great. Our flight lands at three," she tells me.

"Sounds good. I'll see you all tomorrow then."

"Love you," Mom says as we end the call. I drop my phone on the bed and fall back against the pillows. Staring up at the ceiling, I think about living with him every day, taking care of Lexi together. It's what we do now, but I don't live there. I've spent the night a handful of times, but this is different.

"Hey, babe," Evan says from the doorway.

Turning my head to face him, I smile. I can't prevent it; he does that to me. "Hey, Lex with your mom?"

"Yeah, I actually asked her to watch her for a few hours. I thought maybe you and I could get out of here for a little bit."

"Really?" I don't even try to mask my excitement. We've pretty much stuck to the house all week, and not that I don't love his family, but getting out for a few hours sounds great.

"Yeah, it's nothing fancy. Just thought we could take a ride, maybe grab some dinner," he suggests.

"Perfect. When do we leave?" I grin.

This causes him to laugh. "We can go now, baby. You ready?"

I look down at my skinny jeans and sweater. "Am I dressed okay for what you have in mind?"

"You're perfect." He leans in and kisses the corner of my mouth. "Let's go say bye to Lexi and get out of here," he says, grabbing my hands and pulling me from the bed.

Once I'm standing, he laces his fingers through mine and we walk down the stairs side by side. We find his parents in the living room on the couch, Lexi eating up their attention. "We're headed out," Evan says, stopping in front of them. I try to drop his hand, but he holds tight. Bending over, he gets eye level with Lexi. "You be a good girl. Daddy and Kinley will be back in a little while." He kisses her cheek and she shrieks.

With my hand that's not occupied by Evan's, I reach out and tap her nose. "See you soon, sweet girl."

Evan pulls me from the room and out the door. "Where are we going?"

"Well, there's a diner not far from here that my grandparents would always take me to when I would come to visit. They have great home-cooked food—-comfort food." He grins.

It's right on the tip of my tongue to tell him I've had so many meals this week I don't think I will fit in my wedding dress, but then I remember he doesn't know about the wedding dress. "Sounds good."

He opens my door for me like the gentleman he is, only this time, he leans in and kisses me before pulling away and closing the door.

As we drive to the restaurant, Evan reaches over and laces his fingers through mine. My heart flutters in my chest. I never had a chance in hell to not fall for him.

The restaurant is not busy for a Thursday night, so the waitress tells us to seat ourselves. Evan leads us to a booth in the back and I slide into one side as he goes into the other. "It's all good here," he tells me, handing me a menu.

"Chicken and Dumplings," I say with way more excitement than I should have for a simple meal. "It's been forever since I've had that." Decision made, I close my menu and place it on the table.

"That sounds good, but so does the homemade chicken pot pie."

"That does sound good," I agree. It really does, but I'm still sold on the dumplings.

"Are you nervous about the wedding?" he asks after we place our orders.

"No. Are you?"

"Surprisingly, no." He reaches over and takes my hand in his. "You're my best friend, McKinley. You're putting your life on hold in order for me to keep my daughter. The only thing I'm feeling is admiration. You're an amazing person and I will never be able to repay you for what you've done for me and Lexi."

"You don't have to. I love her, Evan. She needs to be with you.

You're my best friend too, and that's what you do for your friends."

"Thank you, McKinley Rae," he says, his brown eyes holding mine.

The waitress brings our food and the conversation moves from how delicious it is to how much extra stuff we have to take home with us. "Really, Kinley, Mom has gone nuts with the shopping. It's a good thing we didn't fly," he says, taking a drink of his water.

"Yeah," I giggle. "She's just doing what grandma's do. She's excited and she knows you're doing this on your own."

"I have you," he counters.

What do I say to that? Nothing. I ignore it like we do most other topics, which we should discuss but don't.

"Try this." I once again change the subject. I scoop up a big bite of my chicken and dumplings and hold it out for him. He doesn't hesitate to lean in and wrap his lips around my fork.

"So good," he says after he finishes his bite. "Try this," he mimics me and offers me a bite of his pot pie.

"Delicious," I say, covering my mouth with my hand.

"Right?" He grins.

We enjoy the rest of our dinner with easy conversation. It's always easy between us. "Where to now?" I ask once we are back in the car.

"I thought I would take you to one of my favorite spots."

"Is that all I get? No hints?" I pout.

"You're cute," he says, tapping my nose just like I do with Lexi. "My grandparents own some property not far from their house. It has a huge pond, and every time I visit, Gramps and I spend a lot of time there. When I came to visit a few months back, Dad came with us. It was good to spend time just the guys. It's always been my favorite spot, and I want to share it with you," he says sheepishly.

"I can't wait to see it," I tell him. I really can't. Anything that's important to him and makes his eyes light up like that, I'm in.

EVAN 39

I thought I would be nervous, but I'm not. I know this is the right thing to do. Her parents think the same thing. Hell, even Aaron agrees with me. This whole situation is surreal.

"Is this it?" she asks as I park in front of the old red barn.

"This is it." I hop out and open the cargo area where I snuck a couple of blankets.

"Where did those come from?" she questions me.

"I put them in there earlier. I was banking on you saying yes to getting out of the house."

"You calling me a sure thing?" she teases.

I close the hatch on the Durango and throw my arm around her shoulders, pulling her close and kissing the top of her head. "Never, baby. I was just hopeful you would spend the evening with me."

"Let's see this pond," she says. She's trying not to get too close; I recognize the signs. I fought it just as hard, but I don't want to anymore. She's going to be my wife, and while she is, for however long that may be, I want this to be real.

I keep my arm around her as we walk down toward the pond. "Watch your step," I tell her when we reach a section of uneven land. There is a wall of trees sheltering this side of the pond. It's great for shade on a hot summer's day.

"You sure you know where you're going?" she asks as we walk through the tree line.

"You don't trust me?"

"No, I do. It's just . . ."

"Right there," I say, motioning with my head. She pulls her eyes from mine and looks in front of us. The huge pond is lit with nothing but the moonlight surrounded by stars.

"Wow," she breathes. "It's beautiful."

"Yeah," I agree with her, but I'm not looking at the pond. My eyes are glued to her. We reach a shadowed edge and I stop her. "Let me lay these down." I spread one thick quilt down on the grass and take a seat. I hold my hand out for her and help her with her balance while she takes her place next to me. I throw the other blanket over us and she snuggles in close.

"This is nice," she says as she takes in our surroundings. "This place is so peaceful."

"Yeah, even during the day it's like that. It's great for fishing. I've spent many hot summer days at this pond."

Turning her head, she looks up at me. "Thank you for sharing it with me." She shivers, but tries to cover it up.

"Come here." I throw back the blanket and spread my legs, patting between them. She doesn't hesitate to climb over and settle against my chest. I cover us back up with the blanket. This time, my arms are wrapped tight around her.

"I did have an ulterior motive for asking you to hang out with me tonight. There are a few things I want to tell you. When we are at my place or even my parents,' it seems like we get sidetracked with Lexi, and I just wanted to spend some time with you so I could get this out." I feel her stiffen in my arms. I bury my face in her neck and place a gentle kiss against her skin. "It's not bad. I just want to get all of this out in the open before the wedding."

I'm glad she's not facing me. I'm nervous as hell, and I'm sure I would botch the speech I'd planned if I were looking her in the eye. "I need you to know this is a real marriage to me. I will respect you and provide for you. You've done so much for me, that I just . . . I need for you to understand, for me, this is real. It's not just some arrangement. I want to share each day with you. I want you in my bed at night. I know it's temporary, and I don't expect anything more than what you've given me, but there will be no one else for me while we're married. It's you and me, McKinley. I just need for you to know that. Need you to know where I stand with all of this. Everything happened so fast, and I just . . . it's more."

I don't say anything else, giving her the time she needs to process what I've said. I just hold her in my arms and wait.

"So . . ." She clears her throat. "So, you want us to be together, as husband and wife, completely until this arrangement is over?" she asks.

No! I want to yell. *I want this for as long as you'll have me. Not just until the risk of losing Lexi is gone.* I can hear the hope in her voice and this arrangement is how she wants it, how it has to be. She needs a man who doesn't have a ready-made family. I know she loves Lexi, but . . . she deserves better than me. However, I'm a selfish prick when it comes to her and I want it all for as long as she's my wife. "Yeah," I say instead.

She's quiet again, the silence surrounding us. "Okay," she murmurs. It's so low I almost miss it.

Excitement runs through me as I realize this is it. She agreed to this. "Hey, can you spin this way?" I ask her.

She moves down and then turns to face me. She's too far away, but I needed to see her face. I grab each leg and pull her to me; her laughter echoes throughout the night sky. I don't stop until I have her in my lap, her legs locked around my waist.

I cradle her face in my hands and bring her lips to mine. I kiss her with all the excitement coursing through my veins, with all the hope for what we could be in my heart. I kiss her, showing her what she means to me. I keep my lips soft against hers, taking my time tasting her. Her hands comb through my hair as she holds my mouth to hers.

She wants this.

I let myself get so lost in the kiss that I almost forget there's one more thing I had on the agenda for tonight. Reaching back to the corner of the blanket, I grab the little black velvet box that I laid there. I do this without breaking our kiss.

Once I have the ring in my hand, I pull my lips from hers and take her in. Her face is flushed and her lips are swollen from our kisses. Her eyes tell me what she won't . . . she wants more. I plan to give her just that. I just have something to ask her first.

My heart is about to beat out of my chest. My palms are sweaty and

I want to wipe them on my thighs, but she's on my lap and then there's the ring I have clutched in my palm. I can feel the diamond digging against my skin.

Leaning in, I place my forehead against hers. I will my heart to slow down, as I open my mouth to speak, but the words won't come. I'm so overwhelmed in this moment that I'm afraid I won't be able to do it. I know what she's going to say, but in my heart, this is real. I want her for a lifetime, longer if possible.

"Evan?" I can hear the concern in her whispered plea.

Lifting my head, her worried eyes watch my every move. I grab her hand, careful to not drop the ring, and bring it to my lips. "I wouldn't change anything about this, McKinley. I have only one regret when it comes to saying our vows."

Her eyes widen, but she doesn't comment.

"McKinley Rae Mills, will you do me the incredible honor of becoming my wife?" I slide the ring onto her left hand. My eyes don't leave hers, and when I see tears begin to fall, I start to worry this was the wrong thing to do. That this was too much for our situation. It's not until I see her blinding smile and she wraps her arms around my neck, sobbing as she buries her face there, that I realize they are happy tears.

I hold her as she cries and fear sets in. What if I read her wrong and this isn't what she wants?

"McKinley, baby, I need to see your eyes." She sniffs and lifts her head.

I cradle her face in the palms, wiping her tears with my thumbs. "Will you marry me?" I ask softly.

Again, the smile—my smile—lights up her face. "Yes, yes, yes, yes!" she says through tears. Then her lips land on mine.

Our kiss is passionate and filled with all the things we've said and all the things we haven't. I roll us over and lay her down on the blanket, never breaking our kiss. I reach back for the blanket and pull it up over us. I don't take it past kissing and neither does she. The moment worked out better than I planned, and I give myself an internal fist bump that this beautiful, loving creature is going to be my wife.

McKinley
40

*E*veryone is asleep by the time we get home. Carol left us a note on the counter saying she has Lexi with her in her room and she moved the pack-n-play.

"I miss her," I say as we're climbing in bed.

"Me too. It's weird to not tuck her in and kiss her goodnight."

"Yeah, she kind of swoops in and steals your heart when you're not looking."

"She does," he agrees. He pulls the covers over us as we lie in bed face to face. I lift my hand to move his hair out of his eyes and my ring shines in the moonlight.

"We're getting married," I say in whispered excitement. I can't hold it back. I'm going into this eyes wide open, but I'm going to relish the fact this man is going to be my husband and cherish each moment until it ends.

"We're getting married," he repeats before his lips capture mine. He starts slow, but I need more. I open for him and he takes the invitation and slides his tongue against mine. We duel and I drink in the taste of him, all the while my hands are roaming over every inch of him I can touch.

I want tonight to be different. Up to this point, it's him giving me pleasure. He never lets me reciprocate. Tonight, that changes. I block out the fact that we're in his parents house. All I see is Evan, and all I can think about is having him unravel from my hands and mouth.

Gently, I push him back on the bed, rising up over him. I take control of this kiss, nipping at his lips. He literally takes my breath away and I need to break the kiss just to catch it. My hands roam over the peaks and valleys of his abs while I place open-mouthed kisses all the way to his collarbone.

"McKinley." My name falls from his lips. The gruff sound of his voice makes me want this even more.

I kiss his chest and travel further until I reach his abs. Let me tell you something about Evan. He's a fucking work of art. His body looks as though it was sculpted. His six-pack abs quiver under the touch of my tongue. This man is as hard as steel and falling apart all because of me. It's a heady feeling.

Feeling brave, I slide my hand over his erection straining against his boxer briefs. "Baby." He runs his fingers through my hair. I love it when he calls me baby.

I continue my journey over the mountains he calls abs and my mouth gets closer to where I really want to be as my hand continues to trace his erection. My mouth reaches the waistband of his underwear and a jolt of excitement courses through my veins. I'm not ashamed to admit I've thought about doing this to him thousands of times. Right or wrong, it is what it is.

Climbing to my knees, I slip my fingers under the waistband and lift it over his erection. He raises his hips, giving me the opportunity to slide them down his legs. I waste no time in taking him in my hand and roaming the length of him.

A gentle tug on my hair has me lifting my head. "Baby, you don't have to do this." His voice is husky and his eyes tell me another story altogether. I stroke him faster, which causes him to clench his jaw. Without releasing him, I move so I'm between his legs and sit back on my knees, still stroking him, increasing my pace.

I don't speak, but lick my lips instead. "Fuck me," he groans as I dip my head and taste him for the first time, one singular stroke of my tongue on the head of his cock.

I run my tongue up the length of him, stopping at the tip and taking him in. His hands find my hair and he holds on tight. Desire like I've never known fuels me to move faster, to take more of him. My hands and mouth work him in tandem. I can't get enough.

Evan keeps his hand in my hair, but never once uses it to guide me. He lets me go at my own pace. I take as much of him as I can, causing us both to moan. "Baby, I'm close." I don't stop. I want to push him over the edge. "McKinley, I . . . can't . . . oh God, that feels amazing," he pants. I quicken my pace, and he pulls on my hair. "Baby, I can't hold off." I take him deeper. I can tell the minute he decides it's okay to let go. Not twenty seconds later, I'm swallowing everything he gives me.

"Come here." He grabs my hand and pulls me up to him. His mouth fuses with mine, his tongue demanding entrance. I've never had a guy kiss me after. He kisses me until we're both gasping for air. His forehead rests against mine, chests heaving.

"I have no words for what that was, how that felt. You . . . wreck me." He pulls away and adjusts us so my back is to his front. He wraps his arms around me and holds on tight. "Two days, Kinley. In two days, you're going to be my wife."

I can't speak without him knowing how his words affect me. Instead, I lace my fingers through his and relax into his hold.

In two days, I will be McKinley Chamberlin.

EVAN 41

aking up alone after having her in my arms for the past week is not something I'm fond of. Yesterday, her family and my dad's parents flew in. The house was full and Lexi stole the show. I love my little girl, but I couldn't take my eyes off McKinley. She likes to talk with her hands and every time the diamond—my diamond—would sparkle. The women gushed over it; Aaron just gave me a nod, the men not saying much at all. This situation is unique. They don't know when I bought the ring, I was thinking of her being mine forever. They didn't see how it took me hours to fall asleep last night because she wasn't there. They don't understand that I fall harder every damn day. And they don't get that the day she finally walks away, when this . . . ends, my heart will be shattered.

With the new members added to the fold yesterday, sleeping arrangements changed. My dad's parents are staying here. The steps were hard for them, but they wanted to be close to Dad. There's a spare room, so it worked out. Jerry, Sarah, and Aaron are staying at a local hotel. Sarah had the bright idea McKinley should stay with them since Dad's parents were taking the spare room. She went on to say it's bad luck for the bride and groom to see each other on the wedding day. I pulled McKinley aside and begged her not to go. Yes, I begged her. I would have given anything for her to stay with me last night. She kissed me like it might be the last time and left with her parents and brother.

I'm man enough to admit I missed the hell out of her. I told her I would. She chuckled and said, "You'll be fine." I am, but I'm not happy. I'm addicted to her, which might make me a whipped pussy, but I

couldn't give a fuck less. If that's how it has to be, how I'm going to be with her in my life, I'll take. I'll take every fucking second of it as long as she's with us.

Lexi is talking her cute-as-hell baby babble, letting me know it's time to get my tired ass out of bed. Throwing the covers back, I make my way to the pack-n-play. "Morning, baby girl." I reach for her and her little arms and legs go crazy. I kiss her cheek and she babbles some more. "I think we need to call Kinley, let her say good morning. What do you think?" She grins and shrieks. Sometimes, I swear she understands what we're saying to her.

After a quick diaper change, I lay her on the center of the bed, grab my phone, and hit Kinley's contact. It rings once before she picks up.

"Evan," she says in greeting.

"Morning, beautiful. I have someone who wants to talk to you." I don't wait to hear what she says. Instead, I place the phone next to Lexi's ear. At first, she goes still, until she hears Kinley's voice. Her eyes look around, searching for her. Whatever Kinley's saying excited her because those hands and legs start to go crazy again. I know it's not what she says, but the sound of her voice. Lexi loves her; it's easy to see that.

Pulling the phone back to my ear, I say, "She misses you."

"I miss her too, both of you," she adds softly.

"Last night was a terrible idea," I grumble.

She laughs. "I know, but how could I tell my mother no. She's set on this 'no seeing each other before the wedding' business. I don't know if I'll ever get married again, so I thought I would at least give her this."

Get married again.

At those words, I want to yell into the phone that she will never be married to anyone but me. I want to demand she never think those thoughts again, but I don't. Instead, I go with the only other form of honesty I'll let myself give her.

"I miss you, babe."

Lexi starts to fuss. I want to say it's because she's hungry, but my little girl, she's a smart one. She knows I'm talking to Kinley and she wants to as well.

"She hungry?" Kinley asks.

"Probably, but I think she's mad I'm talking to you. Let me put you on speaker and see what happens." I switch to speakerphone and stretch out on the bed beside Lexi. I place the phone on the pillow between us.

"You're on speaker, babe," I tell Kinley.

"Lex, are you being a good girl for Daddy?" At the sound of her voice, Lexi stops fussing. She holds still, waiting.

"She's stone still, Kinley. She misses you," I confirm.

"I miss you too, sweet girl. I'll see you in a few hours." Her voice sounds sad. "Evan, do you think . . ." Her voice trails off.

"McKinley?"

"Never mind," she says.

"Not never mind, what were you going to say?" Was she going to ask if I thought we were doing the right thing? Is she getting cold feet?

"I was wondering if, I don't know, maybe I can have Aaron or Mom come get Lex and spend some time with her this morning. I can get her dressed here and bring her with me." I can hear the hope in her voice. I can also hear she's hesitant to ask. Does she think I would be mad? She loves my daughter, and she's the only mother figure in her life. I'm honored she loves Lex enough to want her with her.

"Baby, you're going to be my wife in a few short hours. Lexi, you, and me, we're going to be a family. This is real, baby. We talked about this. You never have to ask to spend time with her, even when . . . you never have to ask, McKinley."

"I miss you both so much, and being close to her will make me feel close to you," she murmurs.

If I didn't already know I was falling in love with her, that right there sealed the deal. She's not using Lexi as an excuse to get close to me. She wants to feel close to me, to both of us.

I'm falling hard.

"Send Aaron on over. I'll feed her breakfast and get her bag packed."

"Thank you, Evan."

"I can't fucking wait to see you walking down that aisle," I blurt out.

"Yeah?"

"Yeah, I'll see you soon, babe."

"I'll be there," she says with conviction.

"Let's get some breakfast. Then you're going to go see your m—"

Shit! I almost referred to Kinley as her momma. It's true in every sense that matters, and today she becomes my wife, but we need to talk about that first. When . . . when this is all over, will she still want that title and the responsibility with it?

The kitchen is quiet, which is strange, but I go about making Lexi her bottle and settle in at the table to feed her. I nibble on a pastry while she eats.

"You're going to spend the day with Kinley, baby girl. Then, in a few hours, you'll come back here while Kinley and Daddy get married." She coos like she likes the idea. "Can I tell you a secret?" I whisper next to her ear. I should feel ridiculous confiding in my infant daughter, but I know she can keep a secret. She stops eating and lets the bottle fall from her mouth, a grin gracing her lips. I swear she understands every word. "Daddy loves Kinley very much." It feels good to say it out loud. "I know you love her too. She's going to be living with us, Lex. Daddy's not sure how long he will be able to do that and not beg her to stay with us forever."

"So the truth comes out."

Shit! Looking up, I see Aaron standing in the doorway. "I didn't hear you come in."

"Obviously." He's not giving anything away. He takes the seat beside me and grabs Lexi's foot. "Morning, sweetheart."

She grins and coos at him. "I have her bag packed. She just needs to finish eating." I ignore the fact I'm pretty damn sure he heard me tell my daughter I'm in love with his sister.

"I'm in no hurry, although don't be surprised if Kinley calls wondering where I am," he laughs.

I don't say anything. Instead, I offer Lexi her bottle and watch as she once again starts to eat.

"Fuck, man. Your fucking eyes got all soft just at hearing her name. You're really in love with my little sister?"

And there is it.

Lifting my head, I meet his gaze. "Yes." I don't offer an explanation or an apology. Just the cold hard truth.

"Does she know?"

"No, and I don't plan on telling her."

"Why the fuck not?"

I sigh in frustration. I've been through this a thousand times in my head. No one else was supposed to know besides Lexi. "She deserves better, man. I'm a selfish bastard for letting her go through with this. I'm scared as hell that, when this is all over, she's going to pack up and move back in with your parents. I know that's what's best for her, but I'm fucking dreading it."

"Don't you think she deserves the chance to make that decision?"

"She loves her, Aaron. She loves my daughter like she would if she were the one who gave birth to her. I don't want her to stay for just Lexi, man. I want her to stay for the whole package."

"How do you know she won't be?"

"I guess I don't. Maybe living together will change that. I don't know, but as for now, I can't tell her."

"Stubborn ass," he retorts. "You really love her?"

"Yeah, man. I really do."

"So the proposal?"

"It was real."

"Wow."

"I'm in deep, man. I know she's your little sister, but she's here." I place my hand over my chest.

"I'm glad it's you. I mean, it's still weird to think about my best friend and my sister, but I know you, and you'll be good to her. I just wish you would tell her, man. What if she feels the same way?"

I shrug. "I think I'll choose heartbreak because when what she thinks is just an arrangement is over, heartbreak is better than her rejection. I don't think I could live with that, Aaron. It's going to be hard enough letting her go when this all settles. To think she never really wanted me . . . this is the better option."

"I think you're wrong, but it's your call."

I don't reply as we sit in silence, both watching Lexi finish her breakfast. "She's a cute kid, man," Aaron finally says.

"Yeah, she's my world."

Lexi spits out her bottle and grins. "All right, baby girl, let's get you cleaned up and then Uncle Aaron is going to take you to Kinley." I try like hell to not be jealous of my daughter.

McKinley
42

$\mathcal{A}$aron left forty-five minutes ago; he should be back by now. I'm pacing back and forth in my room. Mom and Dad shared a room as did Aaron and I. So there is no one here to witness my crazy. I know Aaron and Evan probably got caught up shooting the shit, as they refer to it, but they could at least send me a damn text so I don't worry.

Just as I pick up my phone to call them, the door opens and Aaron waltzes in with Lexi in tow. "Finally!" I say, dropping my phone on the bed and taking Lexi, seat and all, from him.

"Hey, the little bugger had to finish her breakfast."

Lexi smiles when she sees me. "Hey there, sweet girl. I missed you," I say as I unstrap her from the seat. Her arms and legs are flying when I pick her up. She grabs for my chin, my hair, anything her little hands can latch on to.

"I think it's safe to say she missed you too," Aaron laughs. "She's not the only one," he mumbles under his breath.

I pretend I don't hear him. "You ready for a today, Lex? You have the prettiest little dress," I tell her.

"You ready for this?"

"Of course I am."

"No reservations? You know it's not too late to back out."

"Why would I want to do that? This was my idea, after all."

"I don't know. Just thought I would put it out there."

"Well don't. There isn't anything that could change my mind," I tell him.

"Really? What if you finally face the truth that you love him and this is going to end with you having a broken heart? Is that reason enough to call it off?" he asks.

I can feel my face flush from his words. "Listen, Aaron, I care about Evan, more than just as my friend, I will admit that, but those feelings are not going to stop me from going through with this. I love this little girl like she were mine. I can't let them take her. Whatever is going on between Evan and me, we will either work it out or we won't. My eyes are wide open, Aaron. I know I'm risking my heart with both of them. Evan is a great guy. He would never keep Lex from me. I know that. If he's just my friend when this is all said and done, then so be it. At least they will both still be a part of my life. I don't think I could accept a world where that isn't the case."

"You love him." Aaron smiles cockily.

My big brother is so damn frustrating. "Fine, yes, I love him. My heart skips a beat when he walks in the room. I don't sleep when his arms aren't wrapped around me. You happy now?"

"You're sleeping with him?" His voice is deathly calm.

"Aaron, come on. We've slept in the same bed a few times, all this week actually, and a few times before that."

"That's not what I asked you," he fires back.

"Look, I'm sure this is not a conversation you want to hear about your little sister."

"You're right, it's not, but it's also about my best friend. I thought Evan had more respect for you than that," he seethes.

"He does. No, we're not having sex!" I raise my voice, causing Lexi to jump. I bounce her in my arms. "Look, Aaron, I'm going to say this once, and then we're never talking about it again. I mean it. You can't even bring it up to Evan. Yes, we've done more than just a few kisses here and there, but I have not had intercourse with him. Does that mean I won't? No, it doesn't. This does not involve you, Aaron. Please, just let it go. Evan treats me like I'm precious to him. Never once has he done something I was not fully on board with. Now drop it."

"McKinley—" I raise my hand to stop him.

"Don't! Just let it go. I'm in this, Aaron. Nothing you say can change my mind. I know I'm your sister and he's your best friend, but what happens between Evan and me is just that, between us. You need to stay out of this."

He runs his fingers through his hair. "Fuck! All right, I'll try my best." He sits down on the bed. "Now give me the munchkin. Her dad was hogging her and Uncle Aaron needs his fix." He changes the subject. He's frustrating as hell, but I love him and it's nice to know, above all, he has my back.

"But I just got her," I whine.

"Too bad, go shower while we play." He takes Lex from my arms and waves his hand toward the bathroom. "You do have a wedding to get to in just a few hours, you know."

He's right. Today, I marry my best friend, who just also happens to be the man I'm head over heels in love with, but too afraid to tell him. There are times when I think he feels it too, but it's not worth the risk. Not having him and Lexi in my life in any capacity is just not an option for me. I'll love him silently.

"Oh, sweetheart, you look beautiful." Mom has tears in her eyes.

"You ready for this?" Dad asks.

"Yeah, I really am. This is the right thing to do. Evan is a good man, you know that."

"I know, honey. He confirmed it when he asked for your hand."

Wait! What? "He . . . what did you just say?"

"Evan stopped by a few days before you all left and asked us both for your hand. Said he wanted to do things right, even under the circumstances," Dad explains.

Holy shit!

"I take it you didn't know?" Mom asks.

"I had no clue. I mean, yeah, he asked me." I raise my hand to show them my ring, as if they needed the proof. They've already seen it.

"If I didn't know any better, I would say that boy's in love with you," Mom comments.

"Knock, knock," Aaron says, coming into the room. He's carrying a smiling Lexi in her little white dress. "This squirmy little monster is hard to dress. We made it happen though, didn't we, Lex?" She coos and reaches for his chin. He acts like he's going to bite her fingers and she grins.

"You dressed her?" I ask in disbelief.

"Yeah, Mom was here with you, and I thought I would help. Easy-peasy once we got the damn thing over her head. Well, and the tights, that was a task," he says with a laugh.

"I would have paid good money to have seen that, son," Dad laughs.

"Damn! I should have recorded it. Evan probably would have too. Lexi girl, we could start a side business." Aaron kisses her cheek.

"Well, looks like we're ready to go. We don't want to keep them waiting."

"Um, hello, minister here, the show can't start without me," Aaron says.

"Um, hello, bride here, the show can't start without me either," I mock him.

"Good thing you're all pretty and shit, or I'd be giving you the biggest noogie," he jokes.

"Let's go, you two," Dad laughs.

I reach for Lexi, but Aaron turns away from me. "No way, sister. Mom would kill me if you get wrinkled or something . . . baby on you. I got her."

"What about you?" I counter.

"I'm just the guy who says the words. No one's going to be looking at me."

"It's a very small group, Aaron, of course they will."

"McKinley, have you looked in the mirror? You're beautiful. I can say with absolute certainty that all eyes, no matter how many are in attendance, will be on you."

"Stop before you make her cry and mess up her make-up." Mom smacks his shoulder and Lexi repeats the action.

"Let's get you married, baby girl." Dad loops his arm through mine and leads me out to the car.

EVAN

We're getting married in my grandparents' church. It's a private service and the pastor was completely fine when we explained the brother of the bride would be the one marrying us. My grandparents have been members for over fifty years. They handed them the keys and said to clean up when we're done. Originally, it was going to be in the backyard, which is where McKinley still thinks it's going to be, but I wanted more for her. I want this to be a day she will remember.

So, we got the church. Mom and a few other ladies took care of decorations and I took care of the photographer. I mean, come on, I'm marrying a photographer who has a true passion for capturing memories. I can still remember that day months ago when she told me why she chose photography. How can I not hire the best to give her pictures—her passion—to remember this day?

I contemplated inviting a few of our friends, but selfishly, I decided not to. I like the idea of an intimate setting, the idea of saying our vows in front of just our immediate family. I hinted around to McKinley about inviting others, and she pretty much said the same thing. The wedding is for us, to pledge our lives—well, for me, my love—but she won't know that. She said it's not for the showboat of the event. We share very similar beliefs, and that just made me fall a little more in love with her. I am admitting it in my head now, especially after this morning. Confessing to my daughter and having Aaron overhear it all, there's no sense in denying it in my head. I know how I feel.

Everything came together seamlessly, and now, I'm sitting in a back

room of the church waiting for my bride and my daughter to arrive. I'm not nervous, anxious maybe, but no nerves.

"Come in," I say to the knock on the door.

"Hey, son." Dad slowly enters the room and takes a seat on the bench beside me. "You ready?"

"Yes."

"I'm proud of you, Evan."

"Yeah, your son who knocked up his girlfriend who ended up wanting nothing to do with him or the baby. The son who has to marry his best friend's little sister, who also happens to be his best friend, to keep his daughter." I don't know where that came from. I guess I'm a little ticked off at the circumstances. I would rather be able to tell McKinley how much I love her as we stand at the altar today.

"Evan, you love that girl. Everyone can see that. You two might be hiding behind this arrangement, but anyone with eyes can see this is more than that."

"Evan you ready?" Mom asks through the door.

"You can come in," I yell back.

She slowly pushes open the door, peeking her head around the corner. "They just arrived. To say she is surprised is an understatement."

"Good." I gently pat my father's shoulder. "Let's do this." I grin at my parents. Dad doesn't say any more about our conversation and neither do I. This is just how it has to be.

I follow my parents to the main area of the church where I see Aaron standing. The grin on his face relaxes me.

"Dude, I can't wait for you to see Lexi. Kinley bought her a little dress. Man, she's a cute kid."

I'm excited to see my daughter, but even more so my fiancée. I don't know what she'll be wearing, and I don't care. She could walk down that aisle in jeans and a ratted old t-shirt and she would still be beautiful to me. I would still be having an internal celebration that she was just minutes from being my wife.

Grandma Lexington takes her place behind the piano and begins to play. I suck in a deep breath, my eyes glued to the doors, willing them to open. As if there was someone there to answer my silent plea, they do, and in walks McKinley, my baby girl in one arm, her dad escorting her with the other. She is wearing a white, sleek, sleeveless wedding gown and she's . . . breathtaking.

"Breathe, man," Aaron whispers in my ear.

Realizing I've been holding my breath, I breathe deep. I hear Aaron chuckle beside me. I want to glare at him, but that would mean taking my eyes off McKinley, and well, that's just not an option for me.

Taking her in, I commit every single second of this to memory and have to fight back the swell of emotion raring to break free.

She's going to be my wife.

She stops before me, and her dad leans over, kissing her cheek. I watch as he also kisses Lexi before turning and taking his seat. McKinley steps forward and I reach for Lexi.

"I want her with us," she whispers, although, with so few in attendance, everyone can hear no matter how soft you keep your voice.

"Absolutely," I whisper hoarsely. What I really want to do is lean in and kiss the hell out of her for including my daughter. However, I assume it's frowned upon to kiss the bride before I'm told to do so.

"Uh, guys, you're kind of stealing my thunder," Aaron jokes. Our parents laugh. "Now, dearly beloved . . ." Aaron rambles on, but I don't hear what he's saying. I'm too busy looking at my bride. Her hair is curled and off to the side, leaving one long, slender side of her neck bare and begging for my lips to kiss every inch of exposed skin. She's not wearing much make-up, which I love. She doesn't need it. The neckline of her dress, is low, but not indecent. Just enough to tease me with the temptation of the swell of her breasts.

Her lips are . . . moving. I blink to focus back on the moment. "Evan?" she says.

"Yeah, baby?" The endearment falls from my lips effortlessly. McKinley sucks in a breath and I realize my mistake. Our families can hear me. It takes me about two seconds to determine I don't care. I don't care if they know how I feel about her. I want our time together to be real. I will cherish her and every moment I get to have her as my wife. Our families need to get used to that.

McKinley tilts her head toward Aaron, and he's smirking at me. "I think this is where you say I do, man," he chuckles.

"I do," I say, my voice strong, full of promise and conviction.

McKinley
44

I always thought I would be nervous on my wedding day, full of jitters for the future. I was wrong. As I stand here, my hand in Evan's and him holding Lexi, I have not one ounce of nerves. All I feel is . . . complete happiness.

"McKinley, do you take Evan to be your lawfully wedded husband?" Aaron repeats to me.

I tear my gaze from Aaron to look at Evan, his eyes are shining with an emotion I can't name. Lexi decides it's time to let out one of her shrieks, causing me to laugh as a lone tear flows down my cheek. Evan brings our combined hands to gently catch it with his thumb. "I do." The words fall from my lips effortlessly. I have no regrets. I just hope my heart can heal when this is over.

"I now pronounce you husband and wife. You may kiss . . . wait," Aaron says, causing me to gasp. He grins and reaches for Lexi, taking her from Evan. "Now, you may kiss your bride."

Evan doesn't hesitate. He steps into me, slides one hand to the back of my neck and the other lands on my waist. He closes his eyes and we're kissing. It's not just a peck. It's a long, closed mouth kiss, ending with his forehead resting against mine. I close my eyes and take it all in.

We're married.

I'm not sure how long we stand like that, with our immediate family there to witness, but little Miss Lexington decides she needs some attention too and starts to babble. Evan and I pull away from our

embrace, both wearing huge smiles. I reach for Lex and she grins. Tapping the end of her nose, I look at Evan. "Now what?"

He chuckles and places his hand on the small of my back, leaning in close to my ear. "Now, my beautiful wife, we eat." He guides me down the aisle and into a back room of the church. It's set for a mini reception. There's a small wedding cake sitting on one table. On the other is an array of finger sandwiches and picnic type foods. The sight brings tears to my eyes. When Evan and I talked about weddings and the meaning, I made the comment I would want it to be relaxed like a picnic, not some overpriced meal no one even likes. He took my words and created that today.

I look up to find him watching me. "I hope I got it right," he says sheepishly. "I wanted today to be special."

Standing on my tiptoes, I place a quick soft kiss on his cheek. "Evan, this is special. The entire day's a huge surprise and it's perfect. I couldn't have planned it any better myself."

"Let me have her. You all will be leaving tomorrow and I don't know when I will see her again," Evan's mom says, taking Lexi from my arms.

"Hungry?" Evan asks.

I nod and follow him to the food. We each make a plate, Evan carrying mine to the table. Everyone is laughing and talking, and Lexi is soaking up the attention she's getting. As I take it all in, trying to memorize the sound of their chatter and the happy laughter, I slip my hand into Evan's under the table. He links his fingers through mine while turning to give me a questioning look. "Thank you, Evan. This day is amazing."

He leans in—to everyone else it looks as though he telling me a secret—and he is, but he also places a wet open-mouthed kiss on my neck. "You're amazing and so fucking beautiful. Aaron had to remind me to breathe." He pulls away, his eyes sparkling.

I raise my eyebrows, telling him I'm not buying what he's selling. Evan places his arm on the back of my chair and leans into me, looking at Aaron who is sitting on my other side. "Aaron, tell your sister what you said to me as she walked down the aisle."

Aaron grins, swallows a drink of his sweet tea, and wipes his mouth. Taking his sweet-ass time to reply. "He stopped breathing when he saw you. I was afraid he was going to pass out."

The look on my face must show my surprise. "He's a goner, that husband of yours." Aaron winks and stands from the table.

"You two ready to cut the cake?" Mom asks.

"Yes." Evan stands and offers me his hand. We make our way to the cake and go through the tradition of cutting the first piece together. We feed each other the first bites with no mess. When I thought about us getting married over the past couple of weeks, I never thought about any of this—the traditional wedding events. I just figured we would be in the backyard, say I do, and go on as usual. Clearly, my husband had other plans.

We spend the next hour talking, laughing, and eating. I could not have asked for a more romantic wedding. It's intimate and personal and everything I could ever want.

"Guys, we got you a gift." Mom hands me an envelope. I look at Evan and he nods for me to open it. Inside, I find a room key. "We thought, under the circumstances, it would be good for appearance's sake for the two of you to have a 'honeymoon,' even for one night. We are going to stay at the house in Evan's room and keep Lexi with us." She motions to Carol. The grandmothers are already staking their claim.

"I've never left her overnight," Evan blurts out.

"I know, but she knows me," Mom says gently.

"With Sarah being there, she will feel more comfortable since she spends a lot of time with her. You two need to do this," Carol adds.

Evan looks down at me. "McKinley?"

"She'll be fine. She's already used to your parents and mine. As far as appearances go, we don't know if they are watching us. I wouldn't put it past them." Evan's attorney filed a petition to have the custody case dropped. By now, Misty's parents have been notified. We can't slip up now.

Evan still looks unsure. I reach out and slide my hand into his. "She'll be fine. They'll call us if they need anything," I reassure him.

He nods and reaches out to take Lex from his mom. "Baby girl, you're going to have fun with the grandparents tonight. Daddy and M . . . Kinley are going to spend the night in a hotel. I promise we will be there bright and early to see you." Lexi just chews on her fist and babbles, not a care in the world. He kisses her on the forehead and bends

down so I can do the same.

We say the rest of our goodbyes and Mom informs us we have a change of clothes already in the room. They really did think of everything.

When we step outside the church, there is a limo waiting. Lifting my head to look at Evan, he shrugs his shoulders. I shake my head at his cheeky smile as we climb into the limo. As soon as the door closes, his lips are on mine. The kiss is . . . hot . . . wet . . . passionate. It's all consuming. His lips never leave mine until the limo stops and we hear the driver announce through the speaker that we've reached our destination.

EVAN 45

I groan when the driver announces we've made it to the hotel. The last thing I want to do is stop kissing her. A few more soft pecks and I climb from the car, holding my hand out for McKinley. We make our way into the hotel and are immediately greeted. "Mr. and Mrs. Chamberlin, we've been expecting you. Your stay has already been taken care of. Please let us know if you need anything," a young concierge says from behind the desk.

I nod and smile, all while pulling McKinley toward the elevator. Unfortunately, an older couple follows us in, so I have to restrain myself. "Congratulations," the lady says.

"Thank you," McKinley answers softly. I watch as a slight blush tints her cheeks, and I can't fucking help it, I lean down and kiss her lips. I don't devour her like I want to, but I needed to feel her lips against mine. The remaining floors took too long to wait.

McKinley places her hands on my chest and pushes back until my back hits the elevator wall. Instead of keeping her distance, she walks toward me and slides her arms around my waist. Her head rests on my chest, and I wrap my arms around her, holding her tight against me.

My wife.

The older couple seems to sense we don't feel much like small talk and the remainder of the ride is silent. When the elevator dings at the sixth floor, all four of us exit. We turn one way and them the other. McKinley is still in my arms, where I want her, as we walk slowly down the hall.

"Room 628," I say.

"There." She points to the door just ahead. I hand her the key then lift her up into my arms. "What are you doing?" she laughs.

"Carrying my beautiful wife over the threshold," I tell her.

"You're crazy," she laughs, and I swear I want to bottle the sound. I love hearing her happy.

She manages to get the door unlocked and I shuffle us inside. Kicking the door closed, I set her on her feet and then step forward until her back hits the door. My hands caress her cheeks, and her eyes lock on mine.

"We did it." Her words are soft.

"We did," I confirm as I brush a loose tendril of hair behind her ear.

"We're married."

"You're my wife," I say, needing to hear the words, needing to repeat them so I can verify this isn't a dream. She's opens her mouth to speak, but my lips mold to hers, cutting her off. I can't wait any longer. I need to kiss her like I need to breathe.

Her hands find their way around my neck, pulling me close. Mine, which were cupping her face, are now on a mission to roam every single fucking inch of her body. Her bare shoulders are soft against the skin of my rough hands as I trace circles on the delicate skin of her back until my hand reaches her dress. Her wedding dress, which I wanted to memorize her wearing just hours ago, is now in my way. I want to remember what it looks like lying on the floor of this hotel room. My mind is working overtime to remember every fucking second of this day. I never want to forget.

"Need you out of this dress, baby," I say in between kisses. I don't give her time to answer before my lips are back on hers. I find the zipper and gently pull until I reach the stopping point. Stepping back, I give her my hand. "Step out." She does, and I lift her dress, tossing it across the room, then turn my attention back to McKinley.

Un-fucking-believable.

Standing before me is the most beautiful creature I've ever seen. Her tan skin is a contrast to the barely there white thong. That's it. That's all she's wearing. If I had known . . . let's just say our little "reception" would have been a hell of a lot shorter.

"Fuck," falls from my lips.

"Surprise." She smiles. "I couldn't get the bra to work, so I just went without," She shrugs.

I can't take my eyes off her—the way her hair falls over her bare shoulder, the swell of her breasts as her tight nipples point toward me, begging for my attention. Then there's the thong, if you can call it that. It's a thin scrap of white material that leaves nothing to the imagination. That's the thing about white clothing, when it's wet you can see through it.

I can see all of her.

My eyes travel over every delectable inch. When I reach her red, swollen lips, I step forward and kiss her, my tongue gliding past her lips. Her hands tighten in my hair and I'm suddenly not close enough. My hands find her ass, gripping tight as I lift her. Her legs wrap around my waist and my cock settles against her wet, barely there thong. I'm still fully clothed, but I can feel her heat. I want inside of her so damn bad.

"Evan," she mumbles against my lips.

Tearing my lips from our kiss, I rest my forehead against hers. "Yeah, babe?"

"Can we . . . ?" She stops. That's not going to work for me.

"Can we what?" My eyes are closed as I focus on the sound of her rapid breaths in sync with my own.

"It's just . . ." She stops again.

Lifting my head, I see her eyes are also closed. "McKinley, look at me." She shakes her head no. "Please?" I kiss the tip of her nose. Her eyes flutter open. "Tell me," I say softly.

"We're married now, so it's not wrong," she blurts out.

"What's not wrong, babe?" I watch as she bites her bottom lip. "McKinley, you can ask me anything," I say gently. I mean every fucking word. No matter what it is, I would try like hell to give it to her.

"Will you make love to me?"

Her voice is soft, like she's afraid I'm going to say no. Does she not realize what she does to me? "Is that what you want?" My heart tells me I need to make sure she really wants this. My cock is screaming to be unleashed.

"I want you." Her voice is no longer soft. Her words are strong as her eyes bore into mine. "You said you wanted this to be real, the time we're together."

"I did say that and I do. You're my wife," I say it again because I'm fucking excited as hell to call her that. Regardless of the how and why, she's McKinley Chamberlin.

With her hands still in my hair, she tugs me close, her lips a breath from mine. "Make love to me, Mr. Chamberlin."

"With pleasure, Mrs. Chamberlin," I say, pressing my lips against hers.

McKinley
46

*T*his kiss is different than all the others. I feel this one all the way to my toes, like a bolt of lightning thrashing through my veins. I was scared as hell to ask for this, afraid that when— not if—when we cross that line and this . . . arrangement ends, we won't ever be able to go back. Back to being Evan and McKinley, two good friends who did what they had to do to keep a little girl with her daddy. Two friends who have shared laughter, intimacy, and . . . love.

I don't ever want to lose that.

Evan pulls us away from the door, his lips never leaving mine. I feel the soft mattress hit the back of my legs, as he climbs onto the bed, me still wrapped around him like a monkey. I pull my hands from his hair and start working on the buttons of his shirt. He sits back on his knees and rips the last two free, pulling his arms from the sleeves and tossing it across the room. Leaning down, he kisses just above the hem of my thong, a wet open-mouthed kiss before sliding off the bed and making quick work of discarding his pants. With one knee on the bed, he freezes.

"Shit," he mumbles and looks up at me. "I don't have a condom."

"Oh." I want to tell him it doesn't matter, that I want him inside of me anyway I can get him, but I don't. "Check the nightstand," I say, hopeful that maybe the hotel started leaving condoms in the nightstand instead of mints on the pillow.

Evan pulls open the drawer and his eyes go wide. I watch as he pulls out a box of condoms with a note card attached. He reads the card with a look of awe on his face.

"What's is say?"

He hands me the card.

Evan—

Take care of her.

Aaron.

"Holy shit!" Aaron knows how I feel about Evan, and he thought ahead. I'm sure this was hard for him, watching us get married, knowing my heart is on the line. I don't know many older brothers who would do what he did. I'm shocked, embarrassed, and grateful all at the same time.

"One of a kind, my best friend." Evan grins.

"Brother-in-law," I correct him. His eyes lock on mine.

"That's right." He rips open the box. "Enough talk about brothers. I promised my wife I would make love to her."

Finally!

Evan grabs a strip of condoms from the box and tosses them on the bed before throwing the box back in the nightstand. A shiver of anticipation runs through me. "You cold, babe?" He doesn't wait for me to answer; instead, he reaches back and pulls the quilt, which was folded at the foot of the bed, over us.

I notice right away it's not something that fits in with the décor. "Where did that come from?"

He chuckles. "My guess is my mother and grandmother. They go to Quilting Bee's on a regular basis."

I run my fingers over the stitching. "It's a wedding ring quilt," I say.

"Yeah, Mom's made them a few times as wedding gifts growing up."

"It's ours," I say, trying to fight back tears.

"It is," he says, burying his face in my neck.

I fear he has changed his mind with all of my chatter, until I feel his lips against my skin. His tongue traces the column of my neck, and I tilt my head, allowing him better access. He hums in appreciation.

"I need you naked," he whispers in my ear. He sits back on his knees, his hands finding my hips. "Lift." I do as I'm told as he moves his body down the bed, my panties sliding down my legs like a magnet being pulled with him. I feel the material slide over one foot and then the other. I watch as he tosses them over his shoulder, his eyes roaming over me. Closing my eyes, I will my racing heart to slow its rhythm.

I shudder when I feel his lips against the side of my foot. I keep my eyes closed tight as he places open-mouthed kisses up my left leg. When his lips leave my skin, I take a breath, exhaling loudly when I feel them on my right leg, repeating the same slow torture.

"Evan." My voice is pleading.

"I'm not going to rush this." He rises above me, his eyes locked on mine. "Never thought I would be inside you, I would get to taste you, and I would be with you like this. I'm taking my fucking time."

I have no reply for that. If I could speak, I would say hell fucking yes! However, his words have rendered me speechless.

I bury my hands back in his hair as his lips slide over my breasts. I bite back the moan that lingers at the back of my throat. His tongue works over my nipple, his teeth gently nipping as he soothes it with his tongue. His fingers pinch and roll the other, sending electric currents throughout my body like a damn on and off switch.

The room is quiet except for the sound of my rapid breaths and his lips against my skin. It's erotic and paired with the feeling of those lips as they devour me, yeah, I'm ready for him.

"Please," I whisper. I need more; more than what he's given me to this point. We've had months of foreplay, and I'm ready for the grand finale.

He releases my breast with a pop, his eyes finding mine. "I want you, McKinley. More than anything or anyone, I want you. I want to know how it feels to slide inside of you, to feel you from the inside. I want to watch you and feel you as you come apart for me." He leans down and kisses me, soft and slow. "I want all that, but I also want to cherish you, show you . . . I want this to be a night neither one of us will ever forget."

He continues to trace every inch of my body, kissing, biting, and soothing the pain with his tongue. I writhe beneath him, biting my lip to keep from begging for more. He's made it clear that slow and steady is his game plan.

EVAN 47

My cock is hard as steel. I've never been this hard in my life, but I ignore it as I kiss just above her pelvic bone. Sliding my lips lower, I settle in between her legs and trace my finger through her folds. She moans, the sound causing my cock to twitch with hunger.

Leaning forward, I slowly taste her. One small stroke of my tongue and that's all it takes for me to second-guess this 'let's go slow' shit I've started the night with. Almost. I fight the urge to give both me and my cock what we want, what we've been craving. The wait will be worth it. This is McKinley after all.

I work my tongue and my fingers in tandem. Feeling her body quiver, I know she's close. I need her there, need to feel her come undone, need to taste it. Only then will I allow myself to be inside of her. I promised her a night we would both never forget.

Her hands tighten in my hair and she pulls, trying to move me. "Evan, I . . . I can't take any more, please," she breathes.

I don't stop, can't stop. I'm addicted.

"Please," she says again, only this time she holds my head in place, thrusting her hips. "Don't . . . stop," her words spur me on.

She's close.

Before I even finish the thought, she's screaming my name, fingers tight in my hair, legs locked around my head. I don't stop until I feel her relax against the mattress. Satiated.

Rising to my knees, I wipe my mouth with the back of my hand, all

while taking in the sight before me. Her eyes are closed, a small smile graces her lips. Her body is flushed, hair spread out across the pillow. As long as I live, this image of her will always be with me. No matter what happens between us, how long she stays mine, no matter how the future pans out, I will never forget what she looks like in this moment.

Her eyes flutter open. "What are you doing?" she asks.

"Taking in the view," I tell her. The tint of her cheeks reddens, but this time it's not from her arousal. She lays an arm over her breasts, trying to cover herself. That's not going to work for me. "Don't." I lift her hand and place it back on the bed. "You're stunning. Don't hide from me. Ever." Her reply is silence, but doesn't try to move her hand back either.

I reach for the strip of condoms by the pillow and rip one off, tearing it open with my teeth. Her eyes follow my every move. As I stroke my steel length a few times, her eyes widen and she licks her lips. I stop my movements and take a deep breath. I could unload on her just like this, but I want to be inside her when I do. I make quick work of sliding the condom on and settle on top of her. My elbows rest on the bed on either side of her head as my hands push her hair back from her eyes.

"Make love to me, Evan." Her voice is soft, but full of conviction. There is no doubt she wants this.

My lips take hers. Softly, I kiss her, tracing my tongue across her lips. She buries her hands in my hair and slides her tongue inside my mouth, deepening this kiss. It's in that moment that I slide inside.

Tight.

Wet.

Warm.

Life-changing.

I'm buried deep inside her and can't move. My orgasm is there. I'm right on the edge of bliss, and it's too soon. Never. It's never felt this good. I bury my head in her neck and take deep, even breaths. Her fingers trail softly up and down my back.

"Evan?" I can hear the question in her voice. I'm about to lose my shit just from entry. If I could form words, I would tell her she's ruined sex for me. That from this point forward, it will never be the same.

When I finally feel like I've got myself in check, I trail kisses from her neck up to her ear. "McKinley," I whisper her name; it's all I'm capable of. Her body shudders beneath me. That's when I pull out and slowly slide back in. Repeating the process over and over again.

She pulls her legs up and fastens them around my waist. Her hands are digging into my shoulder blades.

"Please," she whimpers.

I know what she wants, but as soon as I give it to her, this will be over. I never want it to be over. "I won't last," I tell her.

Her hands leave my shoulders and find their way to my face. She holds my stare. "We're married, Evan. This isn't a one-time thing. We both agreed to this. Until this arrangement is over, I'm yours."

I kiss her hard as I slam home. "Yes!" she screams as her hips rise to meet mine thrust for thrust.

"I'm close, babe."

"I'm . . . don't stop," she pleads. I sit back on my legs, holding onto her hip with one hand and running my fingers through her folds with the other, never losing pace as I bury myself inside of her over and over again.

"I need you there," I pant.

Her eyes close, teeth dig into her bottom lip, two more thrusts and, "Evan!" she screams for me as she falls over the edge at the same time my body lets go inside of her. I run my hands over her thighs, her breasts, and her arms. I touch every inch of her I can while I'm still inside of her, the aftershock of her orgasm squeezing my cock.

I want it all.

Not ready to lose our connection, I pull her up, so we are chest to chest. Her legs wrap around my waist like she can read my mind. I work my legs out from underneath me and slide off the bed, her in my arms, me still inside of her.

"What are you doing?" she laughs.

"I need to get rid of the condom."

"You're crazy. Put me down."

I ignore her and carry her to the bathroom. I carefully sit her on the counter and reluctantly pull away from her body. "You're still . . ." Her eyes are on my cock.

"Yeah, only with you."

She watches with rapt attention as I remove the condom and toss it in the trash. Reaching in, I turn on the shower. I wait for the water to warm before holding my hand out for her. "Come here." My voice is gruff.

McKinley doesn't hesitate. She hops off the sink and takes my hand. I help her step into the shower, following in close behind. Turning to face me, her hand closes around my still hard cock. "You're dirty," she whispers.

I glide my hand down her ribcage, across her belly, and sink two fingers inside her. "So are you." I kiss her, and from there, our hands and mouths are everywhere. I can't get enough of her. We stand under the spray, exploring each other until the water turns cold. After a quick cold rinse to get rid of the soap, I turn the water off and step out first, wrapping a towel around my waist. I hold another out for her. Carefully, she steps from the shower and raises her arms. I place the towel around her before reaching for another for her hair.

"Sorry," she says, covering a yawn. "I didn't sleep great last night."

I kiss her lips. "I didn't either. My bed was cold."

Her face lights with my smile, causing my heart to skip a beat. "Let's get you dried off and into bed."

We make quick work of finishing and brushing our teeth before flicking off the light. I lead her to the bed and hold the covers back for her. Once we're settled, I pull her naked body as close to mine as I can get her. She moves her hand to cover mine and the moonlight shines off her ring.

My wife.

I'm holding my wife.

"Goodnight, Mrs. Chamberlin," I whisper in her ear.

She giggles. "Goodnight, Mr. Chamberlin."

McKinley

48

I wake up to the sound of Evan's whispers as he talks on the phone. My head is resting on his chest, and he has one arm holding me tight. "Did she sleep good?" I hear him ask. I smile, knowing he's asking about Lexi. He's such a good dad. "Is she okay?" I raise my head up and look at him when I hear the concern in his voice. "Okay, well, we'll be heading out soon." He listens on the other end. "Thanks, Mom," he says and hangs up.

"What is it? What's wrong?" I ask immediately.

"Good morning." He kisses the top of my head. "Nothing is wrong. Lexi's just been fussy this morning. Mom thinks she just misses us."

"Of course she misses you. She's never spent the night away from you," I tell him, climbing out of bed.

He reaches for me. "What are you doing?"

Stopping, I look over my shoulder. "We need to go. She needs you." I continue getting dressed.

I hear his feet hit the floor, and then he's there, right behind me. "I wanted to make love to you again."

"I want you too, trust me. However, Lexi comes first. Let's go get your girl. Today is our last day here. You need to spend time with your family."

He spins me around to face him, his hands holding my face, tilting up so he has my full attention. "You're amazing," he says before his lips find mine.

Although I want nothing more than to kiss him, and more, Lexi misses him. I push against his chest. "Get dressed."

"Yes, ma'am." He swats me on the ass.

It doesn't take us long to pack up our bags. Our family thought of everything, as there was a garment bag for my dress to bring it home in. I know my family can read me like a book. They know this is more for me than just making sure Lexi stays with Evan. It's also embarrassing as hell to know my parents, my brother, and my . . . in-laws set this up. They'll have a pretty damn good idea about what went on in this room last night.

"I called downstairs. They are calling us a cab."

"Great. I think I've got everything."

"Not everything," he says, snaking his arm around my waist.

"What did I forget?" I ask, my eyes roaming around the room.

"This," he breathes as his lips meet mine.

"We have to go," I laugh when he sighs in frustration, resting his forehead against mine.

"Thank you, for everything. For helping me prepare for Lex, helping with her, giving up who knows how much time of your life to make sure I can keep her with me." He tightens his grip on my waist. "For last night. I won't ever forget it. Every single fucking second is burned into my memory."

I love you. "We better go," falls from my lips. I have to remember to keep my feelings from him. When we walk away from this, neither of us needs to have feelings of guilt. I'm going to enjoy this time with him, with Lexi, and when it's over, I pray I can keep my composure and go back to how we were before last night. Before all the foreplay. Before I gave him my heart.

The cab ride is quiet. Evan has his arm around me, my hands resting on his chest. He draws circles on my knee. "It's going to be hard not touching you," he says wistfully.

"What do you mean?"

"When we get back to our families. It's going to be hard for me to keep my hands off you. I just . . . want you close."

Wow! "Is there a reason you don't . . . don't want to? In front of them, I mean?"

232

The hand on my leg moves to lift my chin up to face him. "No. I don't want to hide this connection we have. I know it's our agreement to do this for Lexi, but I just . . . you're my wife."

"I am. There is no reason for you to hide anything, Evan. We're not doing anything wrong."

"I know that, but I wasn't sure. I mean this . . ."

"This is between us. We know this is temporary, but we have a strong connection." It kills me to say the words, but I know he needs reassurance I'm okay. "We're consenting, married adults. It doesn't matter what they think."

"Not so worried about them, more about you. I wasn't sure you would want this, want them to know this."

"Evan, they put us up in a hotel room for the night with one bed. Yes, they said for appearances, but my brother bought us a box of condoms. They can see the chemistry between us. It's natural with as much time as we have spent together. You said it before, we enjoy our time being married, enjoy the benefits of being married, and then, when we know Misty's parents are gone, we go back to the way things were." Without you knowing you hold my heart in the palm of your hands.

He leans in and kisses me. "So you're okay with me kissing you in front of them?" He kisses me softly. "You're okay with me standing behind you with my arms wrapped tight around your waist?" Another kiss.

"Yes," I say, breathless from his kisses.

"I'll try to be as respectful as possible," he says as the cab pulls up to his grandparents' house. "Let's go see our girl." He opens the door and climbs out, offering me his hand.

Our girl. He doesn't even realize he said it. Those two words cause my heart to swell and crack all at the same time. No matter how bad I want her to be, she's not my girl. I know I will get to see her still when this is over, but I want that claim. I love her.

We find our parents and Lexi sitting around the kitchen table. Evan drops our bag and rushes to take her from his mom. "Hey, baby girl," he whispers to her. She coos and grins at him, and he visibly relaxes. In two long strides, they're next to me. "We missed you," he tells her, including me again.

Reaching out, I offer her my finger. "Hey, Lexi girl," I say, leaning in to kiss her cheek. She latches onto my hair and shrieks. Silly girl.

"Have you eaten?" Carol asks.

"No, we packed up and left right after I talked to you," Evan tells her.

"Well, have a seat. We had biscuits and gravy. There's plenty left over."

Evan pulls out a chair and motions for me to sit. I take the seat and he hands Lex to me, dropping a kiss on top of my head as he pulls back. I don't even think he realizes he did it. I see my mom grinning from the corner of my eye.

"Hey, you're back," Aaron says, joining us.

"Yeah, Mom said Lex was a little cranky, so we packed up." Evan brings me a plate and sets it in front of me before going back to make his own. Once he's done, he takes the seat next to me. "You want me to take her?" he offers.

"I just got her," I complain. He grins and shakes his head.

Lexi settles in my arms, watching her surroundings, so I pick up my fork and begin to eat. Evan does the same, resting one hand on the back of my chair.

"So our flight leaves at four," Aaron speaks up. "Before we go, I was thinking you and I could hit that fishing hole you're always yammering about."

Evan's eyes flash to mine, and he winks. "You okay with that?" he asks me.

I'm taken off guard by his question. "Uh . . . yeah, why wouldn't I be?"

He just shrugs and turns to look at Aaron. "Sounds like a plan."

"You want me to keep Lexington?" his mom asks. Again, Evan turns to look at me.

"I'm sure you want as much snuggle time as possible before we leave tomorrow, but I'll be here either way," I tell her.

The rest of breakfast is small talk. Evan, Aaron, and our fathers talk about fishing while Mom and Carol talk about the cute outfits Carol bought for Lexi. When we're done, Evan takes our plates and adds them to the dishwasher. Lexi is now sound asleep in my arms. He stops beside my chair and kneels at my side. "We won't be gone long, a couple of hours." He reaches over and pulls her sock up. I nod and smile, and before I know what's happening, he leans in and kisses me. It's a soft chaste kiss, but it's in front of our families. Pulling back, he winks before standing and turning to Aaron. "Let's head out, can't have you missing your flight," he says, heading toward the door.

Aaron looks between me and Evan like he can't believe what just happened. Did he forget he left us a little present in the hotel room? He finally shakes his head and follows Evan out the door.

"I was hoping, since Evan's gone, I could take a few pictures of the two of you and Lexi," I tell his parents. "I know I've taken a ton this week, but I thought maybe a few that were a little more formal might be a good surprise for him."

"Of course, but I have one condition," his mom says. I smile and nod. "You have to send me copies."

I laugh. "You got it. I'm going to go lay her down, and when she wakes up, we'll take a few. It won't take long," I say, looking over at his dad. He looks worn out from all the excitement.

"Sounds like a plan, young lady," he says, his voice gruff.

EVAN 49

"This is it?" Aaron asks.

"Yep, we need to walk through that clearing." I point through the front window of the Durango.

"Let's do this. We only have about two hours before I have to get back," he says, climbing out of the SUV.

I keep waiting for him to call me out. I kissed McKinley in front of all of them, but it just felt right. She had my daughter, who I know she loves, in her arms and she was smiling at me, my smile, damn it. How was I supposed to resist that? I wanted to kiss my wife and I did. No regrets.

We make it through the clearing and I guide us away from the spot where I proposed to McKinley. We set up our chairs, bait our hooks, and kick back for some male bonding. Aaron and I have been fishing more times than I can count over the years.

"What was that this morning?" Aaron breaks the silence.

I play dumb. "What was what?"

"You asking my sister for permission to go fishing."

Oh that. "She's my wife."

"I know that, but this was supposed to be for Lexi," he counters.

"Plans change."

"Really?"

"You really want to have this conversation?"

"I asked, didn't I?"

"Yes, my plans changed, but hers have not. This is still an agreement with amended terms."

"I see." I can tell my answer aggravates him, but what can he say? Like McKinley said, we're both consenting adults—married consenting adults.

"We got your gift," I say, putting it out there. If he wants to talk about this shit, then we can talk about it. I'd rather do it now than when McKinley is around to hear it.

"I went back to the room three times before I actually left it there. I fought with myself over and over. I knew the two of you weren't planning to spend the night anywhere else and by the way you kept looking at her . . . I just thought better safe than sorry."

"Thank you."

"It's weird for me, seeing you with her like that. I mean, I've watched the two of you grow closer, but since Lex was born, it's just different between the two of you."

"It's been happening for months, man. She's . . . amazing."

Aaron turns to look at me. I can feel his stare, but I keep my gaze on the water.

My phone vibrates and I pull it out of my pocket. It's a text from Kinley, a picture of Lexi curled up on her chest sleeping.

"That my sister?" Aaron asks.

"My wife," I reply. The words falling from my lips. I should have just said yes.

"You told her." It's not a question. I have to tear my eyes away from my girls to answer him.

"No." As soon as the words are out of my mouth, shame washes over me. I wanted to tell her, almost did.

"I think you're making a mistake."

"I just . . . can't tell her okay."

Aaron throws his head back and laughs. Probably scaring all the fish, fucker. "It's easy to see, man. You think I would have left you a box of condoms in a hotel room with my baby sister, marriage license or not, if I didn't know you loved her? She knows me better than that. I'm sure she can see right through you just like the rest of us."

"You can't tell her."

That sobers him up. "No, you need to tell her."

"This is different for her. She cares about me, but she loves my daughter. She reminds me daily that we both will be walking away from this. Until then, I want to hold on tight to every moment she's my wife. Moments like kissing her goodbye and asking if she's okay with me leaving. I don't need her permission, but I want to share it all with her. That all comes with it," I explain.

"I get it, but I think you're wrong. She loves both of you."

How I wish that were true. We could drop this agreement bullshit and just be . . . us. "She's adamant, man. She constantly says that this is just temporary."

"I call bullshit."

I shrug. "I won't pressure her to change her mind. I want her happy. More than anything, that's what matters to me. If leaving me once this shit is worked out with Misty's parents is what she wants, then I have to live with that."

My phone vibrating in my pocket breaks the silence. Digging it out, it's another text from McKinley. This time it's her and Lexi both wide awake, lying on the bed, smiling up at the camera. The caption says, "We miss you."

"Your wife?" Aaron smirks.

"Yes." I hold the phone up so he can see the picture.

"Like I said, I call bullshit. Let's pack up and head out. Fish aren't biting and I really just wanted to get you away from *your wife*, so we could talk."

"Yeah," I say, saving both pictures and then sliding the phone back in my pocket.

We pack up and are back on the road in no time. "Never thought it would be my little sister, man, but I'm happy for you."

I grin at him. "You do realize we are now officially brothers?" I ask him.

He laughs. "Never thought about it, but I guess we are." Reaching over, he claps me on the shoulder. "Welcome to the family."

Family. My foot presses a little harder on the pedal in a hurry to get back to mine.

McKinley
50

*T*his week has been a little crazy. In between shoots at the studio, I've been packing up my clothes and bringing over a few boxes at a time. I'm not bringing everything, because, well . . . I'm just going to have to move it all back when it's over.

Luckily, today I have nothing scheduled in the studio, so Lexi and I are hanging around the house. I'm working on getting my clothes unpacked. Thankfully, we have a furniture delivery coming around eleven. We decided to go ahead and buy a bed for one of the extra bedrooms as well as another dresser to match the suite in the master. Evan insisted I have a place for my clothes. "I don't want you living out of boxes," he said.

"Honey, I'm home," I hear Evan yell from downstairs.

"Daddy's home, Lex," I say as I finish changing her diaper. "He's home early."

"There you are." He stands in the doorway of her bedroom. "How are my girls?"

I love it when he does that, when he calls us his girls. "Good, doing some laundry and waiting for the furniture delivery. What are you doing home?"

"I missed a call from the attorney, so I thought I would stop here and call him from the landline. Reception has been sketchy the last few days."

"I haven't noticed, but then again, I don't think I've done anything

other than text or email from my phone." I lift Lexi from the changing table and she grins at her daddy.

"Hey, baby girl." He grabs her foot. "I'm going to go make the call. Then I'll hang out with you two for a bit. I feel like all we've done this week is rush around."

"Me too."

He leans in and kisses me. "I won't be long." I watch as he walks back downstairs and toward the office. My gut clenches. We've been waiting to hear from the attorney. Evan faxed him our marriage license from Alabama before we left. Now it's just a waiting game.

Lexi and I are in the living room playing on the floor when Evan joins us. "Has she done it again?" he asks.

"Not today." Lexi rolled over two nights ago and we've been dying for her to do it again. "What did he say?" I ask.

He sits down on the other side of Lexi and props up on an elbow. "Apparently, her parents are furious. They are still going to try to take this thing to trial. Fields says they have no case. It doesn't help their case that he has documentation from Misty saying they were to have nothing to do with Lex."

"They don't love her," I blurt out. "I feel bad for them, losing their daughter, I do. However, that does not give them the right to take ou . . . yours."

"Hey." He reaches over and cradles my cheek. "They won't take her. You made sure of that the day you agreed to be my wife."

"I just hate it! I hate thinking of her living with them. They told her to . . ." I can't even finish the thought.

"I know, babe. Fields mentioned that as well. Misty brought that up the day we signed the papers. He assures me they don't have a case. If they want to waste attorney fees dragging this thing through court, let them."

The doorbell chimes. Evan grins. "That, my wife, is your dresser." Leaning over, he kisses Lexi on the nose and offers me a quick peck on the lips before jumping to his feet to answer the door. We're getting a complete bedroom suite and one additional dresser, yet it seems as though that single dresser is what excites him. I stay in the living room with the baby while Evan shows the men where to go.

Twenty minutes later, Evan reappears. "All done." He grins. "I need to head back out to the stables. We have two new colts being delivered today."

"Delivered as in the momma is ready to deliver or delivered as in coming on a stock trailer?" I ask him.

"Stock trailer."

"Awe, maybe I'll bring Lex out so she can see them."

"Anytime you want, baby. They should be here in the next hour or so."

"It's time for her bottle. Hopefully, she will nap and I can fill up that new dresser. Then," I tickle Lexi's belly, "we will go see Daddy at work."

Evan grins and waves goodbye. It's not ten minutes before Lex starts to fuss and I know it's time for her to eat. "Let's get you fed, baby girl."

While Lex naps, I take full advantage and unpack the last of my clothes into the dresser. I'm just breaking down the last box when I hear her baby babble from across the hall. I wash my hands and then go get her up. After a quick diaper change, we're out the door. I load her up in her car seat and we head to the stables.

The sound of the door opening has everyone turning to look at me. Evan is standing there with his flannel shirt hanging open, sleeves ripped off and those abs, the ones I like to trace with my tongue, are on full display. He really is a work of art.

Evan smiles. He ignores the men in front of him and stalks toward me. Snaking his arm around my waist, he kisses me. Lex babbles, causing him to laugh and pull away. "I see you, baby girl." He taps her nose with his finger. "You ready to see them?" he asks me.

I nod. He takes Lex from me, his arm around my waist, and leads us to the group of men.

"McKinley?" one of the guys says. I turn to look and see Barry Barnes. He and I graduated together.

"Barry, hey." I step out of Evan's embrace and hug him.

"How have you been?" he asks, stepping away.

Evan slides his arm around my waist pulling me into his side. I rest my hand on his chest. "Good, I have a photography studio at Mom and Dad's," I tell him.

Barry smiles at me. "That doesn't surprise me. Seems like you always

had a camera in your hands, even if it was just a cell phone."

"I didn't realize you and my wife knew each other," Evan chimes in.

"Wife, wow, I didn't know. Yeah, Kinley and I graduated together."

"That's right. I forgot you lived here before," Evan adds.

"Your daughter's a cutie," he says to me.

"She is," I reply. It's with those words I feel Evan relax beside me. "You see the horse, Lex?" She couldn't care less, but I still wanted to bring her out to see them.

Evan laughs. "I don't think she cares, baby."

My heart skips a beat at the term. He uses it a lot when it's just us, but here in front of his employees . . . he just keeps stealing little pieces of my heart.

"I think you're right. I won't keep you. I just wanted to stop in and see the new additions."

"I'll walk you out." Evan looks up at the group of guys. "Be right back."

He loads Lexi in her seat and walks me to my side of the car. Pushing me up against the door, his mouth devours mine. "What was that for?" I ask once he breaks the kiss.

"I just . . ."

"You're jealous?" I grin up at him.

"Fuck yes, I'm jealous. He had his hands on you," he pouts.

"Evan, come on. It was a friendly hug."

"I know that, and I kept my cool, but . . . I didn't like it."

"Poor baby," I coo, like I would to Lexi.

"Right? I had to watch another man with his hands on my wife."

"You crazy man. Get back to work. We'll see you later." I stand on tiptoes and kiss him one more time.

When I pull away, he's grinning. "I'll be home soon." He kisses me again before opening my door. I drive away with a smile on my face.

EVAN 51

$\mathcal{S}$ ix months. It's hard to believe my daughter is already six months old. Not only that, but today is my two-month wedding anniversary. Yes, I know this is not usually a milestone that is celebrated, but for me, I don't know how long I will have her. Each day with McKinley is better than the one before. I've almost slipped hundreds of times and said I love you. I do. I love her. She's just as much a part of me as Lexington.

Today, we're taking pictures. McKinley has done a special shoot for Lexi each month. Her newborn pictures are still my favorite. She got her elephant ears for a hat and a diaper cover with an "A" on it. My baby girl is sleeping in a ball with the ears on and a matching diaper cover. The day she gave it to me is one of the days I almost let it slip. I almost let the words roll off my tongue. We had only been home from Alabama for about two weeks. I got home one night and there were frames set up all over the kitchen table. The newborn pictures of Lexi along with month one, two, and three, and then there were the pictures of her with my parents. Not gonna lie, I had to choke back tears when I got to those.

"You ready, Daddy?" McKinley asks. She's standing in the doorway to the living room, camera bag in one arm and my daughter in the other.

"Yes." I reach for Lexi and she holds out her arms for me. This is something new she's been doing. I hold her in the air and blow on her tummy, making her giggle and grab my hair.

"Let's go, you two. Did you get the car seat strapped in on the Mule?" she asks me.

"Yes, ma'am. We're good to go." We make our way outside and I strap Lexi into her seat as Kinley climbs in the front and get her camera bag situated. "Where to?"

"I thought we could go down to the meadow with all the wildflowers. The lighting will be good, with both bright lights and shadows. I also thought it would be cute to put one of the flowers behind her ear and set her in them."

"You know she's just going to try to eat them, don't you?" I ask her.

She laughs. "Probably, but that will just add character to the shot. What did Mr. Fields say when he called earlier?"

Just the mention of my attorney's name causes my blood to boil. It's nothing he's done, but it means I'm still dealing with Misty's parents. Their attorney filed an extension, claiming they were giving the court time to investigate if McKinley and I are good parents. We've met with a social worker twice already.

"Nothing really. The social worker has to make a total of four visits. One planned, which we've already been through, and three unplanned. It's their way of trying to catch us being bad parents."

"She can come every damn day if she wants," she seethes.

I reach over and lace my fingers through hers, "I know, baby. It's just a process we have to go through. You ready to get rid of me already?" I tease her.

"No! It's not that, I swear. I just . . . hate this. I hate that it's still looming over our heads, that they want to try and take her. It's not right."

"No, it's not right. They're playing a game, Kinley. They know they can't win, so instead, they're trying to catch us screwing up. It's not going to happen. They will not win this," I tell her.

She squeezes my hand and we remain silent the rest of the ride to the meadow. Well, we do, Lexi laughs and babbles as the wind hits her face. She loves taking rides on the Mule. Her little baby voice yelling "da da da" flows to my ears and straight to my heart. That's new too. About three weeks ago, she said it for the first time and I was the only one to hear her. McKinley kept saying I was making it up until two nights later when I came through the door after work. She started saying it over and over and over. I didn't stop grinning for a week and still haven't really. Life is good. No, life is great!

We reach the meadow and Kinley goes into photographer mode. I let her do her thing while I get Lexi out of her seat. "Okay, I think we should start with her single shots first before she gets worn out and over the whole process."

"Good angle. Where do you want her?"

"Over there in the wild flowers." As she mentioned earlier, she picks one and hands it to Lexi. She's so interested in it, she doesn't notice McKinley shoves one behind her ear. "Now move back and I'll get a few before she starts to get away," she laughs.

"Da da da," Lexi babbles on while crumbling the flower in her hands. I'm standing close for the minute she tries to eat it. I know that's the plan; she puts everything she can get her little chubby hands on in her mouth these days.

"There she goes, Dad," Kinley giggles. Lexi, done with the flower, is now on all fours, rocking back and forth. Kinley and her mom, even mine, says she's going to be crawling any day now. I baby-proofed the house last weekend just in case. I need my little girl safe when she's on the move.

I grab her and she chuckles, her hands tapping my cheeks. "Perfect," I hear Kinley say.

Lexi and I both look at her at the same time. She continues to snap pictures. "My turn," I say, handing Lexi off to her. Instead of her camera, I reach into my pocket and pull out the one she bought for me when Lexi was born.

"You could have used mine, Evan," she laughs.

"Hell with that. I wouldn't even begin to know how to use that thing. Besides, I like this. My wife bought it for me." I grin. That's something else I never get tired of hearing, her being called my wife.

"What do you think, Lex? You think we should let Daddy take our picture?"

"Da da da da," Lexi rambles on. Kinley tickles her belly and they both have their heads back laughing, wild flowers in hand. I snap a picture or twenty. Capturing memories just like she said I would.

Kinley ends up setting her camera on the tripod and using the remote control to take some portraits of us all. This wasn't her plan, but I insisted. I can't wait to see how they turned out.

"I think our girl is about done," I tell McKinley as she packs up her gear. Lexi is rubbing her eyes with her head resting on my shoulder.

After throwing her gear in the back of the Mule, she walks over to us. "You were such a good girl today, Lex." She reaches out, brushes her cheek. That's when it happens.

"Momma," falls from my baby girls tired lips.

McKinley gasps, throwing her hands over her mouth. Her eyes instantly welling with tears.

I don't hesitate with my response. I reach out to McKinley and pull her close. "That's right, baby. That's Momma," I tell her. It might be wrong of me to do that without discussing it with Kinley first, but damn it, I want her to be her momma. I want to live each day for the rest of our lives just like we have the last two months. I don't want to let her go.

McKinley pulls away, wiping at her tears. "You can't do that," she tells me. "You can't tell this precious little girl I'm her momma. You can't tell my heart I'm her momma. This is temporary, Evan. You can't do that to her, to me," she cries.

"What if it's not? What if this is permanent?"

"Oh, Evan, we both know that's not what this is."

"Bullshit."

"Watch your language around her," she fires back.

Lexi starts to cry and McKinley reaches for her. "Aunt Kinley's here, baby. Let's get you home." She takes her and straps her in the seat. Instead of sitting up front with me like she did on the way here, she climbs in the back to sit with Lex. I don't regret what I said, but it's apparent she still doesn't feel the way I do. My chest feels like a knife has been twisted through it, but I don't let it show. Instead, I drive my girls back to the house and unload McKinley's equipment while she takes Lexi in and makes her a bottle.

I kick the Mule's tire once they are inside, swallowing the scream that wants to tear from my throat. The woman I love, my wife, doesn't love me back. That's a hard pill to swallow.

As soon as Lexi is finished with her bottle, she's sound asleep. I lay her in her crib and walk across the hall to our room. My heart is breaking. Little tiny shards of it fall away each day closer to the trial. When she called me momma . . . devastating. I want that so much.

I curl into a ball on the bed and let the tears fall. I hear Evan downstairs. He agreed with her, but he's caught up in this, in us being real while there is still a threat of Misty's parents. I can't let myself be mom and have it taken away. I just . . . can't. I close my eyes and drift off to sleep.

When I wake a little while later, I feel warm lips press against my neck. "I don't want to fight with you, McKinley," Evan says softly. "I'm sorry I didn't correct her. I will in the future. I just . . . I don't want to fight with you, baby." He sounds broken. "I don't like finding you in our bed with your cheeks wet from tears. It breaks my fucking heart. I just want you happy. Today was amazing and I want that back," he says.

I roll over to face him. "Today was amazing," I confess. His thumb traces my lips. "I love her, Evan. I love her so much, and I just . . . don't want to confuse things—-confuse her. I know she's just a baby and she won't remember today, but can we . . ."

"I'm sorry," he says, pulling me tighter against his chest. "Let's go back. If she does it again, we'll just ignore it or tell her your name. Hell, I don't know. I don't know what I'm doing with her."

"You do. It was impulse from the day we were having. I'm not angry

and I don't want to fight with you either."

"Thank fuck," he mumbles as his lips take mine.

Within minutes, we're both naked and he's reaching into the nightstand for a condom. As soon as he slides in, we hear Lexi whimper over the baby monitor. "Great timing, baby girl," he chuckles, resting his forehead against mine.

"She can wait a few minutes. She's not crying and . . ." I raise my hips.

"Yeah?" he asks.

I nod. Lexi whimpers again. "Hard and fast," I say, biting my bottom lip.

"But this is make-up sex," he pouts.

I smile. "It's with you, Evan, that's all that matters. Now get busy before Miss Lexington decides we're missing the party."

That's all the motivation he needs before he slides out and slams back in. I wrap my legs around his waist and grip onto his back, holding on for the ride. "Help me, beautiful," he pants. I nod and slide my hand between us. The sensation of touching myself while he pushes in and out of me isn't new for us. This isn't the first time we've had to work around Lexi's sleep schedule.

A few rotations of my two fingers and I'm close. "So close," I breathe.

"Me too," he tells me as he sucks a nipple into this mouth. The sensation has me screaming out his name. This, in turn, causes Lexi to scream as well.

Evan stills; then he's resting his weight on me.

"She's not impressed." He grins.

"No, she's not, but we usually run right to her. She's a little spoiled," I admit.

"Yeah," he agrees, lifting off of me. I run to the bathroom and clean up while he discards the condom, throws on some shorts, and goes to soothe a pissed off Lexi.

When I step out of the bathroom, I find them lying in bed. "She looks happy."

"Yep, as soon as I stepped into her room, her tears stopped. I think you're right about being spoiled."

"Yeah, but we wouldn't have her any other way," I say, lying down beside them.

"Can you watch her for a minute while I clean up?" he asks.

"Sure, we'll just go downstairs and look for something to make for dinner."

"Why don't we just order pizza? That new little market down the road delivers to us now. Let's try it out."

"Perfect. Do you have the number?"

"Yeah, there's a menu hanging on the fridge. Just order whatever. I'm easy, but I'm starving."

"Got it." I gather Lexi and the few toys she was playing with and we make our way downstairs. I put Lex in the pack-n-play while I order the pizza.

A few minutes later, the three of us are on the couch watching Shrek. Evan was flipping through the channels and, as soon as the green ogre popped on the screen, Lexi's babble stopped and her eyes were glued. "Who would have thought?" Evan says.

I laugh. "All kids love cartoons. We need to get you some princess movies, Lex," I tell her. She doesn't budge at the sound of my voice. "Looks like we take a backseat to the talking donkey," I laugh.

The doorbell rings. "Shit. My wallet's upstairs. Can you get the door and I'll run up and get it real quick?"

He's already up and moving. I pick Lexi up and she babbles on, reaching for the television. I'm afraid she's going to cry until she sees we're walking toward the front door. The girl loves being outside and going bye-bye, that's for sure.

"Da da da," Lexi says, grabbing my attention as I open the door.

"Sorry, my husband's getting his . . ." I stop talking when I look up and see who's standing in front of me. "W . . . what? H-how?"

"Sorry, man, how much . . . what the fuck?" Evan exclaims as he pushes Lexi and I behind him.

"They told me you were dead," he says, matter-of-fact.

"Hi, Evan. Can I come in?" Misty asks.

"No! You're not coming anywhere near her," he seethes. "Baby, take her inside," he says to me.

I do as he says, not wanting Misty to get her hands on Lexi. She was supposed to be dead. What the hell is going on?

EVAN 53

This cannot be happening.

"Evan, I need to talk to you," Misty pleads.

I hold my hand up, stopping her, and she clamps her mouth shut. Shit! I can't let her in. I don't want her around Lexi, but I need Kinley. I need her by my side for this. Pulling my phone out of my pocket, I call Aaron. "Hey, man, where are you?" I wait for him to answer. "Can you come and get Lex? I'll explain when you get here, but I need you to come and get her, sooner rather than later."

"I'm not here to take her, Evan," Misty says quietly.

"I don't give a fuck! I'm not letting you near her. You can wait out here until Aaron gets here," I seethe.

I send McKinley a text.

Me: Hey, I called Aaron. He's coming to get Lexi. Can you get her bag ready?

McKinley: Yes, everything okay?

Me: I don't know, baby. I just don't want her near her.

McKinley: Okay.

Aaron pulls in a few minutes later. His eyes grow wide when he sees Misty standing on my front porch. "Turns out she's not dead after all," I say in greeting.

"I can see that. Where are the girls?" he asks.

"Inside. McKinley has her bag ready. Thanks for taking her, man. I don't want her here for this."

"No problem, bro. McKinley?"

"I need her here with me," I say honestly.

He nods in understanding.

I open the door. "McKinley, Aaron's here." Not a second later, she

appears with a smiling Lex in her arms, carrying the diaper bag. When Lexi sees Aaron, she reaches for him.

"Hey, baby girl," he says to her. "You get to come hang out with Uncle Aaron for a little while."

"You have a car seat?" McKinley asks him.

"Yeah, I just leave it in all the time these days. She loves to go for rides." He smiles. "Call me," he says and I nod.

I put my arm around McKinley and we watch as they pull out of the drive. "Let's get this over with," I say, turning and holding the door open for both of them.

McKinley leads the way to the living room, Misty right behind her. I take a seat on the couch and pull McKinley down beside me. "Talk." I point to the chair. Misty takes the hint and sits.

"It's a long story, but I assure you, I'm not trying to take her from you."

"We're listening," I say. My hand is squeezing Kinley's so tight I'm sure I'm about to cut off her circulation. I will my grip to loosen so I don't hurt her.

"She's beautiful, Evan," Misty says.

"Talk," I say through gritted teeth.

"Okay." She takes a deep breath. "Growing up in my house was not a pleasant experience. My parents never wanted me, but it was the southern thing to do, for a man in politics—get married and have a family. They had me, and then hired a nanny to raise me." She wrings her hands together, never looking at us. "I never got hugs or kisses, never had my mom or dad lie in bed with me at night and read me a story. I had nannies. Nannies who were instructed to not spoil me by showing me affection."

How did I spend a year of my life with her and not know this?

"I never wanted kids. I was too afraid I would be like my own parents, and no child deserves that. I can admit I'm selfish and spoiled. I was raised to be. I finally got the courage to leave home with their blessing because I was in college. It worked for their social circle to say I was 'off at school,' but what my parents didn't know was I was biding my time until I could get as far away from them as possible." She looks up and her eyes land on my hands gripping McKinley's tightly.

254

"I turned twenty-five about a month after she was born. Every day, I felt guilt for not loving her. What kind of person doesn't love their own flesh and blood?" she sobs. "I was wracked with guilt. I didn't know how to fix it. How to let her know how sorry I was, and how signing over my rights to you was what was best for her. On my twenty-fifth birthday, I got the call. My grandparents, my mom's parents, left me a trust fund. I had no idea. Their rules stipulated I was to not have access until my twenty-fifth birthday. The guy on the phone told me the fund was ten million dollars." She looks up at me, tears in her eyes.

"That's when it hit me. I could make sure you and Lexington were always taken care of. I know you make a good living, but this was something I could do. Not only that, but I could make a fresh start for myself. I could break free from the parents who never loved me as well."

"How did you do it?" I ask her.

"My parents' attorney." She grins. "Money talks and he signed a non-disclosure to not discuss any of this with my parents. Client confidentiality and all that. He helped me with the car accident, my new identity, and setting up an offshore account with five million dollars, and he also helped me set up a trust for Lexi. It was my stipulation that you not be notified until she turned one. I wanted to give you time to not hate me as much, to let some of the pain I caused you fade before you were notified I willed your daughter five million dollars in the event of my death."

"Holy shit," Kinley whispers.

Misty smiles. "It was a great plan, except for the fact it turns out the attorney sleeps with his secretary. She is also sleeping with my father. I was unaware or I would have chosen someone different. However, what's done is done."

"I don't know what to say," I tell her.

"Don't say anything. The less you know about the how and where the better. I got word that my parents found out and were coming after you for custody of her. Turns out, they're in financial trouble and gaining custody of her also gained them the five million dollars I willed to her in the event of my death. As soon as I found out what they were trying to do, I hopped on a plane and here I am."

"They're going to be pissed."

Misty gives a humorless laugh. "Yeah, it's safe to say I will more than

likely be spending some time behind bars for my little disappearing act."
She shrugs. "It's my own fault. I should have put the money into an
account and sent you the information. I thought about it, but I knew
you would never take it, not with me still alive. I knew if you found out
about my death and then the money you would save it for her, for her
future. That's all I wanted."

She looks at McKinley and then to me. "I'm sorry for what the two
of you have gone through. My parents are not nice people, and there is
no way I would let them get their hands on your daughter."

"Thank you," McKinley says before slapping her hand over her
mouth.

"No, it's okay," Misty assures her. "I could see, just from the small
interaction, you love her very much. I can tell from the tears in your eyes
as I told you my story. I'm glad you're her mom. I gave birth to her, but
you are the one who gives her love and affection. I don't have that in
me to give."

"Someday?" McKinley says.

"Maybe. I've been seeing a therapist, which is long overdue."

"I don't know what to say to all of this," I say.

Misty shrugs. "Nothing. I just wanted to tell you myself that my
parents will no longer be an issue. I have money for my legal fees." She
reaches into her purse. "And here is the account information for the
money I want to give her. There are no restrictions on it. It's in your
name and hers."

She holds it out for me, and I stare at her hand.

"Evan, take it. I want to do this. I don't know how to be a mom and
I know I wouldn't be good at it, but I want her to be whatever she wants
to be. College, backpacking through Europe, whatever her heart
desires—I want her to have the means to do it. I know you, and I know
you will let her live her life, not hold her back. I want her to have this."
She shakes the account book at me. "Please," she says softly.

I reach out and grab the book, setting it on the table. The doorbell
rings and McKinley jumps up. "That's the pizza. I'll get it." She turns to
walk away.

"Babe," I yell for her. When she turns, I toss her my wallet and she
catches it with ease before quickly wiping the tears from her cheeks.

"You love her," Misty says.

"I do."

"Good. She's good for you and your daughter."

I need a break from this. "You need something to drink?" How can I stay angry with her when she did this for Lexi? She's going to jail to keep my daughter safe with me.

"Sure, water if you have it."

"I'll be right back." I flee from the room in search of McKinley.

McKinley
54

I find Evan in the kitchen pulling three waters out of the refrigerator. He reaches for the boxes of pizza. "I guess it's a good thing I ordered extra," I tease him.

"Come here," he says gruffly. He pulls me into his arms and buries his face in my neck. "I just need to hold you for a minute."

I wrap my arms around his waist and hold on tight. I can only imagine the thoughts running through his head right now.

When he finally pulls back, he kisses my temple. "You think we should let her meet, Lexi?" he asks.

I want to scream no, but I believe her, she doesn't want to be a mom, not right now anyway. "I think giving her the option would be nice. She's had a rough life from the sound of it, and she did the right thing. They have no case now." That also means our agreement will be up. A few more weeks, I would say for appearance's sake, and then I will be leaving. I push that thought out of my mind for now.

"I wanted to ask you before I offered," he tells me.

"It's your choice, but I think the offer would be nice. Who knows when we will see her again, and Lexi is too young to remember her." I know that sounds mean, but psychologically on Lexi, this will mean nothing, but it could mean everything to Misty.

"Will you call, Aaron? I'm going to have her come and make a plate, if she will," he adds as an afterthought.

"Yes." I kiss his cheek and he hands me his phone.

I dial my brother. "Hey, bro, everything good?" he asks.

"It's me," I say into the line. "Everything's good, but it's a long story. I hate to ask this, but can you bring Lex back? We have pizza," I say to sweeten the pot.

"She still there?" he asks.

"Yes, but it's really all good. I'll explain when you get here. We are going to let her meet Lexi," I tell him.

"Okay, I'll wrangle her away from Mom and Dad and be right over." The line goes dead as Evan and Misty enter the kitchen.

"Aaron is going to wrangle her away from my parents—his words not mine—and be right over," I tell Evan.

"Thanks, babe," he says.

Fifteen minutes later, Aaron and Lexi join us. She sees Evan and grins, reaching out for him. "Hey, baby girl," he says, taking her from Aaron. "There's someone I want you to meet." Lexi just pulls at his lips, not a care in the world. He pulls her hands down and turns to face Misty. "Lexington Rae, I would like you to meet Misty. She's a friend of Daddy's."

I can see him flinch slightly at the word friend, but what else is he supposed to call her? Not that it matters, because Lexi won't remember this meeting, but for the four other adults in the room, this will be hard to forget.

"Hi." Misty waves awkwardly. I can see tears pooling in her eyes. "Evan, she's beautiful."

"Thank you. She's a good baby. Hardly ever cries." His eyes find mine and he winks.

I set my plate of half-eaten pizza aside and reach for Lex. "What do you say we go show Misty your room?" I ask her. Misty looks relieved at the suggestion. The awkward silence was killing me. "You two finish eating while we girls take a tour," I suggest.

Evan leans down and kisses me. "Thank you," he whispers only loud enough for me.

I lead the way upstairs and into Lexi's room. I sit her in the middle of the floor on her play rug and scatter some toys around her.

"How long have you been married?"

"Two months."

"I'm happy for him, for both of you. You have a happy family."

What am I supposed to say to that? I decide to go with manners. "Thank you."

We spend about twenty minutes in Lexi's room. Misty stacks blocks and Lexi knocks them down. She could play this game for hours.

"Da da da." She points toward her bedroom door.

"You've been up here for a while," Evan says in greeting.

"Just playing with blocks," I tell him.

He smiles. "She could do that for hours."

"Did Aaron leave?"

"Yeah, just a few minutes ago."

"I need to be going too." Misty stands from her spot on the floor. "I already called my parents' attorney, who is no longer mine. I hired my own as well. You should be receiving a call within the next twenty-four hours letting you know the case has been dropped."

"Thank you," Evan says sincerely.

"You're welcome. She bends down and pats Lexi on the head before turning back to Evan. "Take care, Evan. Thank you for being the father that little girl deserves." Then, surprising me, she turns to face me. "McKinley, thank you for loving her like your own. Thank you for giving her what I know I never could."

I nod. Words are not possible at this point. Lexi starts to fuss, causing Evan to scoop her into his arms. She rests her little head on his shoulder.

"I'll walk you out," I manage to croak.

"Take care of them," she says when we reach the door.

All I can do is nod, again. My heart is breaking for her, and for me. My time is up. They no longer need me.

EVAN 55

isty was right. The next day, I received a call from Mr. Fields that said the case was dropped. However, Child Protective Services would be by sometime within the next five days for their final visit. Turns out, they have to open their own case and, due to the suit being dropped, the home visits were dropped to one more. Apparently, at this visit, we will be notified if they too will be closing the case with their department.

McKinley cancelled all of her shoots for the week. She didn't even bat an eyelash. She said she needed to be here when they showed up. I didn't argue with her. My mind has been too pre-occupied with all that's happened in the last few days. I'm not worried about the home visit. I know we're good parents, my house is safe, and she's healthy. They have nothing. No, what worries me is that once this is all said and done, McKinley will be leaving. Our agreement was for her to stay until we were sure they could not take Lex from me. That time is now.

I fucking hate it.

I want her to stay.

I too decided to let my crew handle things this week. We've spent all week together, the three of us, soaking up as much time as we can. We don't talk about it, but we both know that's what's happening.

Lexi is asleep in her pack-n-play while McKinley and I are curled up on the couch watching television. Well, it's on, but I'm not paying much attention. The doorbell rings and she sits up. "I'll get it," she says so quiet I barely hear her.

I turn off the television and stand. I hear Lexi greet Mrs. Allan, the social worker. Their voices grow louder as they move down the hall.

"Mrs. Allan," I say, offering her my hand, and she takes it.

"Mr. Chamberlin." She looks over my shoulder and sees Lexi asleep. "She's such a good baby," she comments.

"She is." McKinley steps beside me and wraps her arms around my waist.

"Well, I'll make this quick. My department is closing its case. We've found nothing that would make us think the two of you are anything but good, capable parents. I just need you to sign off on this document stating that and I will be on my way."

She pulls out the papers, tells us where to sign, and shakes our hands. "I'm sorry for what you went through. You have a lovely family."

Just like that, it's over. There is no threat of my daughter being taken from me. Instead, I'm losing my wife.

McKinley sits on the couch and curls her legs up underneath of her. "It's over, Evan. I'm so happy for you," she says with tears in her eyes. "You never have to worry about anyone taking her again."

"Thank you for what you did for us."

"You're welcome. I guess I should start packing, huh?"

"No," I say firmly. "I don't want you to leave. I need you here."

She's quiet for several minutes before she replies. "No, you don't. You're a great father. You know what you're doing. You don't need me anymore."

"I do need you. I can't do this on my own," I tell her.

She smiles through tears. "Yes, you can, Evan. You don't need me. I'm still going to come and visit. Mom and I are still going to watch her for you. I love that little girl. You can't get rid of me that easy."

"What about me?" I ask her. "You love my daughter, but what about me?"

The dam finally breaks as the tears fall over her cheeks. "Of course I love you. We've been through so much over the last year, but it's time for me to go."

"You can't go. I need you," I say again.

"No, you don't. I'm going to go pack a few things and spend the night at Mom and Dad's. The sooner I start this transition, the better."

Her words cut through me. I was just about to tell her how much I love her, but she doesn't love me like that. She cares about me and this is sad for her, but it's not tearing her heart out of her chest like it is mine.

I don't say anything. I can't even look at her for fear I will drop to my knees and beg her to stay, beg her to live the rest of her life with us. She stands from the couch and I turn my head. I listen as her footsteps disappear up the stairs. My blurry gaze locks on Lexington and my chest aches for my little girl. She loves McKinley just as much as I do, and she's leaving. It doesn't matter what I say . . . she's ending this. I knew it would happen, but I didn't know it would feel like this—like I can't breathe, like my heart is physically broken into pieces.

I don't even know how much time passes when she stops in front of me. "I'm leaving. I'll be back off and on over the next few days to move the rest of my stuff." I still don't look at her. "Please give her a hug and a kiss for me when you tuck her in tonight." Her voice breaks, but I still refuse to look at her.

I can't.

"Goodbye," she whispers.

McKinley
5G

I can't breathe. Luckily, the drive to my parents' house is less than five minutes, because I can't see.

When I pull into the drive, Aaron and my parents are sitting on the front porch. One look at me and they know something's not right.

"What happened? Are Evan and Lexi okay?" Aaron asks, meeting me at the bottom step.

I don't answer him. Instead, I throw my arms around him and sob. "Shhh, McKinley, you have to calm down." He rubs my back, trying to soothe me.

"They're fine, but it's over. He doesn't need me anymore," I cry.

"I find that hard to believe," Aaron says. He picks me up and carries me into the house. We sit down on the couch, and I pull the blanket from the back and wrap up in it. "Tell me what happened."

"CPS came today and they dropped their case. As of about an hour ago, there is no threat of him losing Lexi, so I left."

"I see. Did he try to stop you?"

"Of course he did. He doesn't want to be alone. He's afraid he can't do it without me, and he can. He loves that little girl so much."

"He does," Aaron agrees. "What did he say when you left?"

"He said that he . . . that he needed me."

"You don't believe him?"

"No, I don't. He doesn't need me anymore. He knows how to take

care of her. I told him I would still watch her and come by to visit, but I thought it was best if I leave."

"Come here." Aaron pulls me into a hug and another rounds of sobs break free. I can hear him talking to our parents, but I can't make out what they are saying. I lose myself in the pain that is buried deep in my chest. I thought I could handle this.

I cry on my big brother's shoulders, taking comfort in his embrace. "He thinks he needs me, Aaron. He doesn't. He's never really had to do it alone. I've always been there swooping in to save him. I did it when I found out about Misty's parents and he let me. He thinks he can't do this on his own, but he can. I had to leave so he could see that," I explain.

"What if you're wrong? What if he does need you?" he asks.

"I guess only time will tell, but I don't know if I can do it. I love him, Aaron. With all that I am, I love him and I don't know if I can pretend and play this charade anymore. I'll do anything for him, help him with Lexi any way I can, but I had to leave."

"Okay," he says, hearing I'm upset. "Let's sleep on it and see how you feel in the morning."

I agree and head up to my room. The bed is cold and lonely. I miss him. I miss them both and it hurts. How am I going to see him every day? That's my last thought as I drift off to a night of restless sleep.

EVAN 57

*L*exi and I slept downstairs last night, her in her pack-n-play and me on the couch. I couldn't do it. I couldn't sleep in that bed without her. We're up early, neither of us getting a good night's sleep, so when there is a knock on the door at seven, I jump to answer it. Maybe it's her. Maybe she changed her mind. I rush to the door and pull it open only to find Aaron. "Hey, man," I say, deflated.

"Wow, don't break out the welcome wagon or anything."

"Want some coffee?" I ask, ignoring his jab.

"Sure." He takes a seat at the table. "So, how did you sleep last night?"

"Like shit," I say, setting his cup down in front of him.

"Are you going to fight for her?" he asks, cutting to the chase.

"She doesn't—"

"She does. Trust me, she does. I held my baby sister last night while she cried for hours. She does."

My chest tightens just hearing she was hurting. "Then why did she leave? I told her I needed her. I asked her to stay. She refused."

Aaron runs his fingers through his hair. "Fuck! Okay, listen, man. From day one, you've needed her. At first, it was to get ready for Lexi, the room, things she would need. Then after she was born, you were timid and unsure, and you needed her then too."

"I did," I admit.

"Then, when all that shit went down with Misty's parents, you needed

her. She stepped up and did what she needed to do to help you."

"She did."

"Why do you think she did that?" he asks me.

"She loves my daughter."

"Nah! Try again," he says.

"It's true. She's told me multiple times that she loves Lexi, she would do anything for her, and I love her for that," I tell him.

"Just for that?" he asks.

"Are you fucking kidding me? You know better than that shit. I already told you I love her."

"Yes, but did you tell her?"

"No, she didn't give me the chance."

"No, instead you told her you need her. Did you give her a reason?"

Oh shit. I think I'm starting to see where this is going. "No."

"Right." He smirks. "Do you have a reason?" he counters.

"Of course I do. I can't fucking breathe without her. I couldn't even sleep in my bed last night, our bed, because the sheets smell like her," I all but scream at him.

Aaron grins. "That's what you need to tell her. She thinks the only reason you asked her to stay was you're afraid you can't raise Lex on your own. You didn't give her a reason to believe it was more than that," he points out.

Fuck me!

"She loves you, Evan. Her heart is breaking just as much as yours. You have to show her you need her, not because of what she can do for you, but because she is the other half of you."

I stare at him. "When did you get so good at relationships?"

He shrugs. "I'm not really. It's easy to see it from the outside looking in. You both are head over heels, but you can't see through all the bullshit to work it out. She's my sister and you're my best friend. I want to see you both happy."

"She loves me?" I ask, needing his reassurance.

"Irrevocably."

She loves me. I think about everything he said and it makes sense. I never told her how I feel, but begged her to stay because I needed her.

Shit!

"Hey, man, can you do me a favor? Can you keep her busy? I know she mentioned coming to get her stuff, but can you keep her occupied until I text you? I need to do a few things first. Give me a couple of hours?"

"She tossed and turned all night. My guess is she'll hole up in her room most of the day anyway, but I got you covered. Can I do anything else?" he asks.

"No, just when I text you, bring her here."

Aaron stands. "You got it, man." He claps me on the back and waves goodbye.

A plan forms in my mind as Lexi babbles, letting me know she's awake. Baby girl needs a diaper change and some breakfast; then we have things to do.

McKinley
58

"**C**ome on, sleepyhead, get up," Aaron says, shaking my arm.

"Go away." I throw the covers over my head.

"Nope, I need you to wake up. It's three o'clock in the afternoon, lazybones."

"Really, Aaron?" I pull the covers back down and glare at him.

He grins. Then sends a message on his phone. "Yes, really. Now get up. I need you to ride to town with me."

"No."

"Yes, come on, get up. We're going to go grab something to eat."

I start to tell him I'm not hungry, but my stomach betrays me and growls. "Fine, but I need to shower first," I relent.

"Twenty minutes, I'm starving," he says, typing into his phone.

"Who are you texting?" I ask.

"Just the guys. They have some questions about the sale next week. I left early to come and take you to dinner." He grins.

Twenty minutes later, we are in his truck and on our way to town. "I see you kept the ring on," he says. "I went to see Evan this morning," he tells me as if we're discussing the weather.

"How are they?"

"He misses you."

"He's fine."

"I really don't think he is."

I don't reply and he doesn't either. We are silent the remainder of the drive. He pulls into Subway. "This okay?"

"Yeah, I'm not that hungry anyway."

"You think your belly got the memo?" he asks as it growls just as loud, if not louder, than before.

I smack his arm and climb out of the truck. We make small talk while we eat. I get a six-inch and can only eat half. It took effort to get that down. Aaron, on the other hand, ate his twelve-inch and the other half of my six.

"You have anywhere you need to go?" he asks.

"No, just home."

He drives us toward home, only he turns down the road leading to Evan's place. "What are you doing?" I ask him.

"You need to talk to him, McKinley. I'll wait outside and I promise, as soon as you want to leave, I will drive you home. You will regret it if you don't at least hear what he has to say."

"What could he possibly say that hasn't already been said?"

"Did you tell him you love him?" he asks.

"No," I say, crossing my arms over my chest.

"Sounds like a good place to start."

"I can't—"

"Don't," he cuts me off. "Don't make excuses," he pulls up in front of the house I've called home the last few months. "Drop the pretense. Just go in there and talk to him. Listen to what he has to say. Be honest with him, and if you all are still in this same place after that, you will at least know you tried."

"Fine." I climb out of the truck slamming the door. As I walk up the steps, Evan opens the door before I even have a chance to knock.

"McKinley." I can hear the pain in his voice. Was Aaron right?

"Hey, uh, Aaron thought we should talk."

"Yeah, I asked him to bring you here." He opens the door wide. "Come in."

I step toward him and, just as I'm about past him, his arms snake out and pull me close. The door slams shut, but it doesn't faze him as he holds me tight.

Lexi babbles "Dada" from the living room, causing him to release me. "She's going to be excited to see you," he says, lacing his fingers through mine and guiding me into the living room.

"Can I hold her?" I ask as tears fill my eyes. It's only been a day. Not even a full twenty-four hours and I miss them both so much.

"You never have to ask that question."

I rush to her pack-n-play and lift her out. I breathe in her baby smell and more tears start to fall. She watches me as if she knows I'm upset. "I missed you, Lex."

Evan turns on cartoons and her eyes are suddenly glued to the television. He reaches for her, sets her in her exer-saucer, and looks up at me. "I'm not going to be one of those guys, the kind who place their kid in front of the TV or video game, but right now, I need to. I have some things to say and I need to know I have your attention while Shrek has hers."

I nod.

Reaching out for my hand, he guides me to the couch, I sit and he kneels in front of me. "I'm sorry. When you told me you were leaving yesterday, I panicked. I didn't make myself clear."

"Evan—"

"Please, let me say this." He reaches for my other hand and smiles. "You're still wearing your ring."

"I just . . . forgot it was there really. I need to give it back, I know— "

"Shhh." He places his finger to my lips. "I told you I needed you, and that was the truth. However, a wise man brought it to my attention that I didn't tell you why. I let you leave here without knowing why and, for that, I'm truly sorry."

He brings my left hand to his lips and kisses my wedding rings. Then those chocolate brown eyes hold me hostage. "I need you, McKinley Rae Chamberlin, because I can't breathe when you're not here. I can't sleep in our bed because the sheets smell like you. I can't tuck our daughter into her bed at night because you're not there to do it with me."

I can't fight the tears.

"My heart needs you, baby. I love you. With all that I am, I love you,

and I not only need you, but I want you. More than anything, I want you."

"Evan," I say with a sob.

He reaches behind him and grabs a book. "Take it," he urges.

I take the book from him and he wipes my tears with his thumbs. I open the book and it's a picture of me holding Lexi at the hospital. Turning the page I see pictures of me and Lexi sleeping on his couch, the very one I'm sitting on. The next several pages are the same thing—pictures that I've never seen. Pictures of me and Lex and even some selfies of the three of us over the past six months. When I reach the end, it's the pictures from our day at the meadow. The three of us are smiling and happy. Underneath the picture, it says, *We love you.* Tears roll down my face as I try to understand what's happening.

I look up at Evan and he also has tears in his eyes. "Keep going," he urges me.

I flip the page and there is a picture from our wedding, the three of us. Below this one it simply says, *I do.* I trace my finger over the picture.

"Keep going," he says softly.

I turn the page and it's a picture of Lexi wearing a onesie that says, *I love my mommy*

I'm crying so hard I can hardly see the pages. Evan hands me a tissue and I wipe my eyes. I smile at him and he offers me a watery smile in return. The next page is blank except for the words, *Open Evan's envelope.*

Looking up, I see he's holding it out for me. I set the book aside and take it from him. It's not sealed, so I slip the paperwork out and unfold it. It's a legal document. At first, I think it's our annulment papers, but then I keep reading. My hands are shaking as I read the words. I have to read the first paragraph four times before I look up at him.

"What does this mean?"

His hands cradle my cheeks. "What this means is Lexi wants you to be her momma. I want you to be my wife, not just because we had some arrangement, but because I love you with all that I am. I love you. In your hand are adoption papers. All you have to do is sign, and Mr. Fields will file the petition with the court."

"Evan, I—"

"I love you, McKinley. Lexington loves you. I want our family back.

I want you here, home where you belong. I want to raise our daughter together. I want more babies with you. I want every minute of your forever to be linked with mine."

He loves me.

My heart thunders so fast I feel as though it could beat out of my chest.

Adoption papers.

I let the papers fall into my lap as I raise my hand to my mouth to cover a sob. Evan leans in and wraps his arms around me.

"It's okay, baby. I'm sorry I let you leave. I should have never let you get close to the damn door. I need you, my heart needs you. Lexi Rae needs you.

After a few minutes of sobbing against his chest, listening to him reassure me that this is what he wants, I pull away. "Evan, this is . . . permanent. You're asking me to legally be her mother."

"Yes. I want that so much. You are her mother, McKinley. You didn't give birth to her, but you love and nurture her, you care about her. Lexi and I would be honored for you to hold that title. You're my wife," he says simply.

I reach for the papers and skim them again before giving him my full attention. "Do you have a pen?" I ask.

His answer is a blinding smile as he leans in and kisses me. "I do," he whispers. Pulling away, he reaches behind him on the table and grabs a pen. I scrawl my name, McKinley Chamberlin, by the various 'sign here' stickers and place the document back in the envelope.

"I love you, too," I tell him.

To finally say the words to him is . . . freeing.

He crashes his lips to mine. "Say it again."

I smile through my tears. "I love you, both of you."

"I'm so fucking sorry, McKinley. Never, I'm never letting you go."

"I couldn't ask for more," I tell him honestly. Evan and Lexi are all that I want. I want our little family.

Evan stands up and grabs Lex from her seat. He brings her over and sets her on my lap. She grins up at me. "Who's got you, baby girl?" he asks her. "Does momma got you?" he asks, his voice now thick with

emotion.

Lexi studies him, then looks at me. "Momma." She smiles and pulls at my chin.

A strangled laugh escapes my throat as I hold her tight. I'm her momma.

epilogue
EVAN
two years later

"**D**addy," Lexi yells when I walk through the door. I lean down and catch her as she slams into me.

"Hey, pretty girl, where's Mommy?" She points into the living room.

I kick off my boots, so my wife doesn't yell at me for bringing dirt into the house, and head in the direction Lexi's little finger points. "Hey, baby," I say when I see her stretched out on the couch. Her legs are propped up on the table. I set Lex down and she runs off to play in the corner. I take a seat next to my wife and rub her very pregnant belly. "How's my boy?"

"He's ready to come out."

I grin. I've gotten that same answer every day for the last week. McKinley is exactly seven days overdue to deliver our son. Leaning down, I kiss her swollen belly. "Hey, little man, take it easy on your

momma. We're ready to meet you," I tell him.

McKinley just smiles and rolls her eyes. This time around, I've gotten to experience it all. The cravings, the mood swings, her belly growing. I get to feel her belly against my back and my son kicking from inside her. It's all overwhelming and amazing, and I can't wait to do it all over again. McKinley just smiles when I say that. I know she does all the work, but I spoil her. Nightly foot rubs, I hired a housekeeper, and she even hired an assistant at the studio. Her mom keeps Lexi for us and also spoils her rotten.

"Your parents are coming in tomorrow. I'm telling you, he's waiting for them. They need to be here this time."

My dad is doing well. He is responding to the new treatments and, although he's not in full remission, his doctors are hopeful. He's doing well enough that he and Mom are flying in tomorrow to spend a week with us. They were hoping the little man would be here by now, which is why they scheduled this week. It also happens to be the right timing for Dad's treatments.

"You might be right."

Lexi comes running over and stops short of barreling into McKinley. "Easy, baby, your brother's in there," I tell her.

She gets a serious look on her face and nods. Her little lips pucker up and she kisses McKinley's belly. "Awon Alker," she says proudly.

McKinley and I both laugh. "That's right, sweet girl. Your little brother Aaron Walker."

"You sure Aaron's not going to be pissed we're calling him Walker?" I ask her.

She shrugs. "Don't care. He got us back together, so he gets the name sake, but this little man," she rubs her belly, "is Walker Chamberlin."

Lexi climbs up in my lap. "Wove you, Daddy." She kisses my cheek.

My heart melts.

She leans over and I hold tight, so she doesn't fall, and kisses McKinley on the cheek too. "Wove you, Mommy."

Just like they have every time before when Lexi says those words to her, McKinley's eyes fill with tears.

We settle on the couch and finish watching Cinderella, me and my girls. I cannot wait to meet our son, to welcome him to our family, and if I have any luck, in a few years, make him an older brother.

It doesn't take long before Lexi is asleep in my arms. McKinley is leaning into me and my hand is on her belly. "I love you, McKinley Chamberlin."

"I love you, too," she replies with a yawn and it doesn't take long before she and I are napping with our daughter.

"Mommy ouch," I hear Lexi say. I rub my eyes and sit up on the couch. I focus in on Lexi as she sits on the arm of the couch watching McKinley.

"Kinley, what's wrong?"

"Well, I think it might be time."

It takes a few seconds for my brain to register what she's just said. "Now, he's coming now? You're in labor?"

She laughs. My wife laughs at me. "Yeah, I'm pretty sure I am. I only dozed off for a few minutes. A sharp pain in my back woke me up. They started out about fifteen minutes apart. Now we're at nine."

"Shit!" I stand from the couch and pull my phone out of my pocket. "How long did I sleep?"

"Daddy, bad wowd." Lexi points her little finger at me.

"Yes, Daddy said a bad word. Little girls don't say bad words," I say, looking at my watch. Fuck! I slept for two hours. "Were you going to wake me?" I ask, hitting a few buttons on the screen and placing the phone next to my ear. "Hey, man, Kinley's in labor. Can you come get Lex?" Aaron tells me he is on his way and I hang up.

"Aaron?" she asks as her face grimaces in pain.

Fuck! I don't want to see her hurting. "Yeah, what can I do, baby?"

"Evan, this is normal. It's not supposed to feel like a relaxing massage."

"I know, but . . ."

"It's fine. We're twenty minutes from the hospital. The bags are packed, both ours and Lexi's. Take a deep breath."

"Is my sister, who is in labor, giving you tips for staying calm?" Aaron laughs.

"Fu . . . Funny," I catch myself.

"Unca Awon!" Lexi exclaims.

"Here you go. Thanks for coming, man. I'm going to run upstairs and get the bags. Don't leave her." I point toward McKinley. I take the stairs two at a time, rushing into our room and then Lex's to get our bags.

"Okay." I hand Aaron her bag. "Here's her bag. You have a key. Use it if you need it. McKinley, babe, I'm going to go pull the Durango out of the garage and load our bags. I'll be right back."

I hear Aaron laughing and I'm sure a smart-ass comment rolls off his tongue, but I don't have time for that right now. My wife is in labor!

By the time we make it to the hospital, her contractions are seven minutes apart. I pull up to the entrance and run in to get a wheelchair. I'm sure I look like a crazy person because a nurse comes rushing over. "Sir, can I help you?"

"My wife is in labor." I take a deep breath. We made it on time.

She grins. "Got ya. Let's go get her." She follows me out the double doors where we find McKinley standing outside the car.

"What happened?" I rush to her.

She chuckles. "Nothing happened. Sitting was uncomfortable. I told you I could walk inside."

"Not happening, baby."

"Hi, my name is Lisa," the nurse introduces herself to McKinley.

"McKinley . . ." She stops, takes a few deep breaths, and then continues. "Chamberlin. This is my husband, Evan."

"Nice to meet you both. This your first?" she asks while she helps McKinley sit in the wheelchair.

"My first delivery, but we have a little girl. She's two and a half."

"Such a fun age. Dad, why don't you park the car and meet us inside."

I hesitate, not wanting to leave her side for a minute. "Go, Evan. I'm not having this baby in the next ten minutes." I lean in and kiss her quickly before jumping into the car to find a legal parking space.

"McKinley Chamberlin," I say once I reach the reception desk.

"Third floor room 303."

I debate the stairs, but the elevator doors open so I jump in and push third floor and then tap the close door button . . . about fifteen times.

When I push open the door to her room, a nurse is standing by the bed messing with an IV. "Where's my wife?" Even I can hear the panic in my voice.

"In here," McKinley yells from behind a closed door.

I don't hesitate. I crack open the door and squeeze in. "What are you doing?"

"I'm helping." She's sitting on a stool attempting to take off her shoes. I kneel before her and take off each one. "Lift your arms." She does and I pull off her shirt. "Bra on or off?"

"Off." Reaching behind her, I release the clasp and pull it from her arms. Rising to my feet, I offer her my hands and help her stand. She braces herself on my shoulders while she steps out of her yoga pants and panties.

My beautiful wife is standing before me, naked, ready to give birth to our son. I place my hands on either side of her belly. "I love you, Walker. Mommy and I cannot wait to meet you." I kiss her belly one last time before standing. Bringing my hands up, I cup her face. "I love you. Thank you for loving our daughter, for giving me our son." I kiss her lips and she grimaces. Rubbing her back, I let her lean on me until it passes. "Let's get you in this gown so we can meet our son."

We get her changed and in bed. The nurse is hooking up her IV when another contraction hits. "Babe, that was only like three minutes," I say as soon as it passes.

"Yeah," she sighs in relief.

"I'm going to go get the doctor." The nurse scurries out of the room.

What happens next is a flurry of activity. The doctor comes in to check her, which I'm still not a fan of. Funny that it never bothered me with Misty. He says she is fully dilated and tells the nurse to bring in the delivery crew. McKinley and I had already decided we were going to be the only two people in the delivery room. It's something we want to share together.

Two more nurses enter the room with a small incubator looking contraption. Overhead lights drop out of the ceiling and McKinley's legs are placed in stirrups that come out of the bottom of the bed. Everything happens so fast, and before I know it, she's pushing.

"McKinley, you didn't have time for an epidural. I've giving you

something in your IV to help with the pain, but I'm afraid it's not near as effective. When you have a contraction, I need you to push as hard as you can and stop when I tell you to stop. It's going to be painful, but I know you can do this," the doctor tells her.

"Push," he says from between her legs. McKinley latches onto my hand and pushes. "Dad, lift her leg and pull it back to her chest," he instructs me.

"Baby." I look to McKinley. Her face is flushed and covered in sweat. She's beautiful.

"Just do what he says, Evan," she snips. I don't say a word because, one, she is not getting the good pain meds and, two, I can't do this for her. If I could take her pain and have our son, I would. Instead, I'll let her scream, yell, and cut the circulation off in my hands from her grip. Whatever she needs, I'm here.

This goes on for about fifteen minutes. Every time she has a contraction, another nurse and I hold her legs and she pushes.

"You're doing great, McKinley," the doctor tells her.

McKinley grabs my hand with an iron grip, so I know it's another contraction. With each leg pulled to her chest, her hand squeezing mine, she bears down and a scream rips from her throat. My heart breaks. I hate she's in so much pain. Then a scream altogether different echoes through the room.

"Congratulations, it's a boy."

Aaron Walker Chamberlin.

The doctor lays him on her chest and I can't speak. My beautiful wife and our son, yet another moment I will never forget. Leaning down, I kiss Kinley on the forehead. "He's perfect, baby. Thank you. You were so strong, so good. I love you."

Eyes brimming with tears and a wide grin, she looks up at me. "I love you too, Daddy."

McKinley and I are sitting on her bed, Walker in her arms. My arm is around both of them. "I can't wait for Lex to meet him."

"I know. Your mom is on her way. Aaron went to pick my parents up at the airport."

"Yeah, she texted me. I asked her if she would text us and let us know when they're here. I want Lex to come back before anyone else. I want her to meet him and know she's special to us."

This woman, I fall more in love with her every day.

"Daddy," I hear Lex say.

I jump for the door and greet her. I give Kinley's mom a hug. "Thank you. We will just be a few minutes. Kinley wants to give Lex some time with him."

"No rush. She's been talking about this for weeks. We will have all the time in the world to spoil both of our grandkids. You take all the time you need."

"Hey, baby girl, you ready to meet your little brother?"

With a serious look on her face, she nods. "Awon Alker."

"That's right." I walk over to the bed and take my seat next to McKinley. Lex settles on my lap and looks at him, a grin on her lips.

"I wove him." She leans over to kiss him.

"Gently, sweetheart. He's still really little. We don't want to hurt him."

"I not. I wove him." She gives me a look like I'm crazy. My daughter is so much like her mother.

"Mommy ouch."

"Yeah, mommy ouch is all better. I love you so much, Lexi, and now we also have a little brother to love," McKinley explains. "You want to hold him?"

My eyes go wide, but McKinley doesn't pay any attention. "You have to sit really still and let Daddy help you, okay?"

Lexi nods and becomes still as a statue on my lap. McKinley places Walker in our arms and Lexi giggles. "Baby," she exclaims.

She's still for maybe a minute before she squirms. "All done," She announces, causing Kinley and I both to laugh.

I take Walker and lift him from her lap and hold him over her head. She slides down between McKinley and me, giving her momma a big hug and a kiss. I snuggle my boy close to my chest and take it all in.

My wife.

My Daughter.

My son.

What more could a man ask for?

CONTACT Kaylee Ryan

Facebook:
www.facebook.com/KayleeRyanAuthor/

Goodreads:
www.goodreads.com/author/show/7060310.Kaylee_Ryan

Twitter:
@author_k_ryan

Instagram:
Kaylee_ryan_author

Website:
www.kayleeryan.com

OTHER WORKS BY Kaylee Ryan

With You Series

Anywhere With You
More With You
Everything With You

Stand Alone Titles

Tempting Tatum

Levitate

Just Say When

Emphatic

ACKNOWLEDGEMENTS

acknowledgements

To my husband and my son, I love you. I spend hours locked away writing and you are nothing but supportive. Thank you for supporting me in following my dream.

I love the Indie community. I've met some amazing people during this journey and I am grateful for each and every one of you!!

Sommer Stein, Perfect Pear Creative Covers, your ability to read my mind, and produce a kick ass cover is astounding. I love your face, cover girl! Thank you so much for the amazing cover!

Mac Robinson, thank you for agreeing to be the face of Southern Pleasure. I wish you much success and best of luck with your future endeavors.

Golden Czermak; Thank you for doing what you do. Your pictures make a kick ass cover, just saying. ☺

Tami Integrity Formatting, you never let me down. You make my words come together in a pretty little package. Thank you so much for making Southern Pleasure look fabulous on the inside!

Kim Ginsberg, thank you for proofreading you're the best!

Jennifer from Proof This, thank you for proofreading, you too are the best!

Kaylee 2, Jamie, Stacy, Lauren and S Moose thank you so much for taking the time to read Southern Pleasure and give me your honest feedback. The time you take from your families to read for me, I appreciate more than you know. You ladies hold a special place in my heart.

Give Me Books, thank you for hosting and organizing the release of Southern Pleasure. I appreciate all of your hard work getting this book out there.

To all of the bloggers out there . . . Thank you so much. Your continued never-ending support of myself, and the entire indie community is greatly appreciated. I know that you don't hear it enough so hear me now. *I appreciate each and every one of you and the support that you have given me.* Thank you to all of you! There are way too many of you to list . . .

To my Kick Ass Crew, you ladies know who you are. I will never be able to tell you how much your support means. You all have truly earned your name. Thank you!

Kaylee (2) Not much new I can say. You are a constant beam of support and the friendship that we have formed is something that I will always cherish. Thank you for being you! I hope that you fell in love with your country boy just as much I did.

Last but not least, to the readers. Without you none of this would even be worth the effort. I truly love writing and I am honored that I am able to share that with you. Thank you to each and every one of you who continue support me, and my dream of writing.

With Love,

Kaylee Ryan
AUTHOR

CPSIA information can be obtained
at www.ICGtesting.com
Printed in the USA
BVOW06s1058020717
488336BV00012B/154/P